Stuff
&
Things
&
Jam
&
That

J. Haydien Kirke

This is a work of fiction. Names, characters, places, businesses, events and incidents are either the product of the author's imagination or used in a fictitious manner. Any resemblance to actual persons, living or dead, events, or locales is purely coincidental.

ISBN 9781981032570

For Family

Prologue

Sam looked at his phone. It passed the time. It gave information. It was by his own customisation a view into a friendly and familiar world when and wherever he needed it. It reassured him when he felt out of place, it was his friend when he was alone. It was, more often than not, an ass for reminding him no one had messaged.

He opened the map up to see where he was going, a useful gadget. He drifted into the same thoughts he had every time he looked at the map. He zoomed out the view. And again. The rooftops of houses. Lots of houses. Who lived here? What were their lives like? Would he get on with them? Were they doing the same thing, wondering where to meet others? Wondering why there were so many people in the world but so few in their lives? So many houses… why didn't he meet more people? Each house he saw contained its own people, its own story, all of them alive at the same time, so close… so separate… All a mystery to each other.

A buzzing pulled him from his philosophy, easily distracted as always. A fly was bouncing around the inside of the window. Sam watched as it bounced and buzzed, confused and frantic as to what was stopping its progress towards the rest of the world. It had got in here, why couldn't it get out?

The top section of the window was open. The likely entry point. A white wooden frame separated the small panel of glass that could be opened from the larger main panel, a design shared by almost every other window. The fly bounced and buzzed across the larger panel of glass. Each time it reached the top of the panel, Sam felt himself cheer it on, hoping for it to make that final jump across the white wood to freedom. It never did. Each time it reached the wood, it bounced back down the glass again, assuming it had reached the end of the opportunity for escape.

Having to go backwards, to fly away from the glass, around the wooden frame and away from the view of the outside, even slightly, seemed too much for it to comprehend. Perhaps too frightening, to turn away from a goal desired so strongly, which seemed so close… too much of a gamble. If it did, if it dared… it would see it was only an inch away from everything it wanted… freedom from this panicked prison, release into the bliss of the outside world.

Sam walked over to the window to try and help. He didn't like flies, but that was no reason for it to suffer. He wondered why they never flew around the wood. It just needed to take a chance on a direction it was afraid to try, let go of the fear that it was wrong, and everything would work out. It would escape the frustration and panic of bouncing repeatedly off the glass. Cupping his hand around the fly, which was harder than he thought it would be, Sam ushered it to the opening and let it go. He watched as it darted outside, quickly vanishing into the evening gloom, happy to be free. Turning his attention back to his phone, Sam's eyes rested again on the rooftops. Touching the glass on the screen he wondered if he had become the fly. His life had formed into a giant window and he was bouncing. Where was the frame? Which bit did he have to push himself around to feel free?

No time for that now, he was already late. He had to catch this bus. He closed the window, picked up his coat and headed out the door.

1

The sky never looked clearer, the stars shone as if they were all exploding, an almost tangible force burning into his soul. He looked at his shadow cast on the wall by the moon. As he opened his hand to let the soft blue moonlight dance through his fingers, he watched his shadow hand move on the wall. He wasn't sure if he had ever seen anything like this. Not sure if it had ever been this bright at night, or he had just never stopped to look. Really look. Ignore his normal hustle from A to B full of worries about what might happen, what could happen, what should… Mustn't…

Did any of that matter? Bathed in the light cast from a thousand other worlds, a million, and one desolate rock floating in the sky above him he wondered… What did it all mean? What was it all worth? Were there people standing on other planets doing the same things? If there were, maybe they had never before stopped to really look at the light cast from this place.

"Wanker!"

The shout seemed to come from nowhere - Sam quickly stopped thinking of the philosophy of moonlight and looked around. *"Damn I shouldn't have looked"* Sam's thoughts punished him as he turned to see a group of lads stumble out of the pub just down the street.

"Oi! Goth! Wanker!"

The shouts continued, interspersed with illegible words and laughter. He quickly turned and began to walk away.

"Haven't got time for this."

Sam mumbled under his breath as he headed down the street. The bus hadn't been slow, but it didn't make up for him setting out late. As he pulled his long black coat around him he considered that this was the only item of black clothing he was actually wearing. Did this mean the group of drunk people could somehow see inside his mind to the style he kinda liked? No, it meant he was overthinking everything as normal. A long black coat is a bit of a giveaway, or an easy target.

The lads were still behind him, laughing and stumbling down the street. They were harmless enough at this distance; the trick was not to turn it into anything. Not to make it more interesting for them. He felt like running, but that might inspire an exciting chase – and if caught the lads probably wouldn't be able to think of anything else to do but unleash a quick kicking. He lengthened his stride. A trick he had learnt some years before, taking bigger steps makes you travel faster without looking like you've sped up. By the time he reached the junction he had created a good separation. Turning to the right, and once the line of sight had been broken a few jogged steps meant he wouldn't have to worry about those lads again. His thoughts returned to the stars. Breathing heavily from the recent effort, he watched his breath drift up in front of him, making the stars twinkle and glisten through the mist.

"Oof! Watch it mate!"

"Oh shit sorry!"

Startled, Sam put his hands up to steady the man he had just walked into. He had drifted off into the world of stars and breath and otherworldly beauty – and completely out of the here and now again. He was suddenly aware that this street was quite busy, the hustle and bustle of a night out on the town, the ritualistic journey of people from one pub to another, one bar to one club. The drunken dance of the grass is always greener, this place is nice but maybe the next place holds the perfect night out, partner, secrets to a happy life? Probably a good name for a bar that.

Focus.

FOCUS.

"Sorry, are you ok?"

Sam asked as the man brushed himself off, straightening his almost fluorescent shirt with a few strokes of his hands.

"Yeah mate, keep it steady yeah?"

The man's gaze was caught by a woman in a dress that matched the lack of subtly of his shirt.

"Have a good un!"

And he was off.

"Err... you too!"

All Sam could muster as a response. Well that went well, considering. Was this man a well-adjusted fella? Able to understand the lack of malicious intent in the collision? Or was he just more interested in finding someone of the opposite sex to bump into? Or, in fact, was it just that Sam was overthinking everything again? To a ridiculous degree. Again.

Sam took a steadying breath and tried to return to the world around him. All sorts of evening wear were on display on all sorts of people on their Saturday night journeys. A strange kind of uniform, shirts and best jeans for the men, small dresses with matching bags for the women. Some men had added suit jackets to their look, and some women's shoes were so tall and unstable that they had to walk arm in arm across the uneven street to avoid disaster. It was difficult to decide which gender was using more hair products, but if you were counting the bearded ones then the men were winning that battle hands down. Why weren't any of them cold?

An older man, slightly scruffy in an 'I'm not bothered about my appearance' way was walking a bulldog along the pavement, defiantly claiming territory back from the revellers. Sam was pondering how to make his way past as the dog stopped, squatted, and began to piss. Its owner looked like he couldn't be less bothered. The pub goers in their fanciest gear looked like they were extremely bothered. Shocked and disgusted looks shot around as they moved away from the spreading puddle. As Sam was contemplating the scene before him, an opportunist delivery bike shot through the gap in the crowd, a blaze of tight green and black lycra with matching oversized box attached. Everyone gasped to see if the tyres would bring forth a fountain of horror upon them, breathing a collective sigh of relief when no such tsunami arrived. Between the dog and the bike, everyone was united in knowing who the true menace was. It was not the dog.

The crowd began moving again, forgetting the moment of high drama and returning to their wishes for the night that lay ahead. Sam negotiated the puddle and made his way towards the next junction, moving away from the centre of the town, heading for Jess's new place.

The pavement seemed to glow orange as the slabs were bathed in warm lights, mixing from fake Victorian street lights and the windows of bars and restaurants. As Sam moved through the glow he glanced through the windows, partially nosey as to what he might see, and partially curious as to whether he recognised the establishments, or if they had sprung up anew since he last walked this way through the town. New venues seemed to flow into the town like waves of some great ocean of business dreams, keen to prove they were novel, new, stylish… before breaking on the shore of the high street, and slowly fading away to make way for the next incoming wave. Through one window Sam could see a young couple, immaculately dressed and made up. They sat at a romantic table for two, each staring down at their phones, tapping and flicking at their screens.

Not wanting to stare, Sam turned his attention back to the street. There were fewer people around as each step took him further away from the main square, the central hub of nightlife. He was not the only person walking up the hill however, and there began to be a noticeable change in the attire of those who shared his choice of direction. Everyday clothes, super casual clothes, coupled with shopping bags from quick stop mini supermarkets became the dress code of the uphillers. The downhillers, greater in number, were in their finest going out clothes, heading towards the square and their chance at the perfect party night out. A couple were heading straight towards Sam, a girl made almost entirely of bare legs clung onto a boy made almost entirely out of gel held quiff, taking up almost all of the pavement. Sam span to his side to dodge their power walk as they made no acknowledgment that he was even there. They were far too important for such things; did Sam not realise this was their big night out? Did he not know who they were!?

The hill grew steeper. The glow began to fade. Restaurants and bars gave way to darkened shop fronts, sleeping for the night. Hustle, bustle, and dodging of people on pavement slabs shifted to taxies and buses, parked and ready, chomping at the bit to compete for the first people to give up on the evening. Sam could hear the taxi drivers laughing and joking at each other's expense, making the most of the waiting to see if they would earn a living that night. Takeaways began appearing for Sam to stride past, alive with staff preparing for the drunken orders they were soon to begin taking. Sam shot a look at a bicycle delivery fellow as he stood astride his chromed war beast, taking up a large amount of the pavement as he awaited his next package and orders for battle with any pedestrians that dare get in his way.

Turning the next corner the glow was now completely gone, as if an embodiment of the hopes of the people out in the centre of town, and Sam was now too far away to be touched by its fake and desperate warmth. A dull gloom hung over the street as it became relics of a lost time. Old shops long gone, industrial brick long cold to the touch, gutted of their original purpose for better or worse, now mostly empty and hollow. They looked sad and uncared for, an orphanage of stone on show, waiting for would be developers to tour around and declare *"that's the one! That's our new prime location for flats! Or bars! Or both! A new repurposed home for the bearded hipster who wants modern living in an old building with organic coffee and plenty of plug sockets for expensive laptops!"*

Steel fencing marked one of the buildings as lucky. Various diggers and piles of sand indicated it had found its new parents, it was time for its new start in life. Sam had enjoyed playing with diggers and sand when he was small, and a part of him was still excited to see the machinery. As he walked past the site he drank it all in. Caterpillar tracks, pneumatic dragon claw looking things, chrome exhaust pipes, dented and bashed yellow metal all came together into giant versions of his childhood toys. Sam wanted to play with these almost as much as he remembered wanting to play with his tiny plastic replicas.

Lost again in the world inside his own head, Sam very nearly collided with another stranger. A man stood, motionless, staring into the building site. Adjusting his step, Sam dodged this obstacle much more successfully than earlier. The man didn't move or even seem to notice as Sam moved past. After taking a few steps Sam's curiosity took over and he looked back at this unknown silent obstacle chap. He was still motionless, still staring into the building site. Sam looked back into the site to see if there was something he was missing that was so mesmerising. Beyond the diggers were large piles of sand and debris. Beyond that the building was half destroyed, falling in on itself and collapsing. Perhaps the new parents had decided they wanted a different child, this industrial remnant not as lucky as it had first thought.

Perhaps this man also shared a fascination for diggers, reminiscing about childhood toys like Sam. But he was not smiling, he did not seem full of joy. He was just staring, blankly. Perhaps he had some connection to this building? A former place of work? Home? Or the home of a lost love? Was this his past being torn down, regrets piling up along with the sand and debris? He turned to look at Sam and Sam quickly looked away, back up the hill, not wanting to intrude or disturb. As he left the man behind him he pondered what he had seen, more mysteries of life to be left unsolved.

2

The candle light shimmered through the room; the walls seemed to be alive with their own party of dancing shadows, in stark contrast to the awkward sitting of the actual party contained within their joyous walls.

"Well, you see, the thing is…"

Steven straightened in his chair, resting his whisky glass on his crossed leg as if preparing for a grand proclamation.

"*Blah... blah... blah... politics…*"

Kim's attention had drifted again. She assumed he was talking about politics, she didn't really care about the subject, and equally didn't care what Steven was saying, so it was a logical conclusion. Probably.

"Don't the shadows look cool?"

Jake half whispered as he leaned across the sofa.

"I've been watching them too. Best thing about this supposed party."

Kim sneaked out a wry smile as she looked down into her wine glass. Jake seemed more fun than Steven, more approachable. Perhaps that was because when he spoke to her it wasn't a way of showing off how clever he was, which is exactly how she imagined Steven felt when he was about to launch into another rambling debate... A vigorous discussion about why he was always right.

"What do the shadows look like to you?"

Kim shifted awkwardly against the arm of the sofa as she turned to face Jake.

"To me it looks like people dancing."

"Hmm yes."

Jake stroked his excuse for a beard as he looked at the nearest wall.

"Funny, I thought that the people were supposed to dance at a party, not the walls."

Kim's smile returned. She took a sip of her wine to try to disguise it. She wasn't sure why.

"When did it happen? Was it an age thing? Or did it just happen to us randomly?"

There was a slight spark in Jake's eyes as he spoke, as if the flickering candlelight emanated from within those blue circles.

"When did being asked to come to a party stop meaning dancing, shouting and fun, and start meaning sitting, talking, and utter, utter despair for the state of your life?"

"Huh yeah. Maybe the clue is in who is throwing the party."

Kim tipped back the last of the wine a little too quickly after finishing her sentence, nearly spilling the last drops on herself. It was ok, no one had noticed, or so she thought, as Jake chuckled.

"More wine?"

Steven had leaned forward, holding a half empty bottle over the coffee table.

"And what do you think?"

He looked proud, and more comfortable than someone leaning over a table holding a bottle of wine in the air should. His confidence in himself seemed to ooze out of each pore of his too tanned for winter skin.

"Err…"

Kim wasn't sure which question she was going to struggle to answer first.

"Well usually I would say a cat would win the fight, but I guess a dog could hold the knife better in its mouth."

Jake seemed very sure of the answer and cocked his head to one side as he sat back and crossed his leg mirroring Steven's earlier posture. Kim and Steven both turned to face him, with equally startled and confused expressions.

"Sorry…"

Jake leaned forward, placing his clasped hands between his knees.

"What was the question Steve? I was finding it very difficult to care."

3

Across the room, Al was sat on his own, in a tall wooden chair in the corner. He had liked the look of the chair when he arrived, it looked out of place in the otherwise modern designed by TV and magazine experts flat. It's long legs and spindled back made it appear to be a cross between a child's high chair and an old fashioned bar stool. Al felt that it reflected how he felt as soon as he had walked into this party, not quite fitting in with everything else, out of place, as if at any moment someone would turn and say *"Oh, no not in here, sorry, I don't know how this got here, I will just get rid of it and we can carry on."*

Al didn't have a drink, and no one had offered to get him one. He still had his jacket on – partly because he felt he may be leaving at any moment and partly because it was comforting to keep it on. If he put it down, he may lose part of himself and his identity in this place – and so far, that's all he had in this party. Himself and the odd chair.

Maddie stood by the greasy man and his friend, she couldn't remember their names. Introductions had been fast, the greasy man had shaken her by the hand like an old style movie star, leaning down as he held her hand rather too tightly. A bad time to introduce yourself, whilst your mouth is angled away from the person you're speaking to just as they are thinking equally about how the music is just that bit too loud and that their hand hurts from a too tight clasp. As introductions go, it was conceivably worse than not bothering at all.

"When will these two go away?"

She laughed as she realised the greasy man had stopped speaking and was just looking at her, expectedly. He had probably made a joke. Safe bet.

She rubbed her right ear nervously, brushing her hair off her face as she did so. She didn't know what to say at all and found the greasy man slightly unsettling. *"Better to be stood talking to someone…"* she thought. *"Better to look like I'm popular than to be sat all alone like that weirdo on the chair in the corner."* She wasn't at all sure it was better, but she thought she ought to convince herself it was, or she was doing much worse at this party than she had feared she would do as she had put the final touches to her makeup in the taxi ride over here. Doing worse than someone who was literally sat on their own.

"You can do this!"

She had whispered reassuringly to the reflection in her compact in the back of the taxi.

"You can do this!"

She hadn't really believed herself then, and she certainly didn't believe it now.

The mixed buzz of music and attempts at chatter drifted out of the flat like steam pouring off a recently boiled kettle. floating out into the night sky and spreading the story of this flat, this party, merging with the emanations of other parties, pubs, restaurants… All the energy of all the adventures and people across the city, creating the palpable buzz, that special electrical charge in the atmosphere that signified a Saturday night out.

4

The stars couldn't be seen at all on this street, stupid street lights. Well, it was nice to be able to see where you were going. Sam had finally arrived at the location of the party. Fashionably late, as people increasingly realised was no different from normal late. His long coat blew open with the cold wind, simultaneously ruining its use as a coat as it let the wind hit Sam directly, and proving its worth as a *'this is going to look cool'* purchase as it billowed and danced behind him with each step. 16B, The Old Mill.

"Hmm."

Sam stopped and looked at every aspect of the building. It certainly was a building.

"Imaginative naming by the re-developers."

The embossed brass name plate hung on the side of the Victorian mill house that now housed two dozen modern, desirable, inner city but not in the dangerous crime inner city way but the trendy inner city where they can charge you double if you ignore the crime down the road style flats. It had a big metal and glass door, with a buzzer panel set in the wall next to it. Sam hated buzzer panels. He was confident and intelligent when he put his mind to it, but something about buzzer panels tripped his inner nervousness. The feeling that he may stutter, or say something idiotic, or wrong, or shaming, and it was being broadcast somewhere unimaginable to who knows how many people…

"Nope. Not gonna happen."

He whispered as if someone else was telling him it was ok to feel that way about these terrible devices. He reached into his jeans pocket, pulled out his phone and searched for Jess's contact info. As he placed the phone to his ear he briefly considered why he felt more comfortable using this phone than the wall mounted buzzer of doom.

"Well it's obvious."

He reached his well reasoned conclusion as he waited for Jess to pick up.

"Hello!?"

"Jess? I'm here let me in!"

"You're here? There's a buzzer on the wall just press on that!"

Sam looked at the buzzer. He couldn't understand Jess's logic. He was on the phone to her already. She knew he was here.

"It's 16b just press the button and I'll answer it!"

Jess couldn't understand Sam's logic. Why had he phoned from next to the buzzer? They both stood slightly confused by each other, in a bizarre standoff.

Tumbleweed could have blown down the street as the stalemate continued. It was high noon and neither buzzer slinger was willing to press first, neither willing to accept the chance of defeat at the finger tip of the other. Logic and sanity were the only things in danger of getting shot to pieces.

A large gruff looking man brushed past Sam, the waft of exotic spices drifting around him like a cloud of magic from a far off land promising so much more than the white plastic tray he was holding actually contained. Pulling a key from his pocket while balancing his takeaway on one raised knee, the man opened the metal and glass door and headed inside.

"Never mind, be right up."

Sam's eyes had followed every action of the gruff man, and in one fluid motion he lowered his phone with his right hand as he raised his left to grab the handle of the large door before it closed. He slid his phone into his pocket as he slid in through the doorway, a slightly proud sidewise motion that made him feel like a spy that had slipped unnoticed into some foreign embassy.

Despite being pleased to get in, Sam was not impressed with the security of this place. The memory of a summer long past flashed back to the front of Sam's mind, as though he caught its reflection in the glass of the door as he watched it close behind him over his shoulder. In between years at university Sam had tried to gain employment through a recruitment agency in a lavishly tall building just off the city's main square. Every week of the summer he tried. Every week they had nothing for him, saying that with his qualifications he needn't worry, he would be fine. They had a door like this with a buzzer. Sam had never pressed it. Never once entered the building in the proper manner. He was still a bit proud of that hollow victory over the employment agency.

"Ninja style."

He whispered with a wry smile as he turned back to continue into the building. His coat lapped at the back of his legs as he took his first few steps into this new place.

The hall was much less impressive than his mental image demanded. Unlike the crafted brickwork of the building's exterior, lovingly restored to provide a sense of charm and oldie worldliness, Sam was greeted by a plain whitewashed hallway that looked to be constructed out of breeze blocks held together by the disappointment of several dozen tenant's visitors that had entered this place before him. The stairway in the corner was grubby, the metal banister matching each stair's edging, scuffed and smeared.

"Was there such a metal as *faux steel*?"

Sam wondered as he reached the first step. The greyish beige off white who knows what colour it was originally carpet gave way to… erm… Sam had no idea what modern cheap stairs were made of. He stopped to gaze down. Wood? Stone? Fake stone metal kinda thing?

"Huh."

Sam realised he had never stopped to consider what stairs were made from outside of his flat, which were definitely traditional wood, and work which were definitely…

"Huh."

Sam felt a combination of invigorated by the discovery of his lack of knowledge about something so taken for granted, and incredibly thick. This was the kind of lack of basic knowledge that convinced him he was a genius. Only geniuses would have minds so full of important things that things like this wouldn't find a place to sit.

"But wouldn't geniuses have big enough minds for all the knowledge?"

Sam pondered as he kicked one of the stairs with the toe of his boot as he made his way up. This was the kind of existential dilemma Sam often found himself lost in thought about. Sometimes he lost himself to thinking about the thoughts he had, and did anyone else share these thoughts, or was it just him. If it was just him he should double his efforts to answer these questions, for someone must, and if it wasn't, he could be saved a lot of time and find his long lost soul mate a lot faster if people would just tell him.

"Stone-wood."

Sam had almost run out of steps to Jess's floor, and he had to switch his mind to other important issues and topics. Like seeming normal once he reached the party, in case it was just him that thought like this. If he couldn't think of the right answer, or if the question was dull or he lost interest, Sam would think of the most ridiculous answer instead.

"Yep. Stairs are made of stone-wood. Only explanation. Probably grows on cliffs."

5

The waves lapped on the shore. They gently caressed the warm sand, as if the ocean was massaging the stress out of the beach. The soft breeze was rustling through the palm trees, telling them that everything was going to be ok. High in the cloudless sky, the golden sun was keeping its reassuring eye on the beach like a kind parent that had found exactly the right amount of protection their child needed to feel secure but independent. Releasing a deep breath Louisa felt like she had found her home, her destiny. She could stay here forever. Happy. Content. At peace.

"White or red?"

Louisa could feel the warmth of the sun on her face. A sudden, sharp tap in her side came from nowhere.

"Oi! White or red?!"

Disorientated, Louisa turned from the window as the beach faded and swirled out of reach to be replaced by car parks, street lights, and takeaways glistening in the glass.

"Huh?"

The only response she could muster. She thought Jess looked expectant, and slightly rushed. Keen to be a good host, she wasn't really paying much attention to her guests in order to make sure she had time to get everything just right for them.

"You look a million miles away! I'm not going to have to elbow you again am I!?"

Jessica's eyes darted everywhere at once, from meeting Louisa's still slightly bewildered gaze, to the glasses of different coloured wine she held in each hand, to Louisa's dress, the floor. Louisa suddenly felt under a lot of pressure to find whatever it was Jessica was looking for.

"Err… red? Erm… please?"

"OF COURSE!"

Jessica seemed suddenly very relieved. One more host dilemma resolved.

"Thought you'd be a red!"

Neither of them knew what that meant. Neither of them acknowledged that fact, they both just smiled as Jess handed her the glass from her left hand.

"Enjoy! There's plenty more! I will be back in a minute!"

Jess had already started to turn as she handed the glass over. For a moment, Louisa had a terrible flash in her mind's eye of dropping the glass everywhere as Jessica spun away, a catastrophic and unrecoverable crime, a murder of the party with grape based blood seeping everywhere never to be scrubbed clean and forgotten. She managed to grab it firmly in both hands before that premonition became reality.

"Why did I choose red!?"

She spoke softly yet firmly to herself as she watched the swirling liquid slowly come to rest in the glass she had firmly cupped in her hands.

"From now on, always white at parties in case of disasters."

It was a sensible pact to make with herself, one that she probably wouldn't remember until she was handed the next glass of red wine. Had she thought of this before and forgotten? She looked around the room; no one seemed to have noticed her near miss with unrecoverable social disaster. Relieved, she began looking past the people at the room itself.

It was indeed, as she had thought previously, a room. There must be thousands like it, scattered around towns and cities like grains of sand on her beach, remarkably similar whilst trying so desperately hard to be unique, different, special. A sofa, matching chair, unmatching chair brought in for guests, TV that looked modern but not expensive enough to be cutting edge; or perhaps it was this time last year, or last week, who could keep up anymore. The walls were quite nice, you could see the original brickwork of the old factory. Although, they weren't at the end of the building, were they? How could they be original bricks?

She tried to remember when she arrived if she had walked far enough inside to have reached a flat that sat on the outer wall of the building. It was too hard to think about. All she could remember about the walk towards this place was that she was slightly terrified about the whole experience. Meeting new people, having things to say to them, listening to what they said to her, responding without sounding like an idiot, terrifying. She averted her gaze from the mystery bricks that seemed to be triggering such anxiety in her, moving instead to investigate cupboardy shelfy furniture that sat against them. Rustic and minimalistic, each shelf brimmed with DVD's and CD's that defined the uniqueness of the owners. Well, by unique, she thought in fact, mostly the same. As she moved her finger along the cases to better peruse the titles, she found about half of the same things that sat uniquely in her own very non-dissimilar room in her own flat.

She looked around at the other people gathered in this place, she only knew Steven from work, and had briefly met Jess at a work do ages ago. She had no idea about the rest of the people here. She wasn't sure if they all already knew each other, or if they felt as lost as she did, invited to make the numbers up perhaps, to fill a room and make the hosts look popular. Steven seemed embroiled in intense conversation with a man and woman on the sofa. They must be a couple. Couple friends of the host couple. Next to them, stood on a non-descript rug of sorts, were two more men and another woman. She couldn't tell which of the two men was the partner of the woman, but one seemed to be doing all the talking. Must be that one.

"Oh great, it's all couples and me."

Louisa longed for her beach, to escape to its soft sand and warm sun, carefree and untroubled by human interaction. She continued her searching gaze around the room. Jessica was in the kitchen area at the far end of the room, wrestling with wine bottles. In the corner she could see another man she didn't know, sat in a chair slightly too small for his rounded form. He still had his coat on. Unsure of whether this was a very clever thing to do (for you could get up and leave at any time with no fuss) or a weird thing to do (there was a very clear pile of coats in the bedroom down the hall) she took a sip out of her glass.

"Well. There's at least one person I think is on their own, so it's not just me that's still single."

She considered going to speak to him, to ask about the coat logic. Hesitating a second too long, she decided not to. He might think she was trying to flirt and he may take it the wrong way and ask her to go out sometime for a drink... She wasn't sure she liked the look of him that much, and that was going to be an awfully difficult conversation to have. She stayed where she was and took another sip of her wine.

6

The door seemed imposing. It did not seem mysterious. Sam tried his best to allow it to seem mysterious, but he just couldn't. It was a large, wooden door with a pretty standard number plate on it.

"Behind this door lies an unknowable dimension."

Sam cocked his head to one side as he continued to size up the door, whilst thinking of its significance to the world.

"This door… I don't know what is behind it, could be anything. Anyone. I could meet someone behind this door who will change my life forever… perhaps discover a new favourite band playing on the stereo… perhaps even some kind of new crazy stereo… this door…right now nothing exists behind it, and everything."

Sam felt the door was staring back at him, questioning his worthiness to gain passage beyond its frame to the unknown that it held behind its cheap yet sturdy construction. He raised his hand slowly to the doorbell... held it there for a few seconds contemplating the world changing power of the small rectangular button.

"I defy you, electronic mystery concealer!"

Taking a deep breath and setting his feet firmly, he banged his fist several times in the centre of the wood panel. He then stood, triumphant, awaiting the adventures and experiences to properly form so that the door could be opened. The seconds began to pass. Perhaps his knocking was not loud enough to penetrate to the party inside. Perhaps Jess was only listening for the familiar buzz of the doorbell.

"Hmm. Well played Sir Door."

He raised his hand aloft again; he would have to knock harder this time. He was not going to give in and press the doorbell, not now, he had come so far and it would feel like defeat.

A sudden gust of air sucked past Sam's raised fist as the door rapidly swung inward, allowing flickering candlelight to escape into the corridor, discovering new and exciting shapes to caress, spreading dancing shadows across the walls and other nearby doors, accompanied by a kind of soft jazzy music that was both unfamiliar and extraordinarily welcoming. Jess stood silhouetted in the now fully open door, with an expression of confusion and slight disapproval.

"Why don't you ever press doorbells?"

"They alarm me."

Sam answered as he realised he was still holding his fist up ready to knock, which now looked slightly odd in the open doorway. He opened his fingers and gave a slightly awkward wave.

"Not good enough."

Jess's expression lightened as she moved aside and beckoned Sam to come inside.

"It gives me a buzz?"

Sam took the invitation and stepped inside the flat.

"Better."

Jess closed the door firmly behind them, and Sam had officially arrived to explore the mysteries contained in this new place. His coat lapped once more at the backs of his legs as he wandered into the small corridor. On his right, a bathroomy style door probably hid some kind of bathroom, unless it was a clever disguise. On his left, a flimsy looking wood effect door was rested slightly ajar, revealing nothing but a dark void beyond.

"Chuck your coat on the bed in there and get yourself in."

Jess pointed to the void door as she spoke, brushing passed Sam and quickly vanishing into the large open plan room at the end of the corridor.

"But I like my coat… it's all swooshy! It's how people recognise me!"

Sam's complaints were lost to the ether.

"Well, I guess I'm going to look odd if I keep it on if she told everyone the same thing when they arrived."

Complaining under his breath to the universe while pushing

the flimsy door open with his foot (and disappointed that it didn't creak as he did) Sam rolled his shoulders and allowed his coat to slip down his arms, catching it just before it fell. As the door swung open the void inside became dimly illuminated. It was a pretty ordinary bedroom, with some pretty ordinary furniture inside. A small dressing table covered in various boxes and loose jewellery, a chest of drawers with a pile of clothes on top, a bedside table with an alarm clock phone charger combo thing and a small pile of paperback books. After throwing his coat on top of the others in the centre of the bed, Sam pulled the door shut and headed towards the source of the candle light and jazzy music.

Standing at the entrance of the main room of the flat, Sam surveyed the scene. His intention was to walk straight into the room, smiling, waving, greeting everyone warmly and having everyone immediately realise what a jolly good bloke he was. Instead, he had stopped dead in the doorway, overcome with the realisation that he probably wasn't going to manage to make the entrance he wanted and that the more he thought about it the less likely he was to manage it. Instead he was stood completely still, just a little bit stuck. He could see Jess again now, she was heading towards a woman by the sideboard that he wondered if he had met before… but he couldn't place her. She was beautiful, but Sam couldn't shake the feeling that he should know who she was. He wasn't going to go over and make a fool of himself by not remembering. He could see Steven sat chatting with a couple of people. They all seemed to be getting along quite well, lots of hand gestures and nodding, relaxed postures, yep that was all fine, not really space for him to jump in. By the kitchenette there seemed to be a man sat on his own, looking into the room in a similar way to him.

"That's interesting, I'm gonna have to find out what's going on there."

He spoke his observation to the universe just in case it was keeping notes. As he was about to move across to speak to the possible kindred spirit, Sam saw something that sparked every inch of his interest and enthusiasm.

"Ohh now this is perfect..."

He pulled his shirt to make sure it was straight (and that he had done the buttons correctly, you never know...) and started to walk towards two men and a woman stood on the rug by the sofa who seemed to be having a conversation Sam could only describe to himself as *excruciating*.

7

"Wooo!"

Jess appeared as quickly as she had vanished, looking flustered but excited.

"How's the wine? Tasty I hope!"

"Yes thanks!"

Louisa couldn't help but be caught up by Jess's enthusiasm and energy.

"It's a lovely place you have here!"

She couldn't remember if she'd said that already, and this was a flat warming party after all.

"Thanks! Yes I like it here, it's my favourite home so far."

Jess's eyes darted, hinting that she wondered briefly if that was a weird thing to say, but she quickly moved on.

"I see you've found our dvd collection – the romantic comedies are all mine!"

"Yes sorry I was looking and realised I have most of these too."

Louisa became suddenly aware that maybe she shouldn't have been looking so closely at the film collection and hoped she hadn't offended Jess.

"No no don't be sorry, it's fun isn't it? When you go to a friend's place for the first time, and you see their dvd's and books and look for common ground – it's like you're asking them all about themselves without having to ask – finding out if they like the same things and getting to know how much of a friend they might get to be."

Jess beamed with an excited smile as she spoke. She looked so happy, everything was positive in her eyes. Louisa was captivated. She had thought Jess seemed nice when she had briefly met her before at the work party, where Jess had attended as Steven's plus one. She hoped she could properly befriend her, she felt she could have a lot of fun in her company.

"Well there are a fair few here that I have too, but there's some I haven't heard of before."

Louisa felt she wanted to say she had the exact same collection, in case that helped Jess see her as proper friend material. That would be wrong though, inaccurate and trying a bit too hard. Best to be as honest as possible and let the universe fall where it must.

"Excellent. that's the best result, it means we must like the same stuff, but there's some stuff we can debate about and maybe some stuff you haven't seen that I can introduce you to, and vice versa."

Infectious giggles passed back and forth.

"How about you then Lou, what do you like to do? Apart from this kind of thing?"

Jess waved the palm of her hand over the DVD cabinet as she awaited the reply.

"Oh…"

Louisa felt a bit on the spot, and for a second she couldn't remember ever doing anything at all.

"Erm… I like to read."

"Ah me too! Well, when I have the time. Or when there is time, one of the two! What sort of thing?"

Louisa had to think for another second, suddenly feeling strangely vulnerable, like she was being asked to give away her darkest secret.

"All sorts I suppose…"

It was both a vague and accurate answer.

"Cool, what are you reading at the moment?"

"I started a fantasy series, not very far in though so far."

Louisa still felt on the spot and was trying to be vague in case she ruined her new friendship opportunity by saying the wrong thing or seeming too weird.

"Fantasy like elves and magic and things? I haven't read one of those in ages… I like how you can escape to a completely different world with those… let me know if it's good and I will give it a look."

"OK sure."

Louisa beamed a smile at Jess. She had felt a twinge of anxiety mentioning the word 'fantasy', not really sure yet if Jess was the type to think it was cool or laugh at her. It was so hard these days to tell what people liked from the way they looked, or the way their friends looked. Long gone were the days of the small groups of well defined subcultures. Louisa felt she couldn't tell anything about anyone by their appearance anymore. It was one of the reasons Louisa loved the fantasy genre, a long favoured bolt hole from this complex and frightening world, to a place where heroes stood tall to fight for what was right, and evil was easy to spot, and just as easily defeated in the end.

Elvish rogues began to appear in Louisa's mind, but she caught herself, just in time, from drifting away from this world, and this conversation, which she was currently thinking was going 'not completely terribly awful' and therefore should be continued. A sharp inhale of breath, and a quick decision to ask a question before she was faced with having to think how to answer another one.

"So…"

It was a much less inspired beginning to the sentence than Louisa had wanted it to be. Not really the confident cool character she had hoped she would appear to be, capable of wooing Jess into being her new friend.

"What other than this do you enjoy?"

Louisa felt the question was a bit unimaginative, seeing as it was the exact same one she had just been asked.

"Ah yes."

Jess raised her free hand to her chin, beginning to stroke an imagined beard.

"I should have thought when I asked you that I would need an answer myself."

Louisa wondered how Jess was so open, so confident to just say things out loud like that. To admit what she was thinking so easily, as though it didn't bother her at all.

"How can that be?"

"So, we've covered films, and books…"

Jess continued stroking her air beard whilst accompanying it with a thoughtful frown.

"Well… I like crafts… but don't laugh… I can't really do it the way I would like. I mean… yeah."

It was the first time Jess had looked like she lacked confidence in something. It triggered an empathy in Louisa that took her by surprise.

"Oh there's lots of things I'm not very good at, I'm sure you're great really!"

The sentence popped out of nowhere, the second surprise for Louisa in such a short space of time. Not for the first time, she had a slight internal panic over whether she had said the right thing or gone massively wrong.

"Aww that's so sweet!"

Jess laughed. Her air beard disappeared as she moved her hand to stroke Louisa's arm.

"But I am really quite shite."

Louisa felt a warmth and calm spread through her, as Jess's now trademark smile combined with her touch on her arm soothed away all of her panic. She was content to stay like this for as long as she was able, only the slight worry that surely she was the one who was supposed to be doing the comforting threatening to ruin it all.

"See, I read the websites, watch the how too guides online, and I think yes… I can do this!"

Jess's hand moved away, returning to wafting gesticulation to heighten the drama of the story.

"I plan what I'm going to do, plan my trip to the craft shop… there's quite a good one by the way just down by… oh that's not important right now… yeah… oh yeah! So… I plan my trip, get all the bits and pieces, get back here, get everything set up, and then…"

Jess stopped. For a moment she stood completely still. Louisa found it a little unnerving, as she seemed so animated all of the time.

"Well…"

Jess started to look uncomfortable. Louisa was just about to jump in with something calming and reassuring as soon as she could think of such a thing when Jess's animation returned in an explosion of self deprecation.

"Rubbish! For tonight, right, I had it all planned. I was going to do these beautiful handmade invitations. Send them out to everyone like it was an oldschool formal dance or something."

"Ooo that sounds cool."

Louisa couldn't help it, she spoke before she had thought it through. Immediately the feelings of *"Oh crap what did I say, why did I say that, I'm such an idiot!"* flowed over her like a bucket of liquid regret.

"I know right?"

Jess seemed unoffended, continuing her story undeterred.

"So I'm sat at the table, music on, crafting away, making my invitations. Doing the pictures, adding the bows, putting on some glitter, in my head I'm thinking 'Yeah these are amazing! Everyone is going to be super impressed and I will become an awesome legend amongst all of my peers!' But..."

Jess shifted in place a few times, as though weighing up her next sentence.

"I got up to get a drink, all blissful. Walk back to the table to admire my work… and then it hits me."

"What? Had something gone wrong?"

Louisa was feeling some genuine concern for the outcome of this story. Jess was so lively and happy, she didn't want anything to go badly for her. She was a bit surprised how drawn in she was to everything Jess had to say.

"You could say that, well not so much wrong as... well..."

Scratching her head to try and think of the correct way to describe the whole thing, Jess winced a little as she explained.

"OK, so I looked at the table and it hit me. These look like the work of a seven year old. A seven year old who was trying to do what the adults do on a rainy Saturday afternoon."

Louisa wasn't sure whether to hug Jess or laugh. Again, Jess saved the conversation. A warm giggle sneaked out as Jess began to laugh.

"I mean, literally a child could have made these. And I was mortified. I had watched the videos, got all the right stuff, planned it all out, but... yep. No good at actually making anything. Plus, I was covered in glitter. The invites were not."

Louisa smiled. The candle light dancing around on the walls seemed to be a visible representation of Jess's mood, bouncy, happy, never still. All over the room, all at once. Louisa felt at ease talking with Jess, it was weird. She had been so nervous about coming here, and she felt so out of place when she had arrived. She had stayed in her own little bubble even when she was here, as though instead of coming outside of her comfort zone, she had brought a part of it with her. All the other people here didn't really seem real, she felt like she was watching them on her TV, still sat on her sofa in the safe world of her flat.

As she continued to answer as best she could to Jess's surge of small talk, she realised that she still didn't feel like she belonged in this party, the sense of ease and warmth she was getting from Jess's smile laden conversation had not pulled her out of her comfort bubble, it had just extended it to include Jess too. She wanted the rest of the world to fade away, nothing existing outside of the dancing candle bubble.

8

The year after Sam had left university had not been a fun experience. His qualifications neither prepared him for the wider world, nor granted him a high paying job with all the trappings of such. He had, in fact, moved back to his home town in much the same way as the majority of his friends had moved back to theirs. This left Sam pretty much on his own again, and unsure quite what to do. He had found another short course to go on, after all that's how Sam had been trained by school and university – the answer to everything must lie in a course. This had satisfied the career centre at his old university, as now he was enrolled in another course he ticked their box of graduate employability, and they were no longer interested in helping him. This course had not helped him either, and after a lot of soul searching about how unhelpful everything he had spent his life doing was proving to be, and what felt like a world record of job applications, he had managed to find an acceptable job, alongside people that had not bothered to go to university in the first place.

Still, it paid the bills. Where he had really struggled though, was in finding new friends. Without the common ground questions of 'what course are you studying?' or 'hey what do you think about that lecturer?' Sam was lost in how to go about getting anywhere with strangers anymore. And the more time passed, the more ridiculous it seemed to try and reference his university life. Always the determined type, and the self-reliant type, and the overthinking type, he had decided that he must learn everything about friendship and small talk. After all, the answer to everything must be in a course, and if there weren't any more to go on, he would just do it himself. This would provide him with all the answers he needed. It had in fact done nothing of the sort, but it had sparked an entirely unexpected outcome.

Sam had studied psychology, relatively well, and this had

now developed into a fascination for figuring out what made people tick, and how to figure them out. His quest to understand friendship led to an unearthing of material designed to understand social interaction. A large proportion of this seemed to be centred around dating. A curious sort, this had triggered his interest. After all, making friends was surely the first part of dating anyway, so it would all be relevant, he thought. He had started learning all about body language, tricks and tips about flirting, how to read signals, all the self help sites he could find. It had become a fascination for him. He found that almost all of the material quickly left behind the simple question of 'how do I make friends?' Soon he had completely lost interest in the supposed end goal of meeting some new friends. He was immersed in the bizarre world of crazy advice he had discovered – tips and tricks that promised the earth but were so bizarrely cold in their nature. Tips for women centred around how to find the love of your life, tips for men centred around how to have sex with whatever women you wanted, and how ever many you wanted. It was an abyss of horror that both disgusted Sam and intrigued him… like a noise emanating from a supposed empty room on a dark night… you should probably call the police… just after you took a quick look…

Sam found he wasn't interested in the dating tips. They were mostly rubbish, centred around acting to be something you weren't. That was not what he wanted to do at all. He just wanted to know how to make friends with people. He focused on the parts he thought would help him, the body language in particular, and ignored everything else. When he tried to put it into practice, he discovered two things. Firstly, some of the body language tips were true, he could begin to see when people were comfortable in a situation, or uncomfortable, bored, happy… although he wasn't always right. Secondly, whenever he was involved in the conversation or situation, his skills of applying what he had learned fell to pieces. He was never sure if he was reading a situation correctly when he was involved in it.

All of his knowledge and lacklustre insight was telling him that the conversation on the rug was not going well. The girl who was stood there looked unbelievably uncomfortable, and Sam couldn't help his curiosity. He wanted to see for himself exactly what was going on there. He began to move across to the group, searching for a good opening line that would break him in to the awkwardness of the conversation.

9

"Well everyone likes to relax, don't they?"

Maddie was slightly baffled by the question, but she couldn't see any way out of this conversation, so she had decided to just go with it for now and let him talk.

"Oh Yes, there's nothing like relaxing by the beach in Rio, it cleanses the soul…"

The greasy man looked off into the middle distance, as if remembering a fond memory.

"Have you been?"

And without pausing to find out:

"Oh Maddie you should… I shall let you know next time I'm thinking of going."

"Err…"

Maddie couldn't quite work out what had happened, had the greasy man just invited her on holiday? She took a nervous swig from her bottle of beer. It was as unpleasant as this entire experience.

"You're no one if you haven't travelled."

The greasy man continued his monologue. His eyes returning from the middle distance to their previous home in the vicinity of Maddie's chest. She was pretty sure she had answered a previous question about travel stating that she hadn't really been to many places. Had he forgotten? Not been listening? Or was he now trying to make out that because she hadn't she was a lesser person than him?

"But that's ok because someone like you is always welcome to travel with me."

The greasy man smiled and took a swig from his drink. His silent friend giggled as he also took a healthy gulp of beer.

Maddie's mind swirled with a confusion of *"did he just… really did he mean… how dare he… what just happened…"*

"Hello is this France?"

Maddie, the greasy man and his silent friend all turned to look at the man who seemingly appeared from nowhere to stand beside them, a quizzical expression on his face.

"Sorry wh..."

The greasy man seemed simultaneously confused, and very annoyed.

"France? No? sooner or later. I'm Sam, how's you?"

"Hi, I'm Maddie nice to meet you."

Although similarly confused, and still blurry from the awful suggestive conversation with the greasy man, Maddie was very relieved to have someone else to talk to. She shifted her stance away from the greasy man and angled towards this new face.

"I'm Dean, I was just discussing places to relax with Maddie."

The greasy man's name revealed to all parties from an annoyed looking face.

"Oh Dean… that was it"

It was all Maddie could do to not say it out loud. Dean seemed flustered, and very concerned with how she had turned away from him. She didn't remember him discussing relaxing with her and didn't really like how forward it sounded spelled out like that. He was visibly shifting now himself, trying to re-align his body with hers, which was not really possible thanks to her continuing to turn away.

Sam's mind was racing now; he was like a child that had just discovered a new toy shop. Or, in fairness, if he had just now discovered a new toy shop. *"Ok… broke into the conversation with a random sentence that stopped them in their tracks, she doesn't seem to mind, in fact she looks relived, him on the other hand…"* Sam never intended any harm when he decided to mess with people like this, he just wanted to see if he was right and he had found someone that was trying just that bit too hard… and try to make the situation a bit more level.

"Places to relax? Hmm like a sofa? By the fire? …bed? He's

smooth isn't he, your fella."

Sam shot a playful glance at Maddie before settling his gaze back on Dean, who was staring back open mouthed as if Sam had just told him his dog had exploded in a freak toaster accident.

"Oh he's not my fella."

Maddie tapped Sam on the arm as she spoke, a little too quick and dismissive for Dean's liking. Sam was pleased that he had given Maddie an opportunity to state out loud that she wasn't with or intended to be with Dean, and have it witnessed by others in case he wasn't listening when she said it to him directly. He hoped that would help take away some of the uncomfortableness.

"I was just saying I'd been to Rio and it was nice and…"

Dean's eyes were darting between Sam and Maddie; he was part panicked that he had lost his carefully worked out line about relaxing leading to intimacy and part furious that this new fellow had stolen Maddie's attention. His silent friend took another gulp of beer, without losing eye contact with Maddie's chest.

"Oh sorry, I thought… Ah well never mind. I've seen Rio on the TV. It looks… beachy."

Sam looked at the three people he occupied this slightly scruffy rug with. Maddie was smartly dressed and heavily made up. She still seemed uncomfortable in the situation, eyes switching between Sam, her beer, and something over Sam's shoulder… perhaps the door. Dean was awkwardly shifting his weight from one foot to the other, whilst opening and closing his mouth as though he was about to say something but kept changing his mind. He was dressed as though he had walked out of a photograph from the eighteen hundreds, pausing only to put all the product in the world into his hair and beard. He currently looked like a fish trying to look dapper after falling out of its bowl. His silent friend was more casually dressed, perhaps even sloppily. He seemed transfixed by Maddie, as though he hadn't seen a real human woman before. Sam felt that was an exaggeration, his perception of the conversation colouring his impression. This Dean was not a super villain, and this silent man was not his sinister sidekick. They were probably just trying too hard and making fools of themselves. Maybe if the silent guy would stop starring at Maddie's body, Sam would have an easier time convincing himself of this rational argument rather than jump to the easier conclusion.

"So... Sam..."

Dean had mostly gathered himself, although he still looked a bit wobbly and off his game plan.

"What is it that you do for a living?"

Sam thought for a second. On the one hand, he wasn't happy in his job. He knew that most people would say they weren't either, but that didn't help his feelings about his own employment. He was also painfully aware that he didn't earn anything like the amount his teachers and employment counsellors had suggested someone with his qualifications could expect to earn. It had turned out that a large part of the workforce had similar qualifications, and the well paying jobs always seemed to go to people who just happened to have family or friends already working there. It was all such a coincidence.

Sam didn't really care about money, he had just wanted to work somewhere interesting that used his knowledge and skills. He had the not enough money to care about covered, now all he needed was a job that was interesting and used his skills and knowledge. Looking again at Dean though, with his overly slick outfit and hair, he could certainly tell that he *did* care. Quite a lot. And he clearly either earned a lot or spent a lot to look like that. Sam was aware that this question was probably a trap. He liked to dress smart yet casual, but always ended up a little scruffy nonetheless. His hair always looked amazing until he opened his front door, at which point placing a bird's nest on his head would probably be an improvement. He knew he had annoyed Dean and thrown him off his chat up of Maddie. He was pretty sure Dean would try to and regain some male dominance by pointing out how much more money he made than Sam, supposedly so that Maddie would see he was the bigger man, and Sam would be put back into his lowly place.

"Oh now let's not talk about work, it's the weekend! We don't have to think of such horrors!"

Sam tried to divert the topic.

"Are you all enjoying this evening? Had a chance to speak to Jess and Steven? Nice place, isn't it?"

"Yeah it's quite a nice flat."

Maddie seemed happy enough to change topic to something more small talky.

"I had a quick chat with Jess when I got here, she seems to be running around quite a lot, Steven is holding court on the sofa and looks in his element."

Sam followed Maddie's nod towards the sofa, and saw Steven, bottle of wine in hand, serious look on face, talking to a man and woman Sam didn't recognise. It was quite probable that Steven was trying to have an overly serious conversation as normal. Maybe he had found the right audience, Sam hoped so. Steven was a great guy, very smart, very concerned for the world. Very bad at spotting when other people didn't want to talk about world concerns.

"It's a nice starter flat, or place to stop over in the city."

Dean was clearly still trying to make himself sound important. He was in fact beginning to sound more and more like an idiot.

"Dude you're trying a bit too hard..."

Sam had to stop and think if he had said that out loud. He didn't think so.

Maddie seemed more relaxed now, more at ease.

"I love the building, the history. I think it suits them, modern flat for Jess, old historic building for Steven."

"Hey that's interesting, I had not thought of it that way!"

Sam was quite excited by Maddie's observation. It seemed a really obvious parallel, right in line with Sam's way of thinking.

"I will ask them later if they did that on purpose. And then mock them."

Maddie giggled.

The conversation continued with shallow small talk and easy jokes. Sam felt that he had helped settle the awkwardness he had seen when he entered the party, equalled the field a little bit by being a nonthreatening presence. At least that's what he hoped. Dean still seemed frustrated by Sam's presence, but after a few more thinly veiled attempts, he had run out of lines from his playbook.

"Maddie, can I get you another drink?"

Dean's question appeared gentlemanly, and Sam wondered if he had maybe misjudged his conversation to be solely based on hitting on Maddie.

"There's quite a good selection if you would like to come and have a look?"

Dean beckoned Maddie to accompany him to the kitchen end of the room. Sam felt his hope for misjudgement may have been premature, as Dean seemed to be aiming to move Maddie away from Sam and back into his own company. He had not offered to get Sam a drink, or indeed his own friend, whom he had never introduced, who had kept quite quiet for the whole conversation.

"Thanks, maybe in a minute, just have to go to the girl's room."

Maddie dodged the invitation, nodded, and turned back towards the hallway and the series of fake wood doors.

Sam turned and nodded back, too late to be seen. Rotating on his heel he started to turn back towards Dean, a move he thought might make him look cool and smooth.

"Actually I don't have a drink so I…"

Dean and friend had already started walking away.

"Yeah… ok then."

Sam stood for a second. Alone on the rug. On one hand, he was now the king of this rug. On the other hand, his kingdom was empty.

"Better to be king of an empty land than a peasant in a full one."

Sam spoke softly to his empty dominion. He already didn't like the phrase, it seemed to be the opposite of what he felt was the right way to be. He didn't like the idea of kings, peasants, superiority and inequality. He was much happier if everyone was on the same level. However, it was tricky to be equal when there was no one around. Sam was in no way overthinking the situation.

Glancing around, the room seemed smaller than when Sam had arrived. The other people here still seemed to be happily chatting away. The candlelight still danced around, perhaps a little softer now, as if the shadows were a little less full of energy than at the start of the evening.

"Well, I still don't have a drink I suppose."

It was the last address as monarch of the rug kingdom, as Sam turned and headed over to the kitchen area to explore what delights Jess and Steven had on offer.

10

Booze. Booze, tall booze, small booze, fancy bottles, nice shapes. Good colours. Sam's fingers searched for something un boozed. He hadn't drunk anything alcoholic since the second year of university. It wasn't for any special reason, no cause, no drama. He just didn't really like it. He felt he had enough trouble understanding what was going on around and within him without adding an extra layer of haze on the top. It did, however, make finding something to drink in situations like this challenging.

Luckily, Jess and Steven knew him well. There was a bottle of lemonade sat between a tall thin booze and a wide thick glassed booze. Sam quickly claimed this as his very own, reaching for a glass from the sideboard to house his treasure. As he finished pouring his sugary fruit, movement in the corner of his field of view induced a flash of distraction, a rush of interest as his eyes darted to focus on the cause. Sam had been enjoying his drink quest, it was a chance to catch his breath on his own for a few minutes, before re-entering the complex world of talking to people he didn't know. He wondered what had pulled him out of his solitary realm.

A new person had entered the party, walking quickly and confidently through the room, heading straight for Jess. Sam watched as Jess's eyes lit up as she saw this new woman heading for her. Each step was mesmerizing, pulling Sam's eyes across the room, urging him to follow, demanding that he move along with her. After a few of her steps he was completely taken up by her, everything else faded away to nothing, a vacuum of space in which he had been floating without purpose until he caught a glimpse at the only star... burning with a brilliance he could feel in every atom of his being.

Sam caught himself, felt himself breathe. He couldn't quite believe the strength of the reaction he had felt. It seemed so cheesy.

Almost pathetic. His knees had gone a little weak, like a bad song, or narration worthy only of a bad film noir. He had only ever felt this way once before, a long time ago. This woman, she had an energy to her motion that Sam found stunning. She now stood with Jess, flicking her hair as she waved her hands in conversation, smiling and wide eyed. Sam had to meet her. But how could he? He frantically searched for something to say, something he could use to start a conversation with this unbelievable woman. He took a step, then froze, and took a step back.

"Crap!"

Sam hoped he had not shouted out loud, angry at his own indecision on what to do.

"Crap!"

Sam wasn't making much progress. He decided he needed to wait for the right moment to go over. Let Jess talk to her, and then when their conversation seemed to settle, he could go and join. Or was that just an excuse to wait for a few more minutes? He began to feel like he might mess this up, say something stupid, not make a good impression. Well, he was going to say something stupid, that was everything that he said all of the time. He was losing his nerve, the voice inside his head was telling him that he wasn't really good enough to talk to someone like this, someone so mesmerizing.

"Crap!"

Sam realised he was now just awkwardly standing across the room watching her talk to Jess, and if she turned around and saw him he would seem super creepy. He felt he should have gone straight over, that he had already ruined everything by making the wrong choice on how to handle this.

"Oh Crap!"

Sam watched in a panic as Dean and his sidekick slid up and joined Jess and the new woman. Dean was smiling too much and bowing. He did not seem to have hesitated. Sam watched in horror as Dean clasped the hand of the woman and introduced himself. Sam felt he had hesitated too much, and it had cost him. The thought of Dean trying the weird pick up lines on her that he was trying with Maddie, the thought that now when Sam wandered over he would be the third guy to appear and say hello, the situation was getting uncool. Sam was getting overwhelmed inside his head.

That was it, if he was going to do something, it had to be now, before too much time passed. He had to get across that he really wanted to meet her, before it became ridiculous, and before anything else went wrong. Too nervous to take a deep breath, Sam wheezed shallowly and started moving towards the group.

It might have taken one hundred years for Sam to cross the floor. Every conceivable outcome flew through his mind, an angry swarm of wasps, each one buzzing a new variation of failure, a storm of anxiety as he battled his way, foot by foot.

"Hi, how are things over here?"

Sam tried a light-hearted question to announce his arrival. Everyone seemed to stop and look at him, forever. He began to panic.

"Oh no that's gone really wrong…"

Sam's inner voice was unimpressed with the behaviour of his outer voice. Now everything was totally ruined forever.

"Hey there Mr Sam, having a good time I hope?"

Jess's melodic tone rescued Sam from a bad situation. Not for the first time. Probably also not the last time.

"Hi yes, all good thanks."

It was not Sam's best conversation so far. He was angry at himself for not being as chatty as he had been not so long ago, but mostly just a little bit in awe of being this close to this new woman. She was even more breathtaking in this proximity. It was making his mind bendy.

"This is Ellie, Ellie this is Sam."

Jess pointed at Sam and the stunning woman in turn.

"Hi."

It was all Sam could muster. He felt like he needed a school book to doodle in, or a tree to carve.

"Hey."

Ellie's voice resonated in Sam's ears. She turned back and continued talking to Jess, Sam must have arrived mid conversation.

Ellie was answering Jess, but Sam couldn't hear any of the words. He was lost in her motion, her hands circling, her hair swaying, her eyes widening, he was transfixed by her dance. She glanced at him and for a brief second, he saw right into her, and he felt like she saw right into him. Her eyes darted away quickly, and Sam felt a tug of loss emanate from deep inside of him. He wanted her to look at him again, and perhaps never look away. He tried to catch himself, take a time out. He was drifting into the territory of a teenage crush, an unrealistic place that would do him no favours. He tried to regain some sense of perspective. It had been quite a while since he had felt anything for a girl, and a very long time since he had felt such an instant attraction. But that was no reason to lose himself to the realm of bad poetry and dancing fluffy animals. Time to focus. Time to be normal. Well, time to act normal.

"Pay Attention!"

Sam instructed himself. He brought himself back into the world, the sights and sounds returning slowly to focus. Small talk. He asked her simple questions, she answered, she asked him similar things, he answered. Nothing too dramatic, nothing too adventurous. Two people who had just met checking for common ground. Sam felt this was a much more sensible adult approach than swooning from a distance. Dean was still trying his best to steer the conversation towards his own glory, Jess was mocking everyone. Ellie was… difficult to read. She would speak to Jess with enthusiastic motions, showing friendship and comfort. She would speak to Dean with short non-committal statements, perhaps dismissively. When she spoke to Sam, he couldn't tell very much.

Sometimes when she spoke to him, she had a half smile, and glistening eyes. Other times, her face seemed blank, her answers short. Was she flirting? Was she just being polite? Did it depend on the question? Sam's knowledge of body language always seemed to fail him when he needed it most. He knew all too well that trying to infer things solely from someone's body language was a bad plan, as some people just thought differently to how they seemed to read. Was this one of those times? Sam tried to be a bit flirty, but he knew he was rubbish at it. He was also aware that Dean was also being flirty, making him feel that Ellie was being attacked on two fronts. He thought he should back off a bit, try and concentrate on being interesting enough to be friend material, and let everything else fall wherever it must. The thought of not trying tugged at him deep inside. He didn't know what to do.

"Calm down."

The internal battle between the rational Sam, who just wanted to enjoy being here, in this moment, talking with the most beautiful girl, and the emotional Sam, who just wanted to blurt out how amazing he thought she was, and how she should be his girlfriend forever and that they should go on adventures together, stormed inside every fibre. He didn't know quite what to say, quite how to stand, quite what to do. Any slip of the tongue or angular lean could ruin everything. A well placed phrase may be the key to never ending bliss. It was too much pressure. He realised he had started to drift out of the conversation again, he needed to listen to what was being said more closely. Respond more thoughtfully.

Jess was giggling whilst apologising for leaving. She had seen someone with no one to talk to and felt that she should not let that happen at her party. The others were understanding and supportive as she started to walk away. This was an opportunity to refocus the conversation, an opportunity for Sam to try and make a lasting impression.

"What do you think Sam?"

Ellie twirled the ends of her hair in her fingers as she waited for the response.

"Erm… Yes, but sometimes no…"

Sam had no idea what the question was.

Ellie's laughter, at first disconcerting, became warm and charming.

"Good answer! All bases covered!"

She smiled as she spoke.

"I think the two of us will get on fine."

Sam felt a flush of warmth. She could have meant many things with that statement, to Sam, it meant everything. She seemed to glow. He couldn't tell if it was the soft candlelight bouncing around the room, or if it was just her, or maybe his eyes were tricking him into seeing things that were not really there at all.

A sharp forced cough demanded both of their attention. Dean took a sip from his beer, and as he lowered his bottle his eyes drank in Ellie's form. Sam watched as he looked her fully up and down before asking her chest a question.

"I like your top; looks like a corset with a bow… it really suits you. Stunning. I have to ask though, what happens if someone pulls the bow? Does it fall open?"

His eyes returned to Ellie's face, in time to see her slightly startled expression form.

"No, it doesn't… the bow is just decorative…"

She turned to Sam, showing Dean her back.

"I've got a top with a zip down the front, but this sleaze will never see it!"

She spoke in a hushed whisper, touching Sam's arm.

"Walk me away from this guy, let him get the message that I won't ever be needing to speak to him again."

Sam's heart skipped. Did she mean she had him now, and only he could see the zip based top? Or was she just commenting on things and using him as a shield to escape this horrible conversation? He nodded goodbye at Dean, not really sure whether to yell at him for being so sleazy, say something polite but firm, getting across the message that Ellie was done with the conversation, or say something to suggest he and Ellie were together and his advances were in vain. The nod was all he could muster, as Ellie began to move away, still holding his arm. He had no choice but to turn away from Dean and walk with her. Still confused as to what it all meant, he was at least deeply happy that his lack of choice had resulted in her touch and them walking away from everyone else in the room.

"Oh my god thank you for getting me away from there, that guy… wow… how can that be real? How can he think that's ok to be like that?"

Ellie was staring wide eyed at the floor as she walked Sam across the flat.

"Yeah… I don't know?"

Sam was still confused as to his role in this, he had been trying to get Ellie's attention to himself for some time, and now he had it, he had no idea what to do next. He was also feeling rather hot under the collar with her being so close to him. He could see the bow on her top bounce as they walked, and it was making him a little uncomfortable. He wanted Ellie to be this close. He wanted to feel her hand on his arm. He wanted to be closer. He knew It was a thin line between him and Dean. He wanted to get across to her that he was not like Dean, that he didn't treat women like objects, but his mind was blurred by her intoxicating closeness, and he was scared of the line. A line too horrifying to cross.

"Guys, right?"

Sam wanted to say how beautiful he thought she was, how he would like to spend as much time as possible with her, how he would do anything to keep her hand on his arm. His brain spun into a panic of possible outcomes from saying those things out loud. All he could imagine was Ellie's horror at him for thinking he was just like Dean, thinking all men were just sleazy chancers out to use up women for their own enjoyment. How utterly horrific would it sound if he responded to her with:

"Yeah, he was sleazy wasn't he? Anyway, do you want to go on a date? You're really amazing... and can you wear the top with the zip that you mentioned? That would be great."

The room ran out. The moment passed as quickly as it had appeared. As they reached the window at the opposite end of the flat, Ellie's hand left Sam's arm, falling onto the window ledge as she leaned towards the glass.

"What a strange evening."

The window fogged slightly as she spoke, causing the sharp lights from the street to turn to a soft focus.

"I couldn't agree more."

Sam was still in a slight panic about the whole situation. Every time he felt the evening was going in a direction he wasn't expecting, a whole new unexpected direction would show up. He felt that if he was better at talking to people he would be better able to, well, talk to Ellie. It wasn't as complex a revelation as he thought it should be, which he didn't expect.

"Jess said I should come along and meet some new people, that I would enjoy it."

Ellie turned and gazed at Sam.

"I've certainly met some characters."

"Have you enjoyed it? Hopefully not all the characters have been bad?"

Sam glanced back across the room at Dean, who seemed to be trying to talk to another woman. It dawned on him that he might be one of the characters Ellie might be referring to, and his panic intensified. Was that good? Was that bad? He felt his body tense at his inability to quite get what Ellie was saying, not sure if she was sending out mixed messages and vagueness on purpose, or if it was just him trying to hear what he wanted her to say, overthinking the whole situation, trying to bend the conversation into the flirty, romantic, wistful encounter he wished it would become.

"I'm not sure yet, think it will take some time to process it all."

Ellie turned back to the window, lost in the distance.

Sam wasn't quite sure how to take the comment. Was he supposed to agree, or apologise and walk away… he felt frozen in the headlights of an oncoming truck of expected conversational response. Still unsure if she wanted to be chatting to him, or if he was just a tool to escape the previous conversation, he felt like his response could dictate which path this situation could take. He had no idea what to say.

"That's fair."

All he could muster.

Ellie smiled and laughed, placing her hand back on Sam's arm.

"You're so sweet, I feel safe with you."

Sam smiled, all at once lost in Ellie. The rest of the room began to fade away, never existing at all. It had always just been the two of them. Safe.

"Wait... safe?"

Sam's mind suddenly began to race again, his thoughts running away in every direction all at once.

"Safe as in 'I feel safe with you, we should always be together because of the safeness lets date and be married in safety from the rest of the world' or *'I feel safe with you, because you would never try and hit on me like other guys do, like Dean just did, there will never be anything between us and it makes me feel safe knowing that.'"*

Not for the first time in this conversation, Sam felt the pressure of a potential life changing moment – a door to parallel worlds opening – one world with a life full of this amazing new person, and the other full of regret and confusion, with no amazing new person. He knew which world he wanted to inhabit, but which one was he in?

11

"How unfair for a fine lady such as yourself to find yourself in this situation."

Louisa found herself pulled back from her thoughts and into the room.

"Sorry…"

She looked at the two guys who had seemingly appeared from nowhere to stand in front of her. One slickly bearded, one… kinda just there.

"Do you mean it's unfair that you've come over and disturbed me from what I was thinking about? Seems like you're being a bit hard on yourself."

Dean seemed a bit confused.

"Erm no… I mean it's unfair for you to be stood alone with no one to talk to."

"Oh."

Louisa shook her head and took a sip from her wine.

"No I like my own company, know who I'm dealing with, it's fine."

Dean seemed a little flustered. Louisa did not notice.

"Well anyway, I'm Dean, and I'm enchanted to make your acquaintance."

Dean took a slight bow.

"Do people still talk like that? Well I guess you just did so I answered my own question. Yay me!"

Louisa did not bow.

"Well, I think that gentlemen should speak in a manner that suits the occasion and shows the proper respect to ladies."

Dean straightened his waistcoat and seemed to pose as though he was having his picture taken.

"Hmm."

Louisa contemplated the comment. And looked at the pose.

"I think people should speak to everyone they meet the same way, and there should be no difference between how you talk to genders, because that implies there is a difference between the genders that needs to be addressed, and also suggests that there's a part of a person's personality that changes depending on who they are talking to, and I find that unsettling and a bit like lying. Also, is your back ok? You seem to be standing funny."

"No I…"

Dean slumped a little, his eyes darting, searching for something he clearly couldn't find. After a few seconds he gathered himself and shifted to a more relaxed stance.

"That's cool, I get where you're coming from. You're pretty *and* clever, the total package."

Louisa tilted her head slightly to the side, not quite sure how to respond to that.

"What do you like to do for fun? Do you like to travel?"

Dean looked down at his beer, and as he raised the bottle for a drink, his eyes travelled the length of Louisa's body.

Louisa felt a little gross as his eyes dragged across her, a situation she had never quite gotten used too, although it seemed to happen an awful lot. She was not really enjoying this conversation. It was confusing and weird to her. Hadn't this guy seen she was fine by herself? Why had he come over and interrupted her, she was having a nice time thinking about her earlier conversation, sipping on her wine. Oh well, she thought it would be rude to just stop talking.

"Yeah travelling can be quite interesting, although I haven't been anywhere particular for ages. It seems to have become this thing that you should do, rather than a thing that's just nice to do."

"Oh, it broadens the mind, the soul!"

Dean seemed to be quite keen.

"It lets you have an experience that you would never have at home, lets you be more passionate and alive!"

Dean really did seem quite keen.

"Well, wherever you go, you take yourself with you. So, if you are 'passionate and alive' when you travel you should be that when you're at home too? Shouldn't you? It's not like you change into someone else because you're away from home?"

Louisa didn't understand what Dean was trying to say.

"Well, it depends who you go with, and what you get up too."

Dean displayed a smile which Louisa felt was supposed to convey some kind of message that she just didn't understand. She decided to ignore it.

"Well the last few times I went somewhere I went on my own to see things that I found interesting so I'm not sure…"

Louisa's spoken out loud train of thought was interrupted by an over keen Dean.

"Well that's where you're going wrong my dear, you need company!"

Dean's eyes had lit up like car headlights, he spoke with the enthusiasm of a dog that had just found something to chase.

"I often travel the world, you are more than welcome to accompany me! The sights we will see! The things we will do! The places I can show you!"

"That's ok I don't…"

Louisa's voice was not relevant enough to stop Dean's monologue.

"For instance, I know this wonderful little bistro in Madrid, not for tourists… the real thing, off the beaten track, rustic, real people, real locally sourced food. It's beautiful. I will take you there, and we can have a real authentic meal followed by wine and dancing, and the best hotel, of course."

"They saw you coming, didn't they!?"

Dean looked stunned, it was not the response he was expecting in any way. Louisa watched his face turn from a look of excited pride to a confused mess. She continued to watch him get more uncomfortable as she spoke.

"If I was going to do a tourist trap restaurant, you know, to get maximum money from people who wouldn't normally spend money in that way, I would take a standard establishment, make sure I picked one that was a little out of the way… Far enough that people would think it wasn't on the tourist strip but not too far that people wouldn't find it, fake it to make it look a bit run down, offer some different sounding things… You know, the same food as everywhere else, but with different names so it seems more exotic. Find out what buzz words cashed up tourists liked, like 'rustic,' 'local,' then charge a bit more for the 'real experience' and call it *authentic*."

Dean's jaw was flapping again. Bearded fish.

"I mean…"

Louisa continued whilst wafting her hand around the flat.

"Look at this place, it's nice, isn't it? Wood floor, exposed brick, stone walls - do you think this is authentic? It would have been a crap factory if it had all of these stone walls in it when it was first built… huge factory, walled up into little flat sized rooms… segmenting it up, where would the machinery go?"

Dean stood.

"What do you think?"

Louisa turned her question to the guy who had wandered up with Dean, who had not said anything at all, just was also there.

"It is a nice flat yeah."

It was Louisa's turn to be thrown, that was not a response relevant to the question.

"No I mean… oh never mind. Are you having a nice evening? You seem quiet, are you ok?"

Louisa was a bit concerned that this guy had been here the whole time and hadn't said anything, she didn't want him to feel left out.

"Yeah it's nice."

The man looked around at the flat, and then took a swig from his beer without further comment.

"Ok… Are you enjoying your beer?"

"Yeah."

"...good."

Louisa had tried. This guy seemed to either not want to speak to her, or not realise he should say more words in order to have a conversation with someone. Either way, she had run out of enthusiasm for trying to include him. She looked back at Dean, who had an expression she couldn't quite understand. It might be frustration or confusion, or stomach ache. She wasn't very good at reading people. He was quiet too, he did not seem to have anything to add to her observations on modern culture. She was a bit disappointed, she felt the conversation was just getting interesting. Maybe they both wanted to have some quiet time to think about it first. Louisa was happy with that, she could go back to thinking about stuff too. She pulled out her phone to check how much thinking time she had left before she needed to think about going home.

12

"Hey Sam, you and Ellie seemed to be getting on."

Jess had appeared seemingly out of nowhere. Sam was stood, confused and slightly shocked. What had happened? Just as quickly as Ellie had appeared in his life, she had vanished. He felt like he had been hit by lightning. He still had no real idea how the encounter had gone. Surely it wasn't just him that felt the electricity, she must have felt it. Had she? He had nothing but questions dancing through his mind, riding the remnants of the sparks through his body.

"She said she had to go, somewhere else she had said she would drop in."

Sam wasn't even sure if he was making sense. The world was upside down and he was floating somewhere outside of it all.

"Ah yes, she did say she was only going to drop in for a bit I think, well it was nice of her to come and see the place."

Jess smiled as she spoke. Sam had no idea how to respond. Small talk had dissolved, he wanted to take Jess by the hands and shout *"did you see her! She was so amazing!"* He wasn't sure if that was the most grown up course of action. Just as he felt he really needed to say something sensible Jess turned away, her attention taken by someone approaching. This was good. This gave Sam some time to recover. A whirlwind had flown through, turned everything upside down and disappeared just as quickly and unexpectedly as it had arrived. Sam stood, trying to make sense of it all, put all the knocked over objects back in the right places in his mind. He was still spinning when Jess's voice brought his attention back from the news reporter in his head covering the wake of hurricane Ellie.

"Hey you."

Jess spoke with a melodic charm as she beamed a smile at Steven. He walked straight to her, a distant look had laid claim to his usually thoughtful face.

"Are you ok? You look like you've seen a ghost."

"No… kind of, in a way."

Steven lowered his eyes to the floor, his voice seemed even more down than his gaze.

"I was talking to… Jake, is it? And Kim I think. They don't like me."

"I'm sure that's not…"

Jess's sentence fell away as Steven continued:

"Oh Jess, I don't want to be like this, I don't want people to hate me."

Steven looked like a puppy that had its favourite toy ball waved in front of him and then thrown off a cliff.

"I thought I was being clever and witty, smart and charming, and then they started making fun of me and saying horrible things."

Jess placed her hand on Steven's arm, attempting to hold his mental state in place as his mind was tumbling down the cliff after his favourite toy ball.

"I'm sure it's not what they meant, did you misunderstand?"

"It started when I asked them a question and he said *I'm sorry I can't find the effort to care."*

Steven looked mournfully at the floor, through the floor, into a darkened subterranean pit. His ball was lost.

"Oh honey I'm sorry."

Jess embraced Steven, kissing him on the cheek.

"That's no way to speak to someone. Especially when you're a guest in their home."

"Chap, that's rough."

Sam didn't know what to say, but as the scene in front of him was getting more personal and upsetting, he felt he needed to say something, to both reassure his friend and remind them both he was still there. He felt uncomfortable and wasn't sure if he should also hug Steven or walk away. He felt walking away was the right thing to do, to let Jess comfort properly, but it seemed callous to hear Steven say he was upset and then immediately walk off to talk to someone else.

"They laughed at me, at what I was saying, who I was. It felt like…"

Steven seemed to be quite disturbed by the events. Sam felt there was maybe more to this than rude idiots who didn't show courtesy to the co-owner of the home they were in.

"For a moment, I thought about what they were saying."

Steven raised his head and mournfully looked back towards the sofa, where Jake and Kim seemed to be touching and laughing more than was appropriate in a public place.

"It felt like I used to feel, when my dad was embarrassing me in front of my friends, trying to be superior, trying to be the big man, trying to show he was better than everyone else there."

"Jake is an idiot. Full on dickpenis. Don't ever listen to him."

Jess seemed agitated as she glanced at the sofa before fixing her eyes on Steven.

"You are smart, and frankly, you are better than him. He would say anything to anyone if he felt it would have a chance of getting him a shag."

"Sounds like a great party guest…"

Sam's misguided attempt at humour was met by a savage glare from Jess.

"Sorry I…"

Sam still was unsure what he was supposed to do in this situation. He was, at least, now sure joking about it was maybe the wrong thing at this stage. He shot a look at Jake on the sofa, as if to psychically shout at him. Jake took no notice of this ESP attack. Sam watched for a second as he stroked Kim's hair while she tapped her hand on his forearm. Shifting his gaze, he saw Dean and his friend talking to the girl from the window. He wondered if they were trying the same lines that had failed to work on Ellie, and Maddie. For a moment, Sam felt saddened by his gender.

This party, supposedly a celebration of a new flat seemed to have become dominated by attempts to seduce women, whatever the cost.

Sam then felt a new depth of sadness as he remembered being with Ellie, and he wanted nothing more than to be in her company again. To try and become a part of her life. Did that make him the same as these other guys? Was he just another guy in a queue, waiting for a turn at the girl, willing to turn his back on everything to spend some time with a stranger? No. Line in the sand. Sam had never been like that, and he reaffirmed his belief that he would never be like that. He hoped that he would get to speak to Ellie again, but he was not going to chase her. And he wasn't going to go to speak with any of the other women here either, to show them that he was not the just the next guy in the evening's ticket line to try and pick them up. To show them that not all guys were like that. He turned his attention back to his friends, the hosts of the evening, where the attention belonged.

"I didn't want him to come tonight."

Jess was holding Steven. Her face a mixture of empathy for her partner and anger at Jake for causing his sadness.

"He walked over as I was inviting Maddie. He overheard and invited himself, and I was too surprised to say no. Trust me, he is never setting foot anywhere near this flat again. And I'm cleaning the sofa once he's gone. I don't want any trace of him left in our home."

Sam watched as Jess glanced around the room. Her expression seemed to shift to frustration as her eyes surveyed the occupants of her flat.

"I don't think Maddie is even here anymore. She didn't even say goodbye to me. Lesson learned. Actually…"

Jess's eyes continued to dart.

"There's only a couple of people here I want to speak to, the rest I would be quite happy to not bother with again."

Sam hoped he was in the former category. He decided to check.

"Well, then this party is a great success."

Jess and Steven both looked at him quizzically.

"You've managed to get most of the people you know into a room and work out which ones you can get rid of in the space of a single evening. Most people struggle with that for years."

Steven let out a half sigh half laugh, which, given the circumstances, Sam took as a positive sign. Jess just shook her head, which Sam knew from experience meant '*Oh Sam, you're such a dick sometimes.*' His experience did not tell if that was affectionate or a warning.

13

The time had passed, in the way it always did. Nervous glances at her phone checking the time had finally succumbed to actually thinking it was time to leave. Louisa did not want to miss the last bus, and she knew she was a terrible judge of how long it took to walk across town to her stop. She waved across the room to Steven and Jess as she started to head out. Each step felt like it was in some way wrong, but also a relief. She had not been convinced that coming here was a good idea, worried about not knowing people. Worried what they might think of her, if she would be able to present herself as a cool individual, someone worth knowing, someone that would leave an impression. She had contemplated staying in instead many times as the date of the housewarming grew nearer, but each time she sat on her sofa, safe with her warm cup of tea and her book, she had felt like she was missing out on something. She wasn't convinced staying in all the time was a good idea. She worried about not knowing people. Worried what people might think of her for never going anywhere. Worried that she would never leave any impression anywhere.

She was glad she had decided to come. It had been a very interesting evening, fun in places, weird in others, but she felt like she was leaving in a positive frame. Jess had been much nicer than she had thought she would be, after all, she was with Steven, and although Louisa liked him, he could be very… Steveny. Unaware when he had crossed the line from interesting to know it all, sarcastic to a bit pompous. She had wondered if Jess would be the same, if as a couple they would reinforce each other's bad qualities as she had noticed in other couples. She had been in a few relationships like that herself. To her surprise though, Jess wasn't like that at all. She had been kind, supportive, self deprecating and a bit ditzy. Most importantly, she had been open to speaking to her, and that welcoming nature had made Louisa feel calm, wanted even. She wanted to spend more time with Jess, and hoped she was telling the truth when she had agreed that that was a good idea.

Still, she was glad to be going home. It had been a big effort convincing herself and coming along, talking with strangers, not making a fool of herself. Well she hoped she hadn't made a fool of herself. She would no doubt be considering if she had or not over the course of the next week when everything was quiet and she was trying to sleep. She reached the bedroom, and pushed open the door, casting light into darkness. She was disappointed the door didn't creak as it swung open, as the dying embers of candlelight spilled through, chasing away any goblins that may have been lurking in the shadows.

The coat pile was bigger than she remembered. She was struck by how easily the coats were getting along, all in one big pile, not a care in the world, while their owners found it so awkward, separated, distant in the room outside. Perhaps it was easier in the dark. Shuddering, she realised how badly an experiment like that could go. She reached for the pile to recover her coat. She could see one familiar sleeve, poking out, beckoning her for rescue. She heard its call and began to move the coat that was covering it. As it began to move, she noticed it was different from the other coats that lay here. Deep black and long, it was not a style that was currently fashionable. She had not seen it on a website advert, or a TV show, it looked like it belonged in a different era. It was easily the most interesting coat here. Who did it belong to? It didn't seem to suit any of the people she had spoken to, and it wouldn't be Jess or Steven's. She thought about trying to find out. Suddenly remembering the urgency of the bus, she carefully returned the unknown coat to its resting place on the bed and grabbed hers. Heading for the door whilst wrestling her arms into the familiar comfort of her own coat, she was happy. This had been a good night.

14

Shadows had returned to normal as the candles had faded to almost nothing, their dancers were resting after an evening's performance.

Sam cast his eyes around the room. Almost everyone had gone. Only the echoes remained, empty glasses, ruffled furniture, chairs out of place. His eyes fixed on a stool by the kitchenette. Eyes narrowing, as though it would help him see something that wasn't there.

"Who was there?"

His memory grudgingly answered after a few moments. The guy sat in his coat, not interacting. Sam remembered seeing him and thinking he should go over and say hello. Just before he had been distracted, and then… forgotten. He felt a twinge of guilt. He hoped that whoever the man was had had a good time, that he had ended up in deep and exciting conversations. Sam couldn't remember seeing him talking to anyone, but then he couldn't remember looking either. He decided to ask Jess and Steven if they had spoken to him. Turning back around he found the pair in a soft embrace. An uncomfortable feeling urged Sam that maybe it was time to go too. He didn't want to be the awkward third person in this situation.

Realising that he probably couldn't just walk away, he shifted uncomfortably on the spot for what felt like an eternity.

"Hey Jess, Steve, I think it's time to make a move…"

Sam tried to calmly interrupt his friends kissing. He then panicked about his wording, and the potential misinterpretation.

"I mean… I should move… I think I'm going to go home."

Jess turned to face him, smiling broadly.

"OK dimwit, thanks for coming tonight, I hope you had fun."

"Yes, thanks for coming chap."

Steven rested his chin on the top of Jess's head, also brandishing a broad smile.

"Yes it's been really fun tonight, and you two have a great place here."

Sam meant what he said, and was pleased to see Steven smiling again. Jess could cheer anyone up, and she saved her strongest powers for Steven. As a couple, their differences seemed to fit together perfectly, each weakness countered by the other's strengths. Sam hoped to find that for himself one day. A tall order, he felt, as sometimes he changed his mind so frequently asking someone to keep up with him seemed ridiculous.

"Thanks, you're welcome to drop in whenever you like, of course."

Steven nodded along with Jess's words.

"Give me a minute and I can walk you out."

"No worries, I can remember the way, and you two look comfy. Thanks again, and see you soon!"

Sam didn't want to disrupt the embrace, and he also didn't want to have to think of a long drawn out series of goodbyes.

"OK, night then, take care."

Steven raised a hand from Jess's waist to wave at Sam.

"Night!"

Jess never seemed to stop smiling.

"Enjoy the rest of the night, and farewell!"

Sam took a small bow, turned, and strode off in the direction of his coat. He hoped his exit was classy and dramatic, leaving an impression of coolness. He mostly hoped no one thought he was an idiot. Before he really had time to overthink his choice of departure, he had reached the non-creaking door that held his coat. The room was still dark, and it took him a minute to locate his trusty flapping wafting outside armour. He pondered how his coat had moved, were there ghosts in the dark shifting things around? Small sprites playing with the pile while everyone was busy in the other room?

He found his coat. It was quite far from where he left it. It was also placed, carefully, neatly. He almost didn't want to move it. How had it ended up like this? If there were creatures of magic at work in here, then it must have been an angel that had placed this. None of the other remaining coats enjoyed such treatment, lying in a scattered heap.

"A curious mystery..."

Sam spoke to the spirit occupants of the room. They did not answer as he carefully picked up and put on his coat. He hoped to find out how this had happened, it was exactly the kind of thing he liked to wonder about late at night, instead of sleeping. Taking a final look around for clues, he walked past the creakless door and headed out.

As he turned to exit the flat, he was again confronted by the large wooden door. His memory flashed to the start of the night. He had looked at the door and wondered what mysteries it held now. When he first saw this door, it represented the mystery of a night, now it represented both the mystery and familiarity of the world outside. He had found out what lay inside. Friends, a girl. Such a girl. People. People with their own adventures, their own stories to tell. Some intriguing, some baffling. Some he hoped to never see again, and some he had never really seen even though they were there.

He reached out for the door handle. As it began to turn in his hand, he felt a sudden chill. He was about to re-enter the wider world, with all of its random confusion and noise. Out into the city, joining the flow of people leaving their nights out, their adventures, their attempts to enjoy themselves and make their stories as enjoyable as possible. He felt he had had a good night. Sad that Steven had not, grateful to have met Ellie. That was all he felt he could hope for, some good to make up for any bad, hopefully ending up more positive than negative. He felt the people of the city shared his approach, the hopes of the start of the night now beginning to shift to hopes for the future, for the next night out. Outside, beyond the door, was Sam's future.

He was again struck by the idea that until he opened this door, it didn't really exist. It could be anything. Taking a deep breath, he pulled the door open, and stepped through.

The Thinganing

15

Thc TV flickered with a familiar countdown. Sam had lost track of how many episodes had streamed since he sat down with his unexciting meal after his uneventful day at work. He wasn't even sure what was happening in this series, but everyone had said he should watch it. It seemed to be sad people being angry and a lot of violent murder. He wasn't sure why. Maybe he wasn't paying enough attention. Maybe no one understood what was going on but because everyone was talking about it they daren't admit that, and just said *"Yeah it's so good you should definitely watch it."* As the next episode started with a backdrop of a dark and rainy city, Sam half gave up and reached for his laptop.

As the laptop slowly spun into life, and the TV characters spun to their doom, Sam pondered what he was going to do. Check social media was the easy answer. All the combined intelligence of humanity, all of history, dreams for the future, all accessible through this device. But had anyone posted a humorous meme? That was the more important question. He opened his page and started scrolling through the feed. A random generating machine pulling random things out of random bags at random would make more sense than the images and messages on this feed. Tagged pictures of people Sam was sure he had never met, videos of animals doing various things, quizzes claiming to show you which fantasy character you were most like, all set off nicely by adverts for used cars and Russian brides.

About to give up on this distraction, his scrolling finally revealed something interesting. A post from Jess thanked everyone for coming to her and Steven's flat warming party. A couple of photos bullet pointed the festivities. Sam smiled as he remembered the evening, although the pictures were perplexing. There was a nice selfie style picture of Steven and Jess, all smiles, hope and pride for their new place. There was a shot of people chatting, featuring people Sam had no recollection of seeing either there that night or ever before in his life. There was no picture of him. At first, he was pleased, as he hated seeing himself in pictures looking ridiculously hideous in comparison to everyone else in the frame. He then decided he felt left out for not being in them. He stopped to consider why he never quite felt right about things, every time he found something to be happy about he would always find a counterpoint to be unhappy about. He took a deep breath to contemplate why this might be, and to remind himself to focus more on the positive side of things. Exhaling, he contemplated why that wouldn't work.

The post was covered in likes and smiley faces. He felt it deserved to be, they were good people and it was a good night. Adding his own like to the post, Sam even considered the rarest of things for him, adding a comment.

"Great night and all the best in the new place!"

'Too formal?' Sam wondered if his post was right, after he had posted it, as normal. Now it was there for all to see for all eternity, that was the right time to think about what to say. Time to click on something else and not fall into the trap of worrying about things again. Looking at the smiley picture of Jess and Steven made Sam want to be in that kind of situation, all smiles and hugs and togetherness against the uncertain future. Time to check the dating profile. This monthly tradition had started about a year ago, when the number of people suggesting it was a good idea had reached a critical mass, and a profile had been created. He had tried phone apps, but they all seemed so shallow, so focused on short term encounters. He was not against this idea, there was a voice inside of him that was very convincing about how different partners all the time was a fantastic idea, but he knew himself, and he knew he needed time to settle with people. He couldn't do the whole smooth say the right thing at the exact right time thing that he figured those kinds of people would need to be masters of. He knew the kind of men that would be into that kind of interaction,

and he never wanted women to put him into that category. He wanted to have a proper connection with someone. If he met someone he wanted to be with, he would want to be with them for as long as he could be, not walk away the next day.

His profile flickered into life. Roughly once a month, he decided that it was worth giving it a go, that this would be the time it would all work out. The inbox was empty, no surprise there. He clicked on his description, time to ponder if it was any good again. He had tried to read the guides on how to write profiles, he just wasn't sure he was doing it right. How could he figure out how a stranger may interpret the words he put down? How could he get across his sense of humour without sounding like an idiot? He had tried, many times before. He had not felt satisfied yet. And his inbox was empty. He tweaked a few words here and there, cut out a sentence, replaced it with something funnier, checked his picture. It all seemed as good as he could get it to be. Time to have a look at the girls.

Setting the search to this city, and a reasonable age range, he let the algorithm do its thing. A list of women appeared. What was the best way to sort through? He scrolled the page up and down a few times, recognising a few profiles that he had seen before. He had tried messaging a couple of these, and never received a response. He had wondered if he had been too brief, or too long winded, he had tried his best to read their profile and send something interesting, but how could you start a conversation other than hello? Did it seem creepy if he sent a message asking a probing question about their likes after reading their profile? You would never ask someone you had just met such a probing question, but if you stuck with a simple 'Hello, how are you?' how would they know you were any different than the other messages that said the same thing? He guessed that's where his profile would come in, to show how he was a good person with a sense of humour. Shame he was no good at writing profiles to get that across. His mind wandered back to the party, and Ellie. She was so beautiful. Sam couldn't remember a time he had been so amazed by someone. Perhaps she was on the dating site? There was no way he was that lucky. Still, worth checking.

There were pages of profiles, dozens of people. The age range was quite wide, and the closeness of location began to be a bit of a stretch, considering the search parameters he had laboured over. But still. A lot of women were on this site, surely one would be a good match for him. He found two profiles that looked interesting. Both very attractive, both had interests that matched his for the most part. He couldn't decide which one to send a message to. It always felt weird sending messages to more than one woman, like cheating. He clicked back and forth between profiles for several minutes weighing up the pros and cons before making a choice. He picked the girl closest to his age and started typing a message. Deleting the message, he re-read her profile. Typing again, he tried to reference things they both had in common, tried to sound happy and fun, added in some self-deprecating humour. He clicked send. Immediately wondering if he had said the right things, he waited for the sent message screen to load. Confirming his possibly rubbish message had indeed been correctly sent, the page immediately showed him five more women with the tag line 'Here are some more you might be interested in.' This made no sense to Sam, he had carefully considered who he was interested in, that's why he had sent a message. Why would it be showing him different people? Although, one of the pictures was of a particularly attractive woman.

Sam couldn't help but click on this new profile. The woman's pictures were stunning, and quite revealing. Her profile shared this description, but for different reasons.

"No time wasters. No unemployed. Must have good job. Must have nice car. Must have own house. Must know how to treat a lady."

The profile made no mention of the personality traits of any suiter, nor did it mention any likes and dislikes of the woman herself. Just demands and pictures of cleavage. Sam wondered why anyone would put up a profile like that, or why anyone would respond to it. He figured no one would. At least she wouldn't get any time wasters. He clicked back to his own profile. No messages in his inbox. Well, it had only been a couple of minutes, perhaps a bit unreasonable to expect a response so quickly. His mind drifted back to the party. He clicked the other tab, returning to the pictures Jess had posted and noticed that she had liked his comment.

"Success!"

He shouted to no one, pleased in his ability to write a half decent wall post. Flicking between the photos page and the dating site, he wondered why he was trying so hard to communicate with strangers when he was still so mesmerised by the memory of Ellie. There was a girl he had actually met and talked with, in the actual world, and here he was, typing on a screen hoping it would lead to a meeting even half as magical as that had been. Reaching for his phone, he thought it was perhaps time to try to follow up on the feelings which had sparked in him that night.

"Hey nice pics of the party! Didn't see you taking them :)"

The opening text in Sam's gambit with Jess, he wanted to be subtle and casual before asking about Ellie, no need to sound desperate.

"Heya, thanks! If you got here on time you would've seen me snapping and you would have been in them : P"

Jess's response was so fast, Sam wondered if her phone was connected directly to her mind. If he could type that fast, he felt his life would be somehow better.

"Fashionably on time I think you'll find. Is that why Ellie isn't on them either?"

Sam felt he was maybe not as subtle as he thought he was, maybe he should have chatted a bit before asking about Ellie. Surely Jess would just see that as an extension of a natural conversation, nothing desperate.

"AHHH I thought you liked her! Haha <3"

Jess had clearly seen through Sam's intricate and clever plan.

Sam contemplated how to respond, his instinct was to deny any such thing, to be cool and aloof, show disinterest to establish manliness. But he was interested, and if he said he wasn't, Jess may take him at his word. It may be messier than he had intended, but if Jess was already onto him, he didn't have much to lose by being honest.

"She was cool, yeah."

It was one thing to decide to be honest with his intention, quite another thing to actually know what to say.

"Ha I KNEW it! Have you asked her out?"

Jess seemed pleased in her deductions.

"When would I have done that!"

Sam wondered if this meant he had already missed his opportunity, although he couldn't figure out when he would have had the chance to do such a thing.

"Saw the way you were looking at her, and you were speaking to her, I'm sure I saw you two arm in arm :P"

Sam felt that Jess was making some fair points, from an outside perspective, this would all seem to point to ample opportunity. But Sam knew better, he was there, and he had had no idea what to say throughout the majority of the encounter. So there.

"We were just chatting, nothing else."

Sam could almost feel the disappointment in his text.

"ASK HER!! She isn't seeing anyone, hasn't for ages, I'm sure she would be interested if you ask her!! Looked like you were getting on well :) :)"

Jess's message was reassuring, although Sam wasn't sure if she meant Ellie hadn't been dating and would agree to see anyone. Although, if he was the anyone, that still worked in his favour, was that right? He couldn't decide if it was a good or bad thing. There was, however, an issue with this enthusiasm.

"OK but I don't have her number, so…"

Part of Sam wanted Jess to sort it all out for him seeing as she was so keen, and he was sure to mess it up somehow.

"HOW!! I thought men always asked all women for their numbers all the time and for dates and everything! That's what men do! You doof!"

Jess's message baffled Sam utterly. The kind of men that would do that sounded horrible, pushy, sleazy, surely Jess knew he wasn't like that. Also, was she having a go at him for not being like that? Complaining that he wasn't a terrible man? Sense made this didn't.

"I don't sleaze onto women!"

Sam felt his honour needed defending, although he was trying to get help with a date, it was beginning to get confusing.

"You're allowed to ask if you're walking arm in arm"

Jess's response seemed sensible, but he felt that the situation wasn't as clear cut as that. Ellie had asked Sam to pretend, to escape, he had felt conflicted then, and it hadn't really passed as a feeling, and this conversation wasn't shining any light of glorious clarity onto his inner turmoil.

"Yeah that was complicated, it didn't mean anything."

Sam wasn't sure If he was now suggesting reasons why he shouldn't ask for her number. What was he doing? Whose side was he on?

"She commented on the photos, why don't you send her a friend request and a message and just find out for yourself doofus boy. Tell me how it goes, and what your kids will be called! If it's a girl Jessica is a good name :) :) :)"

Sam responded with a series of emoji, it was all he could muster. Excited for Jess's support, yet slightly worried that if he messed it up he would get the extra humiliation of having to explain where he had gone wrong. He was never sure where he went wrong. It just seemed to be the natural progression of him trying to do something. He clicked back to the photo post. Jess was right, Ellie had liked the photos and commented that she would have been in them if she was on time. Sam thought that was a much better way of responding than he had, self-deprecating for being late, but also pointing out she was there despite the lack of evidence. Sam clicked to like the post, then clicked on Ellie's name. Her profile appeared, her picture beaming out of the screen. Outshining any of the pictures he had seen on the dating website, a full moon against a backdrop of city polluted stars. This was his chance; he had better take it before it slipped away in a sea of doubt and worry.

His mind cast back to that moment, that striking first moment, stood on the rug in Jess and Steven's flat. The reaction he had when she walked into his sight. How it had hit him so hard he lost his breath… a part of him still hadn't really caught it yet. It was a rare feeling, part of him was afraid to let it slip away. Another part of him was afraid to feel it again. To lose control of his mind like that, to be so helpless against his emotions. The only other time he could remember something like this happening before was in his first year at university, when he first met Tish.

Tish was Sam's best friend's girlfriend. The first time he saw her was one of the most powerful reactions for someone he had ever felt. He was stood in his halls corridor, chatting away with the other residents. She had come to visit her boyfriend. Sam turned to see her walk up the corridor. Her posture was perfect, she stood tall in boots, a long black dress swaying with each step. Head held high, she smiled with a proud confidence as she walked past Sam and the other students, not making eye contact with anyone, never shifting her focus from her destination, and very aware that that was exactly what she was doing. Her very long hair flowed over her shoulders, seeming to move in synchronicity with her dress, a wave of femininity that flowed down the corridor and vanished, as abruptly as it had appeared, as her boyfriend closed his door behind her as she entered his room. Sam had of course never told anyone of this feeling, and as he got to know Tish over the months of term, they had become firm friends. The better friends they became, the more Sam wished he had met her under different circumstances. But he hadn't. She was inseparable from her boyfriend, for all of their time at uni. They slowly lost touch afterwards, the same story as so many others. Good intentions slowly fading under the weight of time and conflicting schedules. He had never told her how he had felt, there was never any point. And he was proud to have her as a friend. He had never seen or heard from her again.

This time. Sam could not let it happen again. Such a strong reaction, so intense. Only twice in his life… what if it never happened again? Perhaps he was lucky to have felt it again… but now, there was no best friend boyfriend to muddy the waters. There was no boyfriend at all… if he felt this way surely it had to mean there was a chance? The universe wasn't so cruel, was it? He had to try.

The send request button was easy to click, the accompanying message more difficult. Draft and re draft, hair pulling frustration, a couple of prayers to deities, blank staring at the wall, none of it was helping pen the ultimate message, the conveyer of his hopes and dreams, his chance at the happy selfie glimpsed at the start of this debacle. After much deliberation, he settled with:

"Hi Ellie, it was nice meeting you at the party, I missed the photos too!"

Sam felt it was probably the best he could do without seeming to be a massive creep – after all, he wasn't sure if she would even remember who he was. He clicked the send button and sat back to contemplate if he had said the right thing.

Drifting in and out of the TV show in which he now had absolutely no idea what was going on in, while flicking back and forth on his laptop, the evening was returning to normal. Time passing, nothing much marking its departure. A delirium of nothing which could be lamented the following day at work, when plans could be made to make more out of the same drift tomorrow evening. A pinging noise snapped Sam's attention back from the edges of the void. Ellie had accepted his friend request and sent a message in response. Sam sat upright to better deal with this developing situation, his heart rate quickened by the highlighted message symbol. He hesitated over the message button, savouring that at this moment, it could contain anything. It might be a 'who are you? Please don't talk to me' but it could also be a 'hey let's go on lots of dates and live happily ever after'. Either way, it would be the key to how he was going to feel for the rest of the evening. Taking a deep breath, mostly to add drama to the situation, he clicked the message open.

"Hi! Yeah it was a fun party! I guess you were fashionably late too then :) Thanks for saving me from that ass btw!"

Ellie had remembered who he was, sparking a great wave of relief. A wave of excitement joined Sam's emotional ocean, as he typed a new message.

"Anytime you need me to help let me know."

Sam immediately felt that had been the wrong response. He would have fared better by mentioning how awesome and available he was, rather than suggesting she was going to have more awkward encounters with other men.

"Well hopefully there won't be anymore, but thanks for the offer! I've certainly had my fair share of asses trying it on!"

Ellie seemed to have let Sam get away with his comment, although he found himself unsure if her response was suggesting she was onto him, that she felt he was just another ass trying it on. In fairness, he felt like he kinda was. But he was not a bad person, and he did want to spend more time with her, so he felt he had to try.

"Sounds like you've got some stories there! Would you like to go for a drink sometime and tell me the funny ones?"

As soon as he clicked the send button, Sam regretted the message. It was like the send button was tied directly into his nervous system. He couldn't press it without it making him feel he had done something wrong. At least he had a good idea what he was doing wrong, continuing to talk to her about bad experiences with men trying to ask her on dates was probably not the smoothest way to ask someone for a date. It was exactly what he had felt he couldn't do at the party, agree with her that men were terrible dating obsessed sleazes with one track minds, but point out that he was different and better. And would she like to go on a date because she was incredibly hot.

"Pub might be nice. I've been in a work and staying in rut lately. I'm sure you've got some stories too! I think I'm free next week, I will send a message when I find out from work. Night!"

Sam was astounded by Ellie's response. Somehow he had managed it, the unthinkable, despite his best effort to screw it up. He quickly typed a confirmation, and then sat, staring blankly at the screen. He had done it. He had secured a date with a woman that he thought was clearly beyond his reach. His mind raced at the possibilities. He couldn't wait for next week, for the chance to see her again, in a one on one situation. He looked back at her profile picture. She really was stunning. And he was in no way going to click and see what other pictures he could see now they were friends. That would be wrong. Probably.

16

The taxi felt far too big for Louisa. One woman in a vehicle designed for several at first felt like an indulgence but had soon begun to make her feel guilty, like she had somehow failed the expectations of the taxi company by not having enough friends to fill the supplied vehicle. The driver was trying to be chatty, she was holding her responses to 'hmm' and 'oh yeah' in the hope that he would pick up on the signal that she didn't really want to converse. It wasn't really working. She was beginning to feel uncomfortable, and slightly vulnerable, alone on the huge back seat of this van of a taxi.

As they reached the streets of the city centre, the monstrous vehicle slowed to a crawl. Louisa turned her attention out of the window, attempting to distract herself from her situation. The pavements seemed full of people, some rushing, others strolling, back and forth, all sizes, colours, outfits, hairstyles… Through the glass of the taxi door Louisa felt like she may as well be at home watching the TV, some kind of mass dance show perhaps… She felt she didn't belong on this street just as she wouldn't belong on a show like that.

Her eyes joined the dance of feet and motion as she wondered how all of these people had met their friends. What had brought them here? Comfortable in their place on this dance show street. Where were they going? How could she get to be as happy as them? A bunch of lads in recently ironed half matching shirts, a group of girls in dresses that were both too high and too low, and couples, arm in arm, wrapped up together against the cold of the night, and of the world.

"Here we are then love."

The taxi had arrived outside a glass fronted bar, with a large steel sign above the door that was probably meant to be witty, or ironic. Louisa handed the driver a couple of crumpled notes and gathered her things together. After receiving her somewhat small pile of change, she stepped out onto the street. The wind was bracing, as if the world itself was trying to tell her not to go any further, how dare she. Two girls passed by as Louisa gathered herself. They were doing the 'wind walk' – each with one hand firmly pinning their handbags to their sides, the other hand pinning their skirts to their thighs.

"Jeans were a good choice."

Louisa watched them continue up the street for a few moments, wondering where they were going and why they hadn't gone into this bar – did they know something?

"Well, no point in questioning now, I'm here, may as well go in, maybe it won't be as bad as... last time."

She felt herself shudder as the memory of the last works outing flashed before her. Taking a deep breath, she tightened her grip on her bag and started walking towards the door. Glass and steel, the door swung open in the hand of the huge bouncer. All in black, it was hard to tell if he was human at all or some kind of monstrous creation from the mind of a mad scientist's basement.

"Good evening miss."

His voice bellowed.

"Thanks, Hi!"

Louisa dashed in through the opening, glad to be out of the gusts of people and wind billowing up and down the street.

Louisa stepped into the bar, somewhere she had wanted to try since it opened a few months prior. She was pleased that Jess had agreed to her suggestion. Apparently it had sounded like it had the right mix of crazy new cocktails for her and authentic craft micro brewed beers to please Steven. The smartly dressed girl that stood just inside the door gave a warm greeting, and immediately ruined it by stating how this area was not for sitting in without prior booking for food. Louisa looked around at the few empty tables, and felt uncomfortable at the notion that her being here was somehow worse than it being empty.

Ushered through to a dark corridor, Louisa was beginning to feel she had made a bad choice of venue. The girl assured her that the main drinking bar was upstairs, and that it was lovely. Again her smile seemed disingenuous as she practically chased Louisa out of her empty area.

"Yeah I'm going!" she thought as she smiled back at the girl, as though she was happy to be removed for the inconvenience of trying to be a customer in this place. The audacity of trying to give her money willingly.

Why anyone would have an upstairs bar only accessible via an apparently hidden staircase around a corner in a corridor that was painted black seemed a mysterious choice. Two arcade machines stood against the black painted walls, both with 'Out of order' signs hanging from thick string covering their screens. The stairs themselves begrudgingly revealed themselves, painted black to match the walls. Louisa reached for the dark wood of the hand rail to aid her in scaling the treacherously dark mountain that lay between her and the fabled bar she was allowed to go into. Each step carefully placed, echoing off the cold surfaces, she felt that if it was this risky trying to find her footing now, what on earth would it be like trying to get back down after a couple of drinks.

There was no door at the top of the dark mountain, Louisa instead found herself bombarded by colour and light as she stepped into a large room filled with miscellaneous furniture and decorations. A new girl greeted her, again with a beaming smile, this time showing she was allowing her to be in this place by pointing towards a small two person table perched against the large glass plate windows that stretched almost the whole length of the outer wall. Although people watching could be entertaining, Louisa didn't like the idea of people outside being able to look up at her while she sat, it felt very voyeuristic. Pointing out to the second greeter girl that she was expecting several people, she was ushered to a larger table against the opposite wall. Smiling and nodding, Louisa sat down on a distressed red leather sofa, placing her bag on the distressed wood of the table. The greeter handed her a drinks menu and wandered off into the depths of the bar. Louisa wasn't sure if she felt pampered and special, or controlled and unwelcome. Heaven forbid she should actually go to the bar herself to order a drink. She glanced at the menu, a series of thick cardboard coloured to look old tied together with thick brown twine. What exactly was this place trying to be? It had only been open for a few months, the whole building had only been built the previous year. No one would be fooled by the attempts to make it look old and naturally worn.

A quick check of her phone had revealed that Jess and Steve were only a few minutes away, no need to feel awkward sitting alone at this large table for much longer. Soon time to feel awkward with a few people sitting at a large table. Louisa decided to take the few minutes to do a proper assessment of this place. Was it living up to her expectations, or was it hilariously failing to. She wasn't sure which one would be the better result.

The general theme seemed to be 'warm and cosy, a bit worn from all of the years of amazing nights out spent here' coupled with 'we are hilariously funny, aren't we? Look at us, that's so this place'. The aged sofa and table Louisa sat at were not unique, several more lined this side of the bar, along a wall of exposed crumbling brickwork. With this being such a new place, Louisa wondered if the brickwork had been shipped in and specially laid to look like it had been exposed. Between the tables, the walls held posters that she thought were meant to be either quaint, or ironic. The nearest one to her pictured a housewife style woman circa 1950 with the phrase "I'd rather have a cup of tea" printed in a speech bubble just above her ever so gleaming smile.

The last table sat in a corner with more reclaimed brick work, this time forming a high arch that cut across the room and met the sheer glass of the opposite wall. A cherub statue stood guard over this archway, in a classic 'thinking' pose, its chubby fist clenched below its solemn face. A printed speech bubble hung on the brickwork, with thought bubbles connecting it to the top of the statue. 'Hmm… Cake…' read the supposed thoughts of the cherub. Louisa decided that this place was not really working for her. Looking up, she noticed the whole room was draped in fairy lights, none of which were on. Perhaps her presence was not worthy of such illumination, perhaps the building could read her less than enthusiastic thoughts and had decided to give up trying to impress her. A shame, she thought, as she liked fairy lights and if they were on she may have felt a lot better about being in here.

Straining her neck, she could just about see the actual bar. It was next to the tree. Bemused as to why the designer of this place had built fake brick walls and archways, she was now totally confused by the decision to place an actual tree in here. It stood, floor to ceiling, a tree. Was this some reference or joke she was not cool enough to understand? Choosing to pretend she had never seen it, she scanned the bar. A drink would be nice, but she felt awkward ordering from the menu before Jess and Steven arrived. However, if some barman was to catch her eye and see her plight, that would be different. Alas the two waist coated staff positioned behind the bar were busy, eyes down chopping up things Louisa couldn't quite see and placing them in glasses that weren't for her. She wanted to go over and ask for a drink, checking on the tree while she was there, but felt she had been put in her place and she shouldn't be so brazen as to get up and walk around without the approval of one of the greeter girls.

"Hey Lou, nice to see you!"

Jess had appeared out of nowhere, seemingly unaccosted by greeters. Stephen was behind her, holding her coat and waving hello.

"Hey you two, I saved you a seat!"

Louisa shifted down the sofa to make room, even though the table could easily accommodate twice their number.

"Marvellous."

Jessica gracefully swished onto the red leather beside Louisa, without so much as putting a crease in her dress. Louisa was quite in awe of her, as she sat, perfect posture, perfectly turned out, flawless yet subtle makeup.

"I'm here too, hi!"

Steven sat opposite, carefully placing coats beside him.

"Hi Stevey, nice to see you! How're you doing?"

Louisa knew that Steven hated being called Stevey, and she knew that he knew that she knew.

"Good, good, thanks Louie"

He smiled, partly because he was happy to see his friend, and partly because he knew Louisa hated being called Louie much more than he disliked Stevey.

"Oh yes, sorry but my friend can't make it tonight, something came up."

He spoke casually as he reached for the drinks menu.

"Steven!"

Jess's tone startled him, making him freeze on the spot and look up like a puppy caught in the biscuit tin. Jess turned to Louisa, and with a much calmer tone continued:

"Steven invited our friend Sam along, I don't know what he was up too, but apparently this mystery plan failed. Not that we need anyone else to have a good evening!"

Louisa felt that Jess had just expertly removed herself from an accusation of matchmaking.

"Oh sorry Lou, I thought I had mentioned he might be along. Wasn't planning anything, just trying to not feel outnumbered."

Steven's use of the word 'planning', combined with Jess's expert denial, confirmed for Louisa that this was indeed some form of matchmaking scheme gone awry. Good job too, she had not prepared herself for such an eventuality and would have been very disconcerted to have been dropped into such an awkward situation with no warning. She had been really looking forward to her own plan of becoming Jess's new BFF, and any other plans, schemes, or distractions, would be far too much to handle.

"That's ok, I'm sure he's rubbish if he turned down a chance to hang out with us."

Louisa tried to lighten the moment and reassure Steven with a wide smile. It seemed to work as he smiled back and returned his gaze to the drinks menu. Keeping her smile, she turned to Jess and whispered:

"No matchmaking."

Jess rolled her eyes and picked up a second drinks menu.

"Hmm these look interesting, don't recognise any of these, lots to try!"

"True there's some I don't recognise, but most are just a play on words."

Steven's eyebrows were joining forces, helping him solve the marketing puzzle before him through the medium of a concentrated frown.

"You don't have to solve everything you know."

Jess had begun staring intently at her menu, clearly more interested in this new puzzle than she was prepared to let on. Louisa wondered if this was a common dynamic in their relationship as she picked up her own menu to have a look at this for herself, and also to hopefully find something to actually order.

"See this one… 'A cuddle on the promenade' looking at the ingredients, that's a 'Sex on the beach.' Quite clever."

Steven seemed to be enjoying his new game.

"Look a 'Shambler!' That's a 'zombie!'

Jess was enjoying this game as much as Steven. They continued pointing out drinks puns to each other while Louisa wondered if they would be like this thirty years from now, solving crosswords by the fireplace on a crisp winter Sunday morning. Thinking about it, they probably did that now. Louisa felt warmed by the romantic image, but not as warmed as a good drink could provide.

As if on cue, a waiter appeared asking for orders whilst flipping open a small note book. His crisp white shirt gleamed against tight sheer black trousers. A sharp bowtie accented the look, echoing the dark waxed moustache which sat on his otherwise pale face. Not a hair on his head was out of place, sweeping to the side like a wave of some dark ocean. Only the cable of his earpiece gave him away as being from this time period, and not a Victorian gentleman wandering through.

Steven was first to decide, opting with no surprise for a locally brewed ale. Jess was next, ordering what seemed to be a series of random words. Louisa felt a little bit lost on the game of what fake cocktail name could be interpreted to be a nice familiar drink. She glanced to the next page, and as her eyes scanned across the page she couldn't help but exclaim:

"HOW MUCH!"

Jess turned to face her, surprise written across her face. The waiter seemed unflustered, as though this was not the first time such an uncontrolled outburst had occurred.

"I will have a glass of the house red please."

Louisa calmed her tone and smiled at the waiter hoping she had not made too much of a scene.

"A couple of minutes."

The waiter took an acknowledgment bow as he finished writing the group's order, then turned on his heel and walked off towards the bar.

"You ok there Lou?"

Jess had started to giggle as soon as the waiter had turned away, and was now trying hard not to laugh out loud. Louisa held up the menu for emphasise as she repeated her complaint:

"I know cocktails can be expensive compared to other drinks, but come on, how much? Seriously? I could get a whole bottle of wine for that! A good one! Or several bad ones!"

"It's not that bad actually, it's cheap compared to London."

Steven had begun re-reading the menu, looking for the cause of drama.

"No, that just means it's more ridiculously expensive in London, that doesn't mean it's cheap here."

Louisa knew Steven didn't mean to seem condescending in his comment, but she was growing tired of the excuse in this town that doubling the prices everywhere was acceptable because things cost more in places that were elsewhere, places known to be the domain of the wealthy elite.

"It's true, a slap would cost you a tenner in London, but you can have one here for a quid."

Jess was pulling faces at Steven, who seemed bemused as to why his helpful clarifying statement had resulted in such a backlash.

"Sorry, I was just shocked, when did drink prices double?"

Louisa had thrown down the menu in slight disgust, she had a good job on what was considered a reasonable wage, but she was getting annoyed at how many things were slowly rising out of her reach. Tired of being caught in a growing rift between people with incredible amounts of money and everyone else, whose ok amounts of money increasingly got them less and less. She was also tired of the effect it was having socially. She had stopped going to the work nights out, because the executives kept buying rounds and complaining that she was tight when she asked to not be included so she didn't have to reciprocate. She was not tight, she didn't have enough money to buy eight cocktails twice a night. She would happily give everything she had in her purse to others, but when there was nothing in there, there was nothing to give.

"It's ok hun, the prices are ridiculous here, but we can't be out late anyway, so there's no danger of us bankrupting ourselves! Watch how long I make my drink last!"

Jess was an expert in calming situations, seeming to Louisa to be on everyone's side simultaneously.

"So what do you both think of this place then? Aside from the prices, I mean."

Steven tried to shift the topic of conversation to be more positive.

"I'm quite liking it, it's quite stylish isn't it? Really managed to forge a unique identity for itself."

"Hold on then, let's have a look."

Jess began looking around, craning her neck, leaning around the leather sofa, unsubtly taking it all in… gathering her opinion.

"I quite like the fairy lights, but why aren't they on?"

"Yes!"

Louisa was glad she had found common agreement in the fairy light situation.

"Don't know about these signs everywhere though, are they meant to be funny? They aren't."

Jess pointed at the poster of the 50's woman.

"And the cherub? What?"

"I think they are funny, in an ironic sense. They seem out of place, which makes them fit right in."

Steven stroked his chin as if intellectual appreciation was the new laughter.

"So it's pretentiousness makes it work?"

Jess started stroking her chin as she took another look around.

"It's not pretentious if it delivers on point."

Steven folded his arms, perhaps subconsciously a defence against Jess's subtle mockery as she made frowning faces, nodding, and continuing to stroke her chin, as though in deep philosophical thought.

"So how do you explain the tree?"

Louisa was enjoying the banter debate, eager to jump in on the fun.

Steven turned to look behind him, causing the leather to crack.

"Well... I suppose it's representative…"

"Of the fact that this is a bit of a pretentious overpriced hipster bar."

Jess cut Steven off and then began to giggle, quickly infecting Louisa.

"Yeah, I've got nothing for the tree. Looks nice though, different."

Steven couldn't help a slight chuckle. He really did like the look of the bar in general, admiring when venues put effort into how they presented themselves. One of the things that had caused him to bond so deeply with Jess was her ability to remind him not to let those thoughts drift too far. Although he liked the extra effort and style, he didn't want to become a poser, or have people think he was stuck up.

"All this place needs is a guy with a waxed beard and a plaid shirt with suspenders. Oh wait there's one, talking with the girl in the bowler hat."

Jess was pointing behind her hand, flicking her eyes towards a couple sat at one of the two-seater window tables. Lost in each other, they seemed to be enjoying flirting between sips of multi-coloured beverages which resided in old jam jars.

"At least that hat is at a jaunty angle"

"You're not one to comment on fashion, do you want me to get your uni photos out?"

Steven batted at Jess's hands to try and stop her from being discovered by the couple. The couple were lost to the outside world however, oblivious that the universe extended further than their own existence.

"People made fun of me, now it's my turn! And, at least we were trying to be individual, even if we were really bad at it and kinda ended up looking a bit the same anyway. These people are literally the same. The guys, it's the same haircut, the same beard, the same clothes. They even all have sleeve tattoos on the same arm. I don't get the point of looking that identical. Don't they get confused in low light situations who they are talking with? Or if it's a mirror? Like I met this really cool guy at a house party last week, but it turned out to be three different guys and my own reflection."

Louisa couldn't help but laugh at the comment, the more time she spent around Jess the more she liked her. Witty and insightful, comfortable enough with Steven to poke at his comments without being argumentative, she seemed to have it all together.

For the first time in a long while, Louisa felt that she had found a new friend, and a new ideal to aspire to become herself. This was how she wanted others to see her. She had almost instantly felt this role model bond develop when she had met Jess, it was now crystallising into a true life goal.

A waiter appeared beside the table, looking more dashing and immaculate than the last one. Louisa wondered how they managed to maintain this image over their entire shift. Perhaps they all got together behind the bar and groomed each other to perfection like a bunch of chimpanzees. Or perhaps they had a scary manager hiding out of view of the punters, cracking a whip at them all until they sorted their act out. Either way, it looked impressive, but probably wasn't in any way fun for them. With a subtle controlled motion he leant down and moved three drinks from his silver tray to the table, stating their names and waiting for a proclamation of their requester before passing them across to their eager recipient. It was all very nice, very professional. Louisa was struck with a feeling of *"I am really properly out, at a proper going out place, with proper people, doing proper going out things."*

It didn't last long. She joined the looks of surprised confusion that had taken over Jess and Steven's faces. Jess was the last to receive her drink. And yeah. It was a sight to behold.

"What on earth is that!?"

Steven was the least likely to have the first outburst, perhaps Jess was as stunned into silence as Louisa.

Jess turned to the waiter, to see his back moving into the distance. She raised a finger at him, as if to ask a question to a school teacher. It was no use, he was not a school teacher, and as such, couldn't see behind him.

"Err… is that?"

Louisa didn't really have many more words.

"What in the world did you order!?"

Steven looked like an explorer who had just stumbled across an unexpected discovery in a distant land.

"Well…"

Jess's puzzled expression increased as she picked up her drink.

"So… I ordered a cocktail called 'Fairground Prize' because I thought it was a cool name, and I couldn't figure it out like I could with the other ones…"

"Is that what I think it is?"

Louisa leaned in for a good long look as Jess raised the drink up to her eye level.

"No. well, yes… but it's not a real fish."

Jess looked like she couldn't really believe the sentence she had just said.

The three of them spent a good few minutes looking at this alcoholic creation. The 'Fairground Prize.' There was no glass, a zip lock plastic bag contained a subtly coloured liquid. Floating in the centre, a piece of fruit had been quite expertly carved into the shape of a goldfish. A straw was wedged into the corner of the bag, held in place by the sealed lock. It was a sight to behold.

"Is that an orange peel fish?"

Louisa was a mixture of horrified and amazed. She felt slightly disappointed by her uninspired glass of red wine.

"I must say I'm quite impressed by that."

Steven's surprise had turned into admiration. He had never seen anything quite like it.

"But how do I…"

Jess was holding the bag of drink by its corners.

"Don't squeeze it!"

Louisa was beginning to find this whole venue ridiculous. She wasn't sure if that was a good or bad thing.

Jess was trying to grab the straw with her mouth, worried that moving her hands would result in some kind of tragedy.

"I hope that tastes as good as it looks!"

Steven reached across and helped her find the straw.

"Well, it's quite nice."

Jess seemed a little underwhelmed.

"If it was just in a glass I would say it's nice but nothing special."

Several sips followed, just to be sure.

"Also, I'm not too sure I can put this down without it spilling everywhere… How's your drinks?"

Jess looked at Louisa's wine and Steven's beer, while holding her bag of cocktail in front of her.

Louisa commented that her wine was quite nice, despite thinking she had nicer bottles at home that had cost roughly less. Steven talked for at least a minute about every aspect and hue of his locally brewed ale, resulting in the conclusion that it was, in fact, alright. Giggles and mockery emanated from Jess, Steven retorting that one who held aloft a bag of drink containing a fake fish was not in a secure place from which to poke fun.

Louisa tried to join in the fun where she could, trying to be even in her attempts at humour between the two of them, throwing in the odd bit of self deprecation to show she was not any better. She was enjoying herself. Much more than she thought she would. She had hoped the evening would go well, and it really seemed to be. Smiles all round, giggles, small talk, she felt comfortable and relaxed.

"So Lou, are you seeing anyone?"

The question stopped Louisa's sense of comfort and derailed her train of thought. Why was everyone always asking her this? Her co-workers, her family, always with the same question. Why was it so important to everyone else? She looked at Jess, who was cheerily awaiting an answer. She had already displayed discomfort over the whole match making thing, why had this question come back? Had she not made it clear enough that she didn't want people meddling with her single status.

"Well no… but…"

Louisa searched for the right words to escape this dreaded question.

"But? Is there someone you're interested in? sounds like there could be a story here!"

Jess's response deflated Louisa. Far from ending this topic of discussion, she had somehow managed to make it worse.

"No no no!"

Louisa was trying to avoid a full panic. She didn't want to get into it. Not here, not when she was doing so well at becoming proper friends with them. Her inner panic was trying to be outer panic. This was not acceptable.

"Oh honey don't worry!"

Jess was as calming as ever.

"Perhaps it's someone that can't be mentioned, married? It's not one of our bosses is it?"

Steven, was much less good at being calming. And reading situations.

Louisa may have made a small mouse like noise at Steven's suggestions. They were nowhere near the truth, but she had no idea to respond to them. She hoped she hadn't made the noise out loud, that it was just inside her head. A brutal stare shot like a laser from Jess to Steven.

"What! I'm only joking!"

Steven recoiled slightly in his seat from the intensity of the laser stare.

Jess turned off the beam, turning back to Jess with a much gentler expression.

"Don't worry about Steven's super power of saying inappropriate things at the wrong time, I was just curious, the more we get to know you the more we like you and we only want you to be happy."

Louisa felt a warmth rise up as Jess spoke, drowning out most of her anxiety. Jess was amazing at disarming situations whilst somehow turning everything into a positive. Louisa was more convinced than ever that she needed her in her life. She felt she had to say something though, to respond. She decided to be as honest as possible, without getting any further into it.

"It's ok, I just don't like talking about that stuff."

It was a vague and slightly useless attempt, but it was the best Louisa could muster.

"No worries."

Jess smilcd widely.

"Why don't we get some more drinks and see what else we can find to talk about?"

Jess craned her neck and began leaning out of her seat.

"Where are the waiter guys? Drinks! And then I can tell you some fantastic stories about how embarrassing Steven can be!"

Steven raised his drinks menu whilst slumping in his chair in an attempt to disappear from view. His muffled voice emanated from his hiding place:

"Hmm. The sad thing is there's quite a lot of those, I'm quite good at it you see. Well you do see already... yeah... maybe order a couple of drinks... this may take a while."

17

"This is it!"

The face in the mirror seemed to fluctuate between confident and good looking and grotesque and afraid. Flicking and picking at stray hairs, on head and chin, Sam tried to achieve the kind of super image he felt he needed for this night to be all he hoped it would be. Butterflies danced inside, it felt like a salsa… even his butterflies were cooler than him. It was after all the trendiest dance for them to be doing.

Anticipation, excitement, fear, urge to run away, urge to run toward, this night could be the greatest night of his life. In no way was he building himself up for a massive anti-climax and disappointment, a Sunday mind hangover full of *"what if I had done that, gone there, did she mean? Did I mean? What did it all mean?"* Sam had in no way developed a habit of doing that. In. No. Way.

Emotional fear and dilemma were quickly subdued by a more substantial real world crisis, as a glance at his watch resulted in a shouted expletive at the numbers it displayed. A whirlwind ensued, Sam could not miss this bus. Quite how plenty of time had again become less than an adequate amount of time in the blink of a panicked eye was a mystery that Sam had battled with his entire life. Grabbing at any objects he felt were essential, spinning around looking to see if he had forgotten anything, all while slapping his pockets double checking he had the things he thought he had, panicking that the sudden motion was probably ruining his carefully prodded at yet less than amazing hair.

Sam was a picture of chaos. The storm before the calm. Pulling on his coat and dropping his keys, falling out of the door, turning back to check he had locked the door, shouting at the locked door for taunting him like that, sprinting down the street while trying to check his watch. Sam was not going to let something as trivial as time conspire against his night with Ellie. He hoped time agreed with his bold declaration. His coat billowed behind him like the cape of a superhero off to save the world. To Sam, Ellie could be the world he would be willing to risk everything to save.

The bus rolled slowly and calmly to the stop. It was late. Perhaps it was fate intervening to ensure Sam caught it. Perhaps it was driven by someone who wasn't that bothered about timetables. Still catching his breath from the now unnecessary run, Sam hoped that the bus wasn't going to be late into town as well. Perhaps he should have gone for the earlier one. That would have gotten him into town far too early, and, being honest with himself, Sam realised that he would probably have missed that one anyway.

A collection of souls that had gathered at the stop now slowly made their way on board the slightly worn out yet confidently overpriced bus. A young man in a short light blue shirt with a white collar took a final drag on his cigarette before casting it to the floor to burn out its last light feeling used and unloved, without so much as a stomp to end its misery. Sam followed as they all shuffled on board, cards beeping and change rattling. Older people sat downstairs, younger went for the coolness of upstairs. Sam felt he belonged to neither category. He wrestled with the stairs as the bus lurched away from the stop. Although not cool, the roar of the badly maintained engine drove him to seek refuge on the higher deck. A young couple sat about halfway down the length of the bus, although Sam could smell her perfume and his recently deceased cigarette from the top of the stairs. The front of the bus was home to a bearded and hair gelled gentleman and his in depth phone conversation. Sam had no real desire to spend the journey learning all about this man and his plans, opting to sit somewhere between the two parties. Fate suggested this was the correct seating choice as a sharp bend encouraged him to sit via the use of gravity. Slightly shocked by the assisted seating, Sam checked himself for minor injury and object spillage. Assured that everything was ok, he placed his trusty headphones in his ears and settled in for the most frustrating part of the journey towards his possible glorious future with Ellie. He could not control the speed of the bus, he just had to wait, and hope it picked up time as it closed in on the city centre and his destiny.

This bus was taking literally forever. Sam kept checking the time on his watch. And then on his phone in case his watch was wrong. He wanted to shout at the driver to go faster. He wanted to shout at the other people who kept standing at bus stops forcing the progress into the city to halt. Did these people not realise he couldn't be late? They were very inconsiderate, with their smiles all ready for their adventures. Perhaps he should have gone for the earlier bus. The calming music he had selected was also failing in its task. Rather than relaxing him, it was winding him up with its slow pace and meandering instrumentation. Did it not realise how important this was?

"Take a minute and calm down."

Sam recognised the feelings. He was letting his mind run away from him. And not in its normal interesting problem solving genius way, but in an anxious stressed panic sort of way. None of the situation he was in was anyone's fault, it was just the situation he was in. He couldn't go back in time and change bus, he couldn't go forward in time and know if the evening was a success. He couldn't even control the speed of the bus, or if it arrived on time or late. he just had to sit, make the best of it, wait.

"Calm down."

He formed the words in his head slowly and deliberately. The bus started moving again, as its newest arrivals took their seats. They all looked jolly, excited and pleased to be heading out for the night. Sam's mind wasn't clear enough to fill out the usual backstories for them that he would normally pass the travel time with. He continued to look around the deck of the bus, which was already getting a bit cluttered with the flotsam and jetsam of the evening punters. Bits of newspaper lay across a couple of seats towards the back, a few squished chips on the seat on the opposite side. Each time the bus took a turn or encountered a hill a can of some form rolled back and forth on the tide. The seat in front of Sam was covered in glitter. He wondered where it had come from, what the person from an earlier journey must have looked like to have left so much of the shiny debris. He contemplated how lucky he had been to not sit in it. Not the most manly impression he could make on this of all nights. Panicking, he checked to see if the shiny plague was restricted to that seat, or if it had had company. It was ok, his seat was safe. It was quarantined.

The window held the next obvious distraction. He gazed outside, at passing buildings he had seen dozens if not hundreds of times before on his journeys into the city. He wasn't really paying attention as the bus slowed to another stop. The buildings were just kind of there, like always. The woman seemed angry. Quite angry in fact. Her eyes were fixed on Sam and she seemed to be shouting. This was a bit odd. And how was she looking straight at him? Wasn't he on the top deck?

Oh. Sam flustered as he realised his blank stare had brought him into eye contact with someone through their bedroom window. He quickly looked away, around, anywhere else. He settled on his phone screen, embarrassed that the woman thought he was trying to deliberately stare at her in her own home. He daren't look back to see if she was still there, keeping his eyes fixed on his phone lock screen. The bus began to move again, removing Sam from the problem. He began to feel a little like the woman should be well aware that there was a bus stop there, that it maybe wasn't all his fault, but it was a pretty weak argument. Still, it had never happened before. Best to not let it happen again. He raised his head and tried to focus on something else. It wasn't difficult. A young woman had got on at the stop, and she had sat in the seat in front of Sam. The glitter plague seat. Should he say something? He had only just finished being shouted at by one woman for unintended invasion of privacy, he didn't want to risk another. Plus having multiple hostile women on this journey was perhaps not the best omen for the night ahead.

Before Sam could reach a decision on the proper etiquette of stranger glitter infection, the girl noticed herself. Tutting she began wiping at her tight fitted black jeans with her hands, removing the unwanted shiny scourge. Sam felt relieved that the situation was resolving itself without him having to choose which of the available options was the most acceptable form of help, and then inevitably getting it wrong. It was all filling time though. The bus was getting closer to its destination, and he was getting closer to his destiny. A few more stops, and they would all be in town, all these people, ready to take the next steps on their journey. He could spend the next few minutes going back over what he would say, how he would sound cool and awesome, how he would mess it up, no, how he would *not* mess it up.

Movement caught Sam's attention. The bus had stopped again, and a man was walking the wrong way past his seat. Nope, he was not getting on, he was getting off – they had arrived in town. Sam was a little startled that he had no memory of the last part of the journey, he had been lost inside his mind, continuing to play out his scenarios for the evening. He checked his pockets and got up, ready to disembark. There seemed to be more people around him than there were, he had not noticed them get on, which was very unlike his hyper observant self. Perhaps the universe had decided it was not happy with the amount of people going out this evening, and had chosen to spontaneously create a few more. The girl in the seat in front of him got up and started heading for the stairs. Her rear end glistened with undiscovered glitter as she strode along. Sam was amused at the sight, but there was no easy way to relay this kind of information to someone without seeming to be a terrible person: "I couldn't help but look at your ass, and it's covered in glitter." Nope, he was leaving that one well alone. He hoped whenever she discovered it, she saw the funny side. He had to focus on his own problems. He checked the time. The bus wasn't late, it must have made the time up along the way.

No need to panic. He had plenty of time to get to the statue. It was all fine.

Stepping from the bus felt like entering a new dimension. No more watching from behind glass, no more glitter problems. Now Sam was part of the world again. The streets were busy, but this was not the time to observe. Sam was laser focused on getting to the statue and preparing for the date. This was his chance, and he was determined not to let the nerves get the better of him. Determined that he was going to grab the opportunity with both hands, he was not going to be sitting in his flat tomorrow lamenting where he had gone wrong, where the chance had slipped through his fingers like so many before. No Sunday mind hangover. At least that's what he was telling himself to think. Each step on the slick concrete slabs of the square was a chance to hammer the positive assertive thoughts into his mind, stomping on the self doubt and self questioning demons that always lurked in the sides of his mind. It was kind of working, each time his foot left the ground he heard the *"what if she thinks I look stupid"* monsters trying to rise up into the void, a see saw battle of his own wits.

He reached the statue. Where to stand? It was the most popular meeting place in the city centre, located as it was on the central square, visible from distance, easy to find, everyone knew this. Sadly, this meant that there were other people waiting here too. Several men were already stood scattered about the statue. Sam didn't really want to join them, but this was the place he had suggested. He opted to stand a little off to one side, so as to not be too obvious that he was joining the waiting group. It felt a little bit like an auction, each person stood there for the world to see, waiting to be chosen. A well made up woman walked up and joined the group. One of the men looked at her, perhaps trying to figure out if she was who he was waiting for… an internet date perhaps? He didn't move or say anything, and neither did she, not the one he was waiting for. He kept looking, perhaps trying to decide if she was better or worse than whoever he was expecting.

This whole situation was beginning to feel a little uncomfortable. Sam hoped he wouldn't be here for too long.

He saw her. All the way across the square, her presence was unmissable. Each step a sway that emanated a pulse of confident attraction, a wave of sex appeal cutting through the crowd, an ice breaker ship cutting through the frozen lands of the average, sailing unhindered towards him. It felt over dramatic, even a bit cliché, but absolutely accurate. Sam felt his confidence drain, how was he supposed to be with this woman? He quickly looked away, turning his body to face a different direction across the square, worried that she would notice him watching her walking. He didn't want her to feel he was awkwardly stood watching her walk towards him. He also felt he shouldn't walk out and meet her, that might look like he was stalking her from afar. They had agreed to meet by the statue, so he stood, looking in the wrong direction. At least until she got close enough to hear him shout hello. Hours passed in Sam's mind, every possibility played out inside that prison.

After a thousand years she appeared next to him.

"Hi Sam, nice to see you again."

"Hi, You too."

Sam almost responded sensibly, but felt he just about didn't. He was suddenly much more nervous than he had been in a long, long time. He struggled to gain a grip on the situation and his mind. Perhaps he was letting himself get caught up in the fantasy of the situation, the dreams, the wishing, the impact of that first encounter. This was just two people talking, in a town square, like many others. It was no good, his mind was beginning to drift again, gone away back to the possibilities of fantasy.

"Shall we go to The Dungeon? I've not been there for ages, it was always one of my favourites."

Ellie's smile shone as she waited for the appropriate response.

"Yeah, yeah definitely, I really like that pub too."

Was it a sign? Sharing a favourite pub? Was it just that Sam and

Jess had similar tastes, and if Ellie was a friend of Jess's, she may well also have similar tastes? Just like all the other people who frequented this particular establishment? Nope. It was a portent of destiny. Sam was convinced.

They set off on the short walk to the pub, weaving around others heading to their own destinies. Sam tried his best small talk, tried to set a comfortable and welcoming tone. He hoped that his internal discomfort and anxiety weren't slipping through, betraying him in this moment, his greatest need to appear cool and collected, a suitable and in fact irresistible choice for a life partner.

The fire erupting from the torches either side of the entranceway was as dramatic a welcoming as Sam remembered. He felt he should hold the door for Ellie, in a show of gentleman date properness. Sadly, the door was wide open, a gruff but smartly dressed bouncer nodding in welcome as she walked straight through. Perhaps Sam would get another chance to show… well he didn't know what he was trying to show, but he thought he better get whatever it was right. He stepped through and tried to catch up to Ellie as she headed for the bar.

Already catching the eye of the barman, Ellie ordered a beer. Well, that answered the question of chivalry over buying the drinks. To be honest, Sam preferred the idea that everyone just bought their own drinks, split everything evenly. He understood the idea of the man spending the money on dates, but he didn't feel comfortable with the idea that he was exchanging money hoping for things in return. It felt ancient and a bit dirty. He was much happier with people being on an equal footing, no one responsible for things, no one expecting things. He was very aware that a lot of people didn't share this view though, and he would go along where necessary. And sometimes, in situations like this, he felt he should be doing that. It was all very confusing to know what to do anymore.

The barman brought Ellie's beer, and looked across at Sam.

"Lemonade please."

The next of the social hurdles to overcome. Sam prepared the required coins as the barman began filling a glass with the required hose of soft drinks.

"Driving?"

Ellie had a curious expression as she began examining her beer bottle.

"No… I don't really drink that much."

Sam was always a bit nervous about telling people this fact, as sometimes they reacted very badly indeed. As if his not drinking was both an offence and somehow an attack on their beliefs and identity.

"Oh, cool. Wish I could do that."

Ellie seemed unphased. A good sign, and a relief.

"Isn't this place great? It hasn't changed at all!"

Ellie had switched to examining the interior of the pub. Old wood, oddities in glass cases, peculiar pipework and chandeliers – it truly was a unique place.

"Look there's a free table, lets grab it!"

Her hair flowed across her shoulders as she looked from side to side. Sam was back to being mesmerized by her. She was incredible. He couldn't believe he had managed to get to this situation, to be in a place he liked, with a girl he liked. A smile spread across him, inside and out. He couldn't help himself.

"Yeah it's an awesome place for a date."

Ellie froze. She looked a little confused. It was not the response Sam was hoping for. She moved over to the table she had suggested and sat down. Sam followed, growing a little concerned. It felt like the energy in the room had just changed.

"To be honest…"

Ellie had a slight nervousness to her tone. Sam placed the drinks on the table and sat down next to her. She began fiddling with the wrapper on her beer bottle.

"I hadn't really thought this was anything other than a couple of mates hanging out. I mean… my last boyfriend… it didn't go so well so I had decided to swear off men for a bit, you know?"

"Oh… well… of course…"

Sam was a bit confused, when Jess had suggested he ask Ellie out, he had assumed that Ellie was aware of or at least open to the suggestion.

"I thought when I asked you out for a drink that it sounded like, you know, I was asking you on a date…"

Ellie glanced at her phone and then went back to picking at her label.

"If you don't want that, that's cool, it can just be hanging out as friends, there's no pressure. I mean, I'm sorry if I made you uncomfortable."

Sam was sorry if he had made her uncomfortable. He began to question his own ability to sound like a friend or potential suitor, and where the miscommunication had come from. He was crushed. It felt like all of his hopes and dreams were collapsing. How could he have let this happen? How could he have assumed someone like this would be interested in someone like him? It was Tish all over again.

"Oh no, don't worry about that."

Ellie stopped the label torture, instead wrapping her hand around the bottle and taking a drink.

"I mean I'm not very good at sticking to what I swear to."

She looked Sam in the eye and gave a coy half smile. Now he was a mixture of relived, confused, and exhilarated. She shifted her position so that she was leaning ever so slightly towards him.

"So tell me some more about yourself."

Sam took a sip of his drink and wondered if Ellie knew that leaning forward like that made her top open ever so slightly… he should definitely not be caught noticing that kind of thing…

"Well you know, not much to tell really, usual stuff, amazing personality, stunning looks, and always in the middle of some form of utter heroism. Just like everyone else really."

Sometimes Sam's sense of humour made people who didn't know him laugh, other times they just looked at him confused as to whether he was being serious. It made him think that he should take people's advice and try and work on it to make more people fall into the first category. Secretly, he felt like he was more likely to find kindred spirits if he stayed the way he was rather than changing to appease people that he didn't really get on with that well anyway. He sat, in the moment waiting for her response. A heartbeat of time, a thousand thoughts. He was already exhausted from the ups and downs of the evening, and they had only just sat down.

Ellie did neither of the usual things in response to Sam's joke. She just flicked her eyes between her bottle, which she had started to play with, rotating it on the table, and Sam's eyes. He wasn't certain, but he thought she had leaned in a little bit more. A hint of lace could be seen lurking below the open button neckline of Ellie's blouse.

Sam did his best small talk. He spoke about his job, his likes, some of his dislikes. All very briefly. He was flustered, and more than slightly confused as to what was happening. Ellie seemed interested, but at the same time the things she said as he had sat down had stuck in his mind. He didn't want to let himself continue to hope she was interested if she wasn't available. But she was so… He still felt slightly out of breath in her presence.

"So tell me about you! How do you like spending your time?"

Sam genuinely wanted to know more about her, and really wanted to stop talking about himself before either he said something really stupid, or she got bored and left.

"Well…"

She giggled a little and shifted her position straightening her back and placing both hands on the table as if she was about to give a political election speech.

"I'm unbelievably awesome. The best at everything and unstoppably amazing at all times."

She smiled and giggled again. Sam couldn't help but laugh. He found himself leaning closer to her, and she settled back into her previous pose, possibly leaning even further and certainly closer. Sam could feel the heat from her forearm through the few inches of air that separated them, and he had to turn his head slightly to keep her gaze. He wasn't sure which of them had moved more, but they were definitely getting closer.

She spoke of her job, of her likes, and her dislikes. All very briefly. She giggled, a lot. It was infectious. Sam found himself joining in and smiling more than he had in quite a while. She tapped his arm as they shared outrage at a shared dislike of people playing terrible music on buses through even worse speakers. She flicked her hair and laughed loudly at the mention of men in overly tight jeans coupled with big puffy jackets trying to look tough rather than like a child's stick drawing of grown ups. He felt like he was melting towards her, his fears and anxieties falling away as they spoke.

"Would you like another?"

Ellie picked up her empty bottle and pointed at Sam's glass. He had forgotten when he had finished it. He had become lost in the moments of conversation and giggles.

"Err yeah sure."

Sam was amazed how quickly he could revert to being nervous and unsure, He had felt so comfortable a few seconds ago.

"Would you like me to go to the bar?"

He glanced anxiously at the bar and the empty glass and bottle. Was he supposed to go? Was that the man's role? He didn't believe in such things but he also didn't want to appear rude or wrong. He wasn't sure what modern etiquette was at the best of times and for some reason he felt even more adrift this evening.

"Yours doesn't hardly cost anything, and I'm sitting at the edge of the table. You can get the next ones if you really want too you dope."

Ellie shook her head a few times to show her sense of *'you're an idiot'* to Sam as she got up from the table. He felt a wave of sparks fly through him as her thigh stroked his as she wriggled out to a standing position.

"I will be back in a minute, don't wander off like a lost puppy."

Sam couldn't help but keep his eyes on her as she walked away. Her skirt was close fitting and her steps seemed to emphasise her curves as she walked. It was too late for Sam. He quite liked Ellie. He was lost.

Snapping back to the world around him, he took his phone from his pocket, proceeding to pretend to read important and interesting things from the blank screen. The idea of being seen sat alone and doing nothing at a table in a pub was unthinkable. Staring at your date from across the room was creepy. Proper people had important phone based things to do when no one was there, that thoroughly justified their situation. Things had to be checked, despite there being nothing to find. Social media needed to replace the lack of physical interaction at this table. There was very rarely anything on his phone of importance at all, so the chance of something appearing in these solitary pub minutes was highly unlikely. About as likely as an asteroid falling from on high into the middle of the room, revealing hitch-hiking aliens to the astonished and slightly inebriated crowd. Now if that happened, Sam would put it on his various pages and walls. Sam wondered if that would be ironic. He still wasn't sure about this entire situation.

Several minutes passed, Sam's mind drifting back to thoughts of Ellie and her giggle. He was excited about the evening, it's possibilities, and anxious for her return. She was the sort of girl he had always seen across pubs and wondered how people got to be friends with people like that. Always seemed a bit out of reach, a bit above his weight class, out of his league. She seemed to be interested in him, and that was making him feel a lot better about things than he had for quite some time. He was nervous that he might do something wrong and mess it all up. That something he said would make her think *"Oh yeah, I don't go for guys like you do I?"*

He thought about what he should say when she came back, how he should be, how he should sit. His mind flew back to the dating tips he had read when he had first left university, when he knew no one in this place. He had studied, as if there was a code or formula that could be discovered and mastered that would make everything work out. Truth was there was no such code. Truth was there were more people interested in trying to sell the idea that there was a formulaic list of do's and don'ts to social interaction than there were people trying to genuinely understand it. Sam knew that he should be himself and just see where it all went, but Sam's truth was that sometimes he didn't like parts of himself and wondered what that meant for trying to get others to like him.

Ellie emerged from the crowded bar with a full bottle and a full glass. The label on the bottle already showed signs of being torn off when she placed both drinks down on the table and began to sit back down.

"You know what that means?"

Sam pointed at the torn label and then immediately regretted the comment. He felt the sparks again as Ellie's thigh brushed his as she sat, but this time they didn't stop. She maintained the contact as she settled in, and as she began picking at the label again she replied, softly;

"Yes, it means I'm addicted to picking beer labels."

The evening turned to night as the world spun around the bubble of Sam and Ellie in the pub. Nothing else seemed to matter but the closeness, the contact, the smiles and giggles. The other people in the pub faded into a blur of shape and colour, their muffled sound unable to break through into this reality of two. As they continued to talk, about everything and nothing, Sam felt at peace. As they giggled together, the taps to the hand and arm became strokes. Without realising when, he realised one of them had touched the others' hand and not let go. They sat, holding hands on the table and giggling. The rest of the world spun in chaos around this bubble of peace.

The barman's thick tattooed arm broke through as it reached for the empty glasses and bottles that had gathered around the two of them, an art installation in Sam's mind depicting the progress of the evening. A beer mat perched across the top of two bottles, Sam's attempt at a pub henge. The barman seemed less than impressed, and as he flicked it off and gathered the empty vessels, he simply mumbled:

"Time."

Ellie jumped up as if it was the start of a race:

"Oh be right back! Don't let me forget my coat!"

Sam, utterly startled by this turn of events and the crashing collapse of his peaceful Ellie bubble, along with his henge, could barely mumble a reply as he watched her dash off to the ladies. He attempted a smile at the barman, who had already turned away and was off to break any other bubbles he could find on his sinister mission around the place. Sam was left with few choices and a disjointed mind. As he peeled himself from the table, he pulled his coat on and checked his pockets. Everything accounted for. It was as though he was making sure he was still really here, that this was all happening. When he was talking to Ellie he felt comfortable, when he wasn't, he was hyper aware that she was gone, and his doubts returned to fill the gap.

He stared at Ellie's coat. Dark grey and tailored, it was smart and feminine. Should he pick it up? Hold it for her? Would that be weird, as though he had been going through the pockets? If he left it there would it look like he wasn't bothered? How come this had all gotten so unpeaceful and complicated all of a sudden? Sam wanted to be sat back with her, watching the corners of her mouth curl into smiles and feel the warmth of her hand.

She caught his eye from across the pub, pointing at her coat and then the door, tilting her head to show it was time to leave. Another anxiety calmed in a second by her. Sam carefully collected her coat and walked over to her.

"Your coat m'lady."

He attempted a butler impression as he held the collar out to her, expecting her to slip her arms in as he held it there. Very gentlemanly, he thought to himself. Man points to me. Instead, she grabbed it from him and bounced through the door.

"Come on, I'm going to miss my bus!"

Startled again, Sam followed her out of the pub. The cold wind hit him directly in the face as though his confusion of the last few minutes had taken physical form and slapped him shouting *"Have that you idiot!"* The street was bustling with people, their outfits as loud as their drunken ramblings. Ellie was dashing along, weaving between old bald men with red faces and young scantily clad ladies with black heels. Sam kept up, a few paces behind. He wasn't really sure if he was supposed to be doing so, or if he should wave and let her go. He felt they were inseparable a few minutes ago, and now he wasn't sure if she remembered he was there. Weaving past a check shirted fellow with a rather large container of meat based product and chips, he found Ellie standing at a bus stop, waving at him to catch up. The bus was there already, pub dwellers and twilight shift workers filing on.

"You OK?"

Sam asked as he finally caught up to her. She placed her hand on his arm and seemed a little out of breath.

"Yeah, sorry, didn't realise the time!"

Her smile reassured Sam, but he still felt a bit lost. What was he supposed to do now? Was this over, should he ask to see her again, or was he supposed to ask to get on the bus with her? Sam was not inexperienced in dating etiquette; he had messed up lots of times before.

"That was a really fun night, thanks I needed that."

The past tense in Ellie's comment let Sam know where he stood. Her words flowed through her smile, her tone was reassuring. Sam couldn't help but smile back.

"Yeah it was, would you like to do it again some time?"

It was about as smooth and romantic as Sam could manage. He felt his heart racing at the excitement of seeing her again and the sadness of seeing her go tonight. For a second he thought he saw Ellie's smile vanish as she glanced to her feet. He panicked that she might say no, that he was right and she was out of his league, despite the evening they had just had, in the pub that now seemed so far away.

Raising her eyes back to his, her smile returning, she answered:

"Sure, that would be nice."

As Sam's heart raced, she added:

"But, listen, like I said earlier, I wasn't really looking for anything, so is it ok if we take it slow and just see where it goes?"

"Of course, yeah, no problem."

Sam was perfectly happy to go as slow as she wanted, as long as he could see her again. He had gotten more glimpses of happiness and satisfaction from sitting with her, holding her hand and talking with her than he had had in a long time, and that was enough.

"And is it ok if we just keep it between us, until we feel more comfortable? My friends know I've been single for a while and they would go mental at me if they found out I had been on a date and ask loads of questions and I would rather not have that bit right now."

Ellie seemed concerned, her body language had become awkward, less confident than he had ever seen her. Sam wanted her to be as comfortable and happy with him as he felt with her.

"OK, yeah, I get that, I only want to talk to you anyway."

Sam caught himself feeling like he had said what he meant with the wrong words, overexposing himself.

"Err I mean I will leave it up to you to tell anyone else, I'm cool with that."

The last few people had taken their seats on the bus, the driver shouted "You coming love?" towards Ellie. She leaned in and kissed Sam on the cheek, which sent him into fits of sparks. The warmth of her body against his left him powerless and suggestible, and he didn't mind at all.

"Night Sam."

Ellie pulled away and bounced up onto the bus, her hair jostling against her shoulders. She gave a wave as the bus pulled away. Sam smiled and waved back, still waving as the bus headed off up the street and away into the night. Turning to face the city and the crowds, Sam was alone again. But, for the first time in a long time, he didn't feel alone. Warmed by the encounter and full of hope for the spark filled future, he joined the flow of people trying to get home at the end of the night. The best night in a long time.

18

The mist hung like the memory of the forest. The call of birds of prey could be heard from the perch on the Cliffside as they soared overhead, trying to find any sign of targets through the density of leaf and vapour. This would be a treacherous path to take, but it was necessary. She had come too far to give up now. Too many hard choices, too many friends lost along the journey to allow the scene ahead to waver her resolve. Beyond the forest she could just make out the high stone walls of the city. An ancient fortress, it still looked pristine as the golden rays of sunset caught the battlements and towers. She hoped the rumours were just that. They told of an ancient evil that protected the stone, the tight clasp of a demon holding the walls together, preventing entrance to any who may try to best its master. If the battered and moth eaten scrolls she had wrested from their dusty resting place deep under the capitol were accurate, she might, just might, have a chance of avoiding certain death - or worse - in this attempt. As she finished her descent from the Cliffside thc calls of birds grew louder. And louder.

Before she realised the danger, one of the birds was on her, long talons digging for purchase on her leather clad shoulders. Instinct kicked in, and she tried to roll to her side whilst reaching for her dagger. Feathers the size of forearms battered her back as she tried to adjust, wrenching just free enough to get a grip on her trusted blade. An almighty crack of blue light pierced the air from nowhere, forcing her to close her eyes and wince at the brightness. The sound of screeching, the release of talons, an almighty thump as the bird hit the ground beside her. Bemused at what had just happened, but thankful, she turned to see the cause of her salvation.

A shadowy figure stood at the edge of the forest. Dark robes and hood hiding intentions. Cautiously, and still with her hand on her blade, she rose to her feet. The hooded figure moved closer. Each foot fall brought extra chance to discern the identity and intent they brought nearer. She peered through the shadows of rock and branch.

"Could it be?"

The words escaped her as her mind began to race. The stranger stopped, a muscular arm reaching up and pulling back the hood. The piercing green eyes were unmistakable. She felt a tremble through her being as she comprehended what had happened, who had saved her.

"Lord Vaiyn?"

No longer tensed for battle, she felt her body clench with a different form of nerves.

"Hello again Drusilla, it seems I was correct when I stated you needed me by your side."

The energy of the magicks cracked between his fingers as a wry smile crossed his lips.

"There's no need for that now is there?"

Vaiyn's green eyes fixed on Drusilla's hand, still gripped on the hilt of her blade.

"Unless you are planning to remove something perhaps?"

Drusilla's heart skipped, she could fend off Vaiyn's attention if she wanted, but she wasn't sure she wanted to in the face of the dangers that lay ahead. Perhaps she

"Louie, the cupboard's still a mess, but there's tea here, do you want some tea?"

"Piss off I'm at a good bit!"

Louisa's frustration betrayed itself in her tone.

"Oh get you! How dare I offer missy a free tea!"

Nia's pitch raised in mock grovelling at the offence of unexpected favours.

"And don't call me Louie! That's a boy's name!"

Louisa felt flustered as her concentration was broken. She had lost herself in the pages, immune to the reality of the world around her, lost in her own world. It slowly dawned on her what Nia had said, and how badly she had reacted.

"You're a boy's name!"

Nia's voice echoed off the tiles of the kitchen, seemingly giving extra gravitas to her statement.

"Thanks for the tea! Sorry! One sugar please!"

Louisa smiled widely in appreciation, a consolatory act that was completely lost on the kitchen door. Had she taken her eyes from the pages, Louisa may have noticed how unimpressed the door remained.

Mumbles could be heard emanating from the kitchen, followed by stomps of increasing volume and then the unceremonious thud of a mug on the coffee table.

"Here you go grumpy, here's your piss."

"Thanks… sorry it's a good bit! I'll let you borrow it after me."

Louisa smiled again and waved the paperback in the air as a compensatory prize for the beverage, as well as a kind of apology for being snappy.

"Err... thanks? Not really my thing though is it, all wizards and dragons and make believe."

Nia gracefully slumped into the chair across from Louisa, mug in hand.

"About as believable as those TV shows you watch that claim to be reality…"

Louisa mumbled as she adjusted her position on the sofa for maximum comfort before returning to the land of magick and the adventures of the dark rogue Drusilla.

"What?"

"Nothing sweetie, reading aloud."

Louisa curled herself up and let the edges of the world fade away, in their place the cold stone of castle walls and sunset over a distant realm.

"Let's have a look then."

Nia reached her hand across the small table of drinks,

requesting the promised look at the book much sooner than Louisa had expected. The castle was again snatched from view.

"Oh… yeah."

Louisa passed over her source of escape. Grumpily.

"Hmm."

Nia looked at the cover. She flicked the pages. She looked at the back. She returned to flicking the pages, stopping in random places. Her lips moved as she read sections out quietly to herself.

"Hmm."

She returned to the cover, scouring every detail before revealing her judgement:

"So… what I don't get here, she's the main character yeah? A bad ass rogue warrior that fights and kills monsters and things, right?"

"Err yeah, that's not all of it but yes she is the heroine and a pretty cool one at that."

Louisa wasn't sure if she was going to have to defend her favourite genre or answer genuine questions. She kinda just wanted to go back to reading it for herself.

"Right, so why is her outfit so revealing? If she's going to battle why is she wearing basically a fur trimmed bra? How does that help anything? The dude in the background has full armour and a cloak on… what's the weather like? Is he really hot dressed like that or is she really cold? Really cold, and going into a fight with huge amounts of exposed skin for monsters and things to stab at?"

Nia was frowning at the picture. Louisa recognised the argument, because it was a ridiculous picture. But she wondered why Nia was asking such a question.

"Yeah that's bullshit, but they draw it like that to sell copies I suppose, sex appeal like everything else, just like the TV shows where the men wear a full suit and the women wear the skimpiest skin tight excuse for a dress ever."

Nia considered the response.

"Yeah sex sells, and all that shit, but why does it cross into this? It's a book about a strong woman, and it's actually putting me off reading it."

Louisa felt she should defend the book series she was thoroughly enjoying, but she wasn't sure she wanted to defend that particular part of it too much.

"It's escapism, I don't pay much attention to that, I suppose. It doesn't read like she's dressed like that, I guess, but still… she's feminine and when it's romantic it…"

"Oh it gets sexy does it? Sexy monster slayers?"

Nia started flipping through the pages again, a sudden ironic spark of curiosity.

"I haven't finished it yet!"

Louisa's concern that Nia was flipping to pages beyond those she had read, and that she might let out a spoiler, added a tremble to her voice. Nia's eyes were wide as she wafted the book in Louisa's general direction.

"And you of all people, reading something like this… a dirty book… tsk tsk missy!"

"It's not! You nutter! Shut it!"

Louisa chucked one of the cushions from the sofa at Nia in an attempt at expression via non verbal communication.

"Oi! Watch my tea you spanner!"

"And what do you mean 'you of all people!' what people!?"

Louisa was flustered at this entire situation. Although she had gained a cup of tea, she had lost her nice cosy escape from the world. This world that was full of fluster causing flatmates.

"Well you're not exactly out on the town making all the romance dirty stories for yourself are you dear."

Nia placed the additional cushion on her lap and spoke with the tone of a disapproving parent.

"In all the time I've known you, you've never once mentioned a partner, date, sneaky rendezvous, drunken mistake…"

Louisa's flust had not and would not subside.

"Well, that's not the point is it! And I've not known you that long!"

Nia was unimpressed by the retort.

"You've not even been out for ages, not since that work party housewarming thing, and that was indeed ages ago."

"Hey, that's not true, I've been out since then, with Jess and Steven, I told you about that! I even asked if you wanted to come along once!"

Louisa defended herself and her actions, which she felt was unnecessary given the circumstances that she wasn't that bothered what Nia or anyone else thought of what she did. Well, that's what she told herself. She was in fact quite deeply bothered. But why let that get in the way of a good strong denial of wrongdoing.

"Yes. You've been out… with a couple. That's not going to fill the pages of a dirty book now is it?"

Nia looked at the book. She looked at Louisa. She held the book up towards Louisa.

"Unless! Louie are you in a weird threesome relationship with a couple!? Are you their bit extra on the side! Ha!"

Louisa's look of shock and horror began deep inside her soul. It rapidly spread across her entire being, focusing with such numbing power that she lost all feeling in her face. Feeling which returned quickly as the cushion landed squarely between her eyes. Nia's laughter caused her to bend double in her chair. Louisa sputtered cushion fluff.

"Now just wait…"

Louisa was unsure which outrage to focus on first.

"I see why they are called throw cushions now, that was so good!"

Nia was struggling for breath between laughs.

"The look… on your face!"

"I am not in a weird relationship!"

"Oh Louie, you're the person I would least expect anything like that from."

Louisa was slightly offended by this latest statement. Despite it being the exact opposite of the last statement which had offended her. This was a very difficult conversation to adapt to emotionally. Nia had managed to calm down, although Louisa feared this would give her the ability to ask more questions. It turned out her fear was not unfounded.

"OK, Ok… no weird threesomeness. Although they do say it's always the quiet ones… But seriously, did you meet anyone else at these things? Or how about at that house party? There must have been people there?"

Louisa thought for a moment. She was not particularly comfortable discussing things like this.

"No, I don't remember speaking to anyone like that. I mean, in that sense."

"Really? No one? At a party?"

Nia shot a look of disbelief from her chair.

"I did see a nice coat, I liked that. I think everyone else were couples or something."

Louisa had remembered the coat. She still wondered where it had come from, she couldn't find it in the shops. Although they were shifting stock to spring.

"A coat? That's what you took away from a party? Seriously? What about guys? Were there any guys there? Did you flirt with anyone? Did they flirt with you!"

Louisa pondered Nia's question. She tried to remember. She knew she hadn't flirted with anyone, because she was rubbish at flirting and didn't really understand how to do it. So that was certain.

"No, there wasn't any of that. Everyone was there for Jess and Steven, couples like I said."

Louisa didn't really want to admit she was trying her best to make friends with Jess, and that it seemed to be working. She liked Nia, and they got on as flatmates. This conversation however, was another example of how she didn't feel she was quite on the same wavelength as her, and she wished she could make it feel better. She just wasn't sure how. She was hoping to learn that skill from Jess, then she could apply it here and everything would be better.

"Hmm. I'm not sure I believe you there. Anywhere there are people there's flirting. It's natural. Even couples do it."

Nia seemed very sure of her statement. Was she right? Louisa tried to think back. She couldn't think of any evidence to back up the statement. She wasn't very good at flirting though. Had she not noticed it? No, that would be ridiculous. She was pretty sure it would be too hard to miss.

"Well either way, I'm not convinced that you don't want to be a part of that, what with your sexy monster slayer books."

Louisa wanted to shrug off the comment with a simple 'whatever' but there was some truth to it. She did enjoy those parts of the book. She would look at Jess and Steven, how they completed each other's personalities, how affectionate they were when they thought she wasn't looking. She did wonder if she would like to have something like that for herself.

"Well…"

It was all she could manage.

"I knew it!"

Nia reacted as though she had just found the critical piece of evidence in a murder investigation.

"So is there anyone? Do they have friends to share? Oh shall we go out on the pull together? Girls night on the town!"

"I'm sure your boyfriend would be thrilled at that suggestion!"

Louisa hoped the formalness of the statement emphasised her disapproval of the entire thing.

"Oh yeah, fair point. Got a little caught up in the moment there."

Nia's disappointment worried Louisa. It didn't stop the conversation though.

"Well, there's other options, you could do online dating? That's what everyone does now… yes!"

Louisa was very unsure about all of this. She did like how happy Jess and Steven looked together.

"Right then you, that's it then. We are making you a dating profile, right now! I will help! It's going to be so much fun!"

Nia was very excited. Louisa was very very unsure about all of this. She wanted her book back now please.

19

The place was almost empty. The music didn't quite fit the venue, a bit too eighties pop for what was normally a metal pub. The girl behind the bar was unconsciously rocking back and forth in rhythm with the happy beat, her bright red hair rolling like waves of cherry pop crashing on the black lace shore of her shoulders.

"Are you eyeing up the barmaid?"

Matt was apparently following Sam's eye line. Sam jumped a little, back into the world and out of his daydream.

"Huh? Yeah, wait no… Not like that! I was just thinking there was this very clear metal fan, dancing along to eighties pop, in here. Seemed a bit out of place!"

"Right…"

Matt seemed unconvinced.

"It's true, I'm all for a pub having a jukebox, free choice and that, great. But if you're a clear style of bar with an identity you're known for, why put out of place music on the jukebox in the first place? Like why put pop music on in here? Why not curate the playlist?"

"Yeah, I don't get it."

It was true, Sam didn't get it.

"Is curate the right word? Sounds like it should be."

"Maybe they have to buy a set jukebox. Like maybe the songs are set. At the shop, the dude is all '*yeah this is the pub 3000, all metal rim. Music included, but you can choose walnut or pine for the side panels*'. Jerk."

Matt shook his head at the thought of the useless jukebox salesman. Sam chuckled as he took a sip of his drink.

"Oh and don't blame you, the barmaid is hot. She follows the law of pubs – the staff are always foxy. I think their general hotness is increased by the role."

Matt bulged his eyes to emphasise his point.

"Does that apply to the men too? Or just the women?"

Sam already knew the crushing answer, but wondered if Matt agreed, or if it was just him that felt it.

"Oh mate."

Matt slumped back in his chair.

"It's worse for the men. The effect I mean. In a place like this? Damn. The men are ridiculous. How are we supposed to compete?! *And* they have all the drinks… It's not fair! *And* they get to hang out with the barmaids… complete with appropriate things to say to them to start conversations. It's so not fair. It's beyond that, it's unjust. And disgusting, frankly."

Matt's head shook in sorrow.

"Imagine the interviews to work in places like this! *Sorry you have to be at least a 7 out of 10 to work here.*"

Matt seemed to have thought this through to a much higher level than Sam had. This made Sam feel better. And a bit worse.

"And obviously once they have the job it adds another 1 or 2 to that score."

Matt's rant continued, Sam had opened the can, and the worms were free. Chuckling again, Sam was relived it wasn't just him that felt it was unfair.

"Yup. Not. Fair. It's disgusting. And unjust. It's disjusting."

Glancing across the mostly empty room, he caught the eye of the red haired barmaid. She turned away and started straightening the bottles of spirits that stood on the shelf behind the bar, passing the time until someone came across and asked for a drink. From the looks of the place, that may be a while.

"Where is everyone? This place was packed last week!"

"Oh yeah?"

Matt perked up considerably.

"In here with your lady? Your mystery friend? Your mystery lady friend?"

He reached for his beer and leaned in.

"Tell me a story Sam, tell me a story of wonder and joy and

mystery women riding horseback across rainbows. You dick."

Sam shifted awkwardly in his mind, and also his chair.

"It's not a mystery, more of a secret."

"Oooh..."

Matt's eyes widened.

"That's better... juicier. Unleash the mystery juice my boy."

"Well secret isn't really the right word... and also eww... sounds so wrong."

Sam's face shifted to show his disgust at all of the things. The right word to describe the situation had been eluding Sam ever since the first night in the pub with Ellie. He knew he would struggle to describe what was going on to Matt if he couldn't explain it to himself.

"It's complicated. But it's fine."

"Complicated, you? Who would have thought!"

Matt's sly smile slightly agitated Sam.

"So is it, or are you just overthinking everything and making it weird? You know, like you do with everything? You know, because you're a dick."

Matt took a long sip from his beer without taking his eyes from Sam. Not even blinking. It was the facial expression equivalent of an exclamation point.

"I am no dick sir! I am a perfectly fine gentleman that gets embroiled in occasional shenanigans and jams as a result of the opportunity for adventure!"

Sam rebuffed Matt's face.

"While you argue that your dickery is the result of external factors, I find myself outraged. Although I would like to remind you that you are the cause of your dickness and my amusement upon many an occasion, I must note that my glass is empty. This I blame you for. This sad turn of events may lay weight to the argument that your penasity is the cause of the ills of the world."

Matt's chair screeched on the floor as he stood up.

"And now, if you will excuse me, I need to acquire a replacement.

I would offer to get you one also, but I find I don't want to."

"I'm sure the barmaid will be happy to see you, even if it's just to judge you as unworthy of her time. And I have plenty of this left, thanks."

Sam held up his glass and swashed the contents in Matt's general direction, willing it to form a beverage middle finger. It did not.

"Indeed, if I get more than five words I will be punching above my weight."

Walking through the empty pub, Matt seemed both excited to be getting a chance to speak to the barmaid and sad about the inevitable outcome of their encounter. Sam watched with a smile as the barmaid wandered over to Matt, nodded, and began to pour the beer. Matt seemed to be trying something. His foot was tapping as he waved his hands about over the bar. Handing him his beer the barmaid looked blankly at him. He handed over a selection of coins, nodded, turned and walked back to the table.

"Well??"

Sam eagerly awaited the response to the complex question he had posed.

"Four words. 'Yeah' and 'four quid mate."

Matt looked both stunned and proud that his attempts at conversation had failed so spectacularly.

"It's ok though, I've decided to live vicariously through your story. So come on, spit it out! Hasn't this been going on for a while now?"

Sam's cackle of glee at his friends' fortune masked his insecurity of how to explain the situation he had found himself in with Ellie. He knew he would have to try and put it into words, and a part of him hoped that doing so would help him make some sense of it himself. He began by saying how they had met, at the party Matt had missed. He tried to explain how he had felt something for her immediately, without sounding unmanly. He knew Matt liked to take the piss. There was no need to give him extra ammunition.

The story continued, how Sam had secured a first date, and a second, and how they were continuing. Slowly. How work schedules made it difficult. How he was trying to help Ellie feel better about it all, how he understood why she was a bit nervous about being out and open. She had told him how her friends would make a big fuss, and she wanted to feel more settled before that happened, after all, she had been single for a while, and in bad relationships before that.

Saying it out loud, it made Sam a little uncomfortable. She was Jess's friend, and he knew Jess would be careful towards Ellie's feelings. After all, she knew that she and Sam were seeing each other to some degree, spending time together at least, and she hadn't gone mental or anything. Never the less, Sam didn't know the core of Ellie's friends, other than seeing their social media posts on Ellie's wall. And he hadn't had a string of bad relationships in his past. It wasn't fair of him to judge her by his experiences. He had to let her settle into it, he had to be supportive. She was worth it, worth the wait, and besides, it was the right thing to do.

The tale was told, the secrets revealed. Adventures laid out for all the Matt to see. Sam looked across the table, ready for the appraisal and review. Nothing. Matt looked deep in thought. Anxiety began to claw up through Sam, as though a grumpy cat was trying to find a comfortable place to sit on his soul, it's claws kneading at his vulnerable innards. After an age of the sharp pressure, Matt stirred himself to respond.

"Mate, what you're saying, basically, is that you went so soppy over this lass that even the water from your own sop was embarrassed to be seen near you. You became a teenager all doe eyed. No. Worse. You became an emo teenager about it."

Matt eyes bulged as he paused for a drink and for the effect of his remark to sink in.

"Now… steady… don't use the E word. Never use the E word."

Sam acted rocked by the accusation. He was a little, he didn't think he had been as affected by Ellie as Matt was pointing out. And he hadn't even told him half of how he really felt whenever he saw her.

Placing his drink upon the table, Matt readied himself for his next onslaught.

"So… emo boy… did you write her a song yet? A poem? Design a tattoo? Ooo a tattoo of a poem?! Yes! That's the fella. How does it go?"

Sam's eyes narrowed as he fixed Matt in unspoken insult. It did not stop Matt, perhaps merely encouraged him. He raised his left hand towards the fragments of street light sneaking into the bar from the grimy window, placed his right hand on his heart, and began.

"She looked like no other person in this room, she was illuminated beyond anyone else. She was shining into the parts of me that had been dark for so long they had forgotten what light looked like. Flowers in winter, starved of the sun, she was melting the snow that had covered them and they were remembering the warmth that they had forgotten they were missing…"

Sam's eyes couldn't get much narrower at this point, but he couldn't help a small chuckle at Matt's words and performance.

"Yeah? Get it in a nice script, on your upper arm, wrapped around a skull yeah?"

Matt started flexing his arm and gesturing to the location.

"Ooo and the skull has a rose in its mouth… and there's blood dripping from the rose thorns… No, no! From the skull's eyes!"

Matt looked impressed by his design idea.

"Oh oh! And you can have your photo taken with it on full display, all black and white, brooding and that! This is the most amazing thing that there has ever been!"

Matt was in full on amazement at his own genius of putdowns.

"Yeah I will get right on that bard boy."

Not Sam's best comeback. He was amused as always by Matt, but a little embarrassed at how he was highlighting that he really did have some pretty strong feelings for this girl. It was time to fire back and deflect from his unconventional dating adventures.

"Hey, you can come to the photoshoot too… you can get a nice tat of the barmaid depicting the time that your charm and smooth social skills won her over and she instantly fell for you."

Matt laughed out some beer he was trying to swallow.

"Yeah, yeah! she can be like leaping over the bar while ripping her clothes off… you know, a historically accurate portrait of events!"

The pair of them broke into laughter, at each other, at themselves.

20

Spring raindrops hit the window with a gentle rhythm, the droplets merging, flowing down the glass in serpentine streaks echoed by the rising shimmer of steam billowing out of Louisa's mug. She watched the falling rain through the rising steam, imagining she was high above the world, watching the clouds below pass over rivers and streams as she flew to some new land, some new place, far away from this flat, away from the confusion, repetition, the predictableness of her life here.

Pulling the mug close to her face, she felt the warmth of the coffee as though it was a sun kissed beach. Closing her eyes, she focused on waving palm trees, rustling in a summer breeze. The rain drops became a decorative waterfall, cascading over rocks into a welcoming pool. She was sat on a wooden stool, at a beach bar built from logs. Beautiful people in beautiful clothes stood on hand to cater for all of her wishes, the warm sun never setting on this wonderful place.

Letting out a sigh of calm wanting, Louisa softly tipped the mug towards her, missed her lips, and causally poured her coffee all over herself.

After jumping out of her seat, and almost her skin, running out of expletives, running around holding her T shirt up like a bowl to catch any excess drink, finding some more expletives, decrying deities, even cursing the origins of coffee beans themselves, she finally managed to end this beverage crisis. Flustered by the experience, she decided she needed something stronger to calm down and get through the rest of the evening. Something more red, something less burny. Returning to her seat with glass in hand, she sighed, and flicked the power button on.

A faint whirring signalled the life returning, and behold… a bright light shone out, bathing Louisa's face in a comforting yet also slightly depressing glow. A loud chink marked a slight miscalculation of distance as her glass hit the desk, causing her eyes to widen and dart to the red waves, luckily remaining within. That would have really not helped with her mood. Letting out another quick sigh, and with appropriate sized glass of wine to hand, her gaze returned to her laptop screen. Maybe this was the time it was ok? Perhaps this was the time there would be a decent response to her profile? Surely this was the time a nice, normal, sane, clothed man would have messaged her.

A series of clicks and swipes, familiar repetitive motions of the modern era, and up flashed her profile.

"Nice girl seeks nice guy, no time wasters."

A straight forward and easy to understand heading. She thought. No chance of misinterpretation.

"Right, here we go… good luck!"

She spoke to the universe more than to herself, attempting to both summon the will to face the potential for heartbreak and heart-warming that lay in the ones and zeros. Twenty-two unread messages.

"Ok, that's an amount."

She wondered how long it had been since she had last checked. A couple of days?

"Is this a normal amount of messages to get when I haven't sent any myself in several weeks?"

Again addressing the universe for reassurance, she felt a kind of faint satisfaction, that her profile and picture were that good, that she was that attractive. She clicked on the first message:

"Hard fuck baby"

And a phone number. Her sense of satisfaction faltered a little. Next message:

"You want this now"

Again with a phone number, and a picture of a man's penis.

"For fuck's sake!"

Louisa deleted the message and reached for her wine.

"What is wrong with these guys?!"

The universe failed to answer. Predictable as ever in its lack of direct assistance. Next message.

"Hey you look sexy, let's meet your place or a hotel msg me back."

"Why not just post that you're married, you creep."

Louisa was rapidly losing the will to continue.

She opened the next couple of messages in quick succession. One more dodgy photo, two more phone numbers.

"I thought this was a dating site."

And with that, her motivation was gone. She deleted the rest of the messages without reading them, and considered deleting her profile too.

"Why the… what is the… how?"

After Nia had helped make her profile, Jess had failed to state It was a terrible idea when she was asked. Instead Jess suggested that she give the site a try, as she had 'several friends' who had found their partners via online dating. Was it a myth? Was 'several friends' code for *'you're not getting anywhere at the moment the way you are you should try that and I'm going to pretend to know people that it worked for to make you want to do it and stop bugging me about not finding anyone whilst also making me sound like I know what I'm talking about and not throwing you to the naked pictured sex wolves of rapeville.'*

Slumping into the sofa, Louisa contemplated her lot in life. How had this happened, how had she arrived at this point. She had done everything she was supposed to, studied, worked hard, helped, cared, how come her reward was sitting by herself surrounded by either silence or random men's unwanted, and extremely graphic, advances.

Nope. No time to sink into self-pity. Maybe she was just looking at it wrong, going about this from the wrong angle. She took a breath, and some wine, pulled herself more upright, and returned to the screen.

"OK, maybe weirdo's send messages, maybe I should try looking."

Louisa tried to reassure herself that it was a good idea. She felt she could only stand to be on this site for so long, both tonight and in general. It was time to try and take more control of the situation. Time to attack the problem head on. She clicked the search options button. Selecting the age range to be roughly similar to hers, and the location to be not too far afield, she clicked on the start button. She felt a slight sense of anticipation as the page went blank as it started its cycle of reloading. Then there they were. A selection of the men on offer. Or, more accurately, a selection of topless posing men. Interspersed were pictures of expensive cars, and a few less expensive cars with aftermarket parts attached to varying standards. Many of the titles of the profiles referenced the word 'fun' in many different ways. 'have fun', 'am fun', 'only for fun', 'king of fun'. Louisa felt herself let out another sigh. Or perhaps it was a bit of her soul escaping.

She began scrolling further and further down the search page, looking for hope. After she saw the third picture of a man with his arm already around a woman smiling at her she finally gave up on the idea as incredibly bad, signed out of her profile, and closed the window. She felt like throwing away her laptop as it had become dirty, a symbol of the horror of navigating modern single life. She wasn't even sure if she wanted to meet someone. Not sure if it was an idea she had agreed with, or one her friends had simply implanted into her mind. She certainly didn't want to meet any of those men.

She thought for a while about her situation. Maybe she wasn't unhappy as she was. She wasn't sure that she actually felt like she was missing anything. TV and the media at large were trying really, really, hard to convince her otherwise. In their opinion, she wouldn't be a happy complete woman until she was 'the other half' of some guy.

And the best way to become that other half was to buy a lot of products. A LOT of products. THEN she would find a man, and THEN she would be happy. It was very important that she remembered that it was not her that was in charge of her happiness, it was magazines, TV, and internet quizzes that determined her state of mind. And the people around her would make sure that if she ever was silly enough to tell them she was actually alright, they would remind her that it was ok, she was in denial. Or that she only felt that way because she hadn't felt the blissful happiness that they had, as part of a loving couple. That was her favourite.

As her mind chased these ideas around and around and let them bounce off each other like some kind of internal dodgem car system she began to wonder if people were actually bluffing the whole time. If the people in the relationships were actually just afraid they had made the wrong choices, jealous of her freedom in singlehood and eager to either live vicariously through her experiences or make sure she got into a relationship like theirs, so they didn't feel so guilty anymore.

"I'm becoming a cynic."

She felt the dodgem cars getting out of control.

"A paranoid cynic."

More wine.

"An alcoholic paranoid cynic."

She felt it was time to change the subject in her head. Perhaps a bit of catching up would do the trick, see what everyone was up to via the glory of social media. The trademarked bland blue on white screen flashed up and began to populate with what appeared to be total, total garbage. People that were once friends posting those awful quizzes, People that went to the same school posting links about astrology clues to wealth and happiness. Louisa felt there was a certain irony in posting astrology 'facts' using state of the art technology, which could so easily disprove such crazy notions with a few clicks on a more science based site.

Her mind cast back to a time when she was younger and thought it was a fascinating idea, that it could give real insight. She had always been fascinated by the immenseness of space…

how people had come to be on this small bit of one corner of a universe. She felt that astrology was based in the understanding of the cosmic machine. She even went to a talk to learn more about it. She had indeed learned more, but not what she was expecting. The speaker had got up and proudly proclaimed:

"Astrology is the oldest form of science; its origins go back over four thousand years."

Louisa had been impressed by this. *"There must really be something to this"* she had thought to herself, eager to learn about the mysteries of destiny and the universe. She awaited the speakers next line avidly.

"The form of astrology we use today was formulated in the nineteen sixties."

"Well. Mystery solved, it's a load of recently made up nonsense."

Louisa had not felt let down by this revelation, in fact she had to bite her tongue to stop herself from laughing. She had to sit on her hands to stop from pointing while laughing. How could this person start the talk with two monumentally contrasting statements? *'this is really, really old and ancient wisdom, made up by my dad one bored Thursday.'*

She had been expecting a real explanation of why this stuff should be believed, how it was compensating for the fact that the distant astrological bodies that form the basis of this belief system would have moved since they were first mapped to their various signs… perhaps gravity's pull on the earth affected us more than we realised, we were mostly water after all, and the moon and tides… but, nope.

She continued to listen, about how it wasn't as simple as just a single sign, but rising moons, ascending planets, moons of planets, dogs on moons on planets. Probably. She had to bite her tongue again when the speaker declared:

"You end up with a lot of information, and it may not seem to have anything relating to you when you read it. But the more you read it, over and over, you may start to see little bits of similarity."

Or in other words, here's a huge page of text, keep re-reading it until you either find a small similarity *'hey it says I won't like Mondays, it's true I don't!'* or you convince yourself that it does. *'Hey it says I wouldn't like to meet a snake in the sea past midsummer! I totally think I wouldn't like that!'* Louisa had left the meeting with the sense of knowing and calmness that she had hoped to gain, but not in the manner she had envisaged. And her tongue was sore.

Wine.

She was aware her mind was drifting. Circling through more memories, and not particularly good ones. Her past misunderstandings, tales of hopes dashed, that time when she couldn't believe she had said that out loud, when she was fourteen, and how everyone who was there would remember it as clearly as she did… they were probably laughing about it now. Whilst swimming with dolphins alongside their luxury yachts.

Her laptop was not keeping her attention. She redoubled her efforts to learn what was going on in her friends lives. She felt it was a thing she should do. Refocusing on the screen, she saw a picture of a sandwich. Hmm. It was apparently very important that she knew what people had had for lunch that day. How had the world gotten by before this invention? This site wasn't cutting it. She pondered what else she could look at. Some friends used other sites. After all, why have all the pictures and words in the same place when you could separate them over several sites. That was the logical thing to do. A couple of clicks and some extra browser tabs later, Louisa confirmed to herself what she had feared the most. The sandwich picture was on all of the sites. It had reached optimal social media. Ultimate internets. Louisa feared for her sanity, but more for the sanity of others. She checked the battery indicator in the corner of the screen. 37%.

"Ooo, that's getting a bit low."

She told herself, unconvincingly.

"Better turn it off and find something else to do."

She clicked shutdown from the menu, and when the screen

went black she slammed shut the lid with a satisfying clunk.

"Total waste of time."

She let out another sigh and slumped back in the sofa. Time to find something else to do.

Wine.

The Jamining

21

"Do you ever get scared?"

Sam asked Ellie as they walked slowly across the bridge.

"Of what?"

Ellie was fiddling with something on her phone, some update, check in, check out, thing. Sam paused and grabbed the handrail of the bridge, looking over the side at the canal below rushing past in a black swirl.

"I don't know, of anything? Of everything?"

Sam felt his legs wobble slightly as he looked over and down at the water. He had never been good with heights. Or deep water for that matter. Leaning back and looking up made the wobble disappear, so he leant to look over and felt its return, taking some strange satisfaction that although he couldn't control the feeling of fear, he could control when he felt it.

"You worry too much, idiot."

Ellie spoke despite still being buried in her phone, oblivious to the raging torrent of water beneath her feet. Sam watched her typing at incredible speed on the glass while he contemplated his response.

"If I worry too much, what does that mean for you? What would happen if you didn't click those phone buttons? Would you worry about what you should have pressed? Whose message you should have responded to instantly? I put it to you, and to the court, that in fact you worry a thousand times more than I do – you just respond fast enough to keep the worrying part at bay."

Ellie looked up from her phone screen, and stared straight at Sam.

"You also think too much, and talk too much."

She started back up the street, putting her phone in her coat pocket.

"You're also an idiot".

Sam felt like he had both won and lost that point. Taking one last glance at the water, feeling the shiver a final time, he let go of the handrail and headed up the street after Ellie.

"Seriously though El, you and that phone, doesn't it bother you? How much time you spend tapping on it when there's all this… stuff… around you?"

Ellie rolled her eyes in Sam's general direction, before smiling out of the cute side of her mouth.

"This phone, keeps me connected to everyone and everything, all the time. This phone is where you asked me to go for a drink, remember? Do you think I should have ignored that then?"

Sam returned her smile.

"Well yeah, but…"

He didn't really have a response that furthered his argument in a favourable direction. He decided to just continue smiling with her as they walked up the street towards the pub. It was a pleasant evening for a walk, still sunny and warm enough. Plenty of other people had similar ideas. The streets were bustling with couples eager to catch every drop of the evening sun, or groups of friends out for laughter and adventure. All smiles, all so keen to enjoy the world. Ellie reached their destination a little bit too soon for Sam. He was enjoying the walk. He felt like asking to go once more around the block, to drink in more of the atmosphere of the city before drinking anything else. She wasn't really into that sort of thing though, didn't quite feel or see the world the same way Sam did, and he wasn't keen on her suggesting he was weird again. If he could only explain it better, maybe he could show her a different way to enjoy it all. The pub doors were wide open, making the most of the season, letting the winter air escape, and the early summer air to take up residence in its place, fresher and happier. They walked in together, Sam nodding as always to the ever present bouncer. Ellie was heading straight for the bar.

"The Usual?"

Her voice beckoned Sam to follow, in the way it usually did.

He agreed. Ellie already had the attention of the barman. She was good at that, getting the attention of everyone as soon as she entered anywhere. As she ordered, Sam took a minute to gaze around the pub. Their pub, where it had begun, where it had continued. This had always been a favourite of Sam, but now it belonged to them both. She had liked it before as well, shared destiny under a dark ancient ceiling.

What secrets did the old wood keep? What other lovers had spent their evenings here, laughing, smiling, touching, holding. The magic of love imprinted into the walls, the beams… to seep back out into the atmosphere each new evening… intoxicating the latest visitors. Aiding their journeys into each other's arms.

Ellie's hair bounced as she laughed. Sam smiled with her, pleased he could still make her laugh when he wanted to, when he felt she needed it, when he needed to see her at her happiest. Sometimes she seemed distant. He wondered what was troubling her, but she was dismissive. Perhaps it was a symptom of her last failed attempts at love. Perhaps she just needed him to be there for her, to continue to make her laugh. She would heal, in time, and then she could tell him. She could tell him anything. He was there for her. He would always be.

Sam's mind drifted, as it often did, to pictures of the two of them together. At night in the darkness and the quiet, he felt the most connected to her. Holding her as she slept, he could protect her. It was simple, physical. Sam wasn't sure how to give that same feeling in the waking hours, he could never explain it to her properly, and she wasn't easy to speak to in those terms. Still a little unready to face it in the light of day perhaps, happy to feel the embrace away from the eyes of the world, in the dark.

The drinks hit the table with a thunk. Why did he always misjudge the height of the tables in here? Maybe they were taller than the tables in other pubs, maybe he was just distracted. A small booth style table, to the side of the room. He felt it was a good choice, felt more private, intimate. An appropriate choice of seating for a date night. As he went to sit, Ellie sat on the opposite side. A little bit disappointed she hadn't opted to sit next to him, Sam finished sitting. Perhaps this was better? This way they could look at each other, after all, this was how couples sat at restaurants. Sam remembered their first trip here, and a main highlight was her sitting with him, the closeness, the warmth of touch.

They began to speak, to continue with the exchange of what had been going on, how work had been, the normal stuff. Sam tried to make jokes out of the characters from Ellie's work. He always made jokes out of his own colleagues. Not in a nasty way, not at all. An affectionate attempt to extend the standard 'can you believe what happened, and what they said?' into a more compelling sit com style yarn. A better story, more chances to make her laugh again, to see that smile. She wasn't forthcoming with new material though. She rarely spoke about her work, or her other friends these days. Sam wasn't sure why. He wondered if she was having a problem somewhere, but she reassured him that she wasn't. Perhaps she was just unsure what to say, maybe nothing had happened recently that she hadn't already texted to him. And she did like to text. Sometimes it was easier to feel he knew how to communicate with her via his phone than he did when they were together. It seemed to make more sense, be more direct.

Sam drifted again. This time, he was back at his favourite pub at university, sat across the table from Tish. He spent a lot of time sat across from her, wishing he could say the things to her that he knew he couldn't, that even if he did all it would achieve would be the loss of one of his closest friends. All that time sat there not able to say those things. Now he was sat across from Ellie, he could say anything. He just couldn't think of the words.

They chatted, they laughed. Ellie tore the label from her bottle, the way she always did. Sam reached across to hold her hand. It was comfortable. Ellie pulled her hand away to investigate a buzz on her phone. Sam waited for her to put it back. He looked around the pub, at the other couples in here. They seemed happy. Enjoying their time together. Sam was enjoying his time too, but something felt a little bit off. Ellie had finished with her phone. Her hand had not returned. Sam knew he over thought things, he couldn't help it.

"El, are you ok? You seem a little bit, I don't know... are you ok?"

Sam waited for Ellie's response, but only time passed in his direction. Ellie looked at the floor, out of the window at passers by... she rubbed at her upper arm, quite firmly. Sam wondered what she was feeling to cause such a response. She seemed to be deep in thought, perhaps an internal struggle playing out on her arm. Sam joined her in gazing out of the window. He could see couples walking along the street, laughing, arm in arm. He pictured himself and Ellie walking along in such a fashion, not a care in the world. Maybe he should suggest they went for a walk? He could take her arm and they could be just like the other couples.

"Yeah, I'm ok. I was just thinking is all."

Sam's picture of walking bliss fell away as Ellie spoke, this was his chance to reach her in the real world, to take the pictures from his mind and make them manifest. She just had to let him.

"If something's bothering you, you can tell me... you know that, right?"

Ellie shifted in her seat.

"Yeah I know."

She checked her phone.

"There's some talk about a bunch of us going to the cinema on Friday."

Sam thought this might be his chance to take things to the next level.

"Oh right, that's exciting!"

"Yeah, anyway I know we had plans for Friday, so..."

Sam was ready for this.

"Don't worry about that, we can do that another time."

Ellie seemed pleased with his response.

"I could come with you if you like, you could show me off to your friends, you know, your amazing catch!"

Ellie shifted again, smiling slightly.

"Yeah, they've booked the seats though, so…"

It was Sam's turn to shift awkwardly in his seat.

"Oh. Oh, never mind. That's a shame though. Next time."

Ellie seemed to be happy with the resolution. The smile returned to her face. Sam wasn't sure if this was all that was bothering her. It was a bummer, but if her friends had booked without asking, there probably wasn't much she could have done about it.

"Was that what was bothering you? Are you ok now, happy?"

Sam was still concerned. He wanted to hug her and tell her it was all ok, but it would be quite weird to try that when she was sat at the other end of the table.

"Yeah, I'm happy. I like things the way they are."

Ellie's response wasn't quite what Sam was expecting. But he was pleased she was ok, and when he thought about it, he was sat in his favourite pub, with his favourite person. He liked the way things were too. He reached for her hand again, he liked being able to hold her.

The evening passed, smiles and laughter. The occasional use of the word 'idiot' in his direction. Sam was happy. This was an excellent way to spend a summer evening. Eventually it was time to leave. The pub chimed its bell, followed by its familiar choice for last song before the bouncers kick you out. Ellie was working tomorrow, so a walk to her bus stop followed by a hug and a kiss. Ellie nearly missed it again, some things never change. He waved at her before turning and heading for his own transport home. The warmth of the sun that accompanied his arrival in the city was gone, but the warmth inside was enough to keep him going despite his lack of coat. A smile kept him company on his short walk.

Before he even realised it, Sam found himself stood in the huddle of people that passed for a queue for the last bus home. He was always intrigued by the characters he saw in this bunch. A few wobbly drunk young guys, their gelled hair starting to point in unexpected directions. An older couple huddled together with rosy cheeks and smiles. A youngish woman with a bag of chips and a mobile phone, unsure which was the more important at that moment. An older guy, with a full beard, just stood, motionless, waiting. And Sam. Three clubbers dashed up to join just as the bus pulled up. People seemed to appear out of thin air to join in the haphazard queue as it began blundering onto the slightly ragged bus. As Sam stepped on board he noticed the driver looked tired, mentally as well as physically, as if he was moaning to himself in his head about how he had ended up with this task again. The familiar beep of Sam's card, and he made his way to find a seat using the special night bus seat acquisition tactics he had developed.

Not upstairs, not on a night bus. That was the domain of the very young, quite drunk, quite rowdy crowd. The journey was too long to have to put up with any grief. So, downstairs. Not the back, again this area attracted those who felt they 'had edge' just like at school. Don't mess with those dangerous folks who sit at the back, they are the coolest, most daring of us all, angels fear to tread in the risqué zone of the back seats. Be wary of the front also, for this is where the most drunk of all dwell, too incapacitated to get any further. This is the zone of rambling conversation, falling over, 'is he about to be sick' and the most dreaded of all, the falling asleep on you. If possible, acquire one of the seats on the wheel arch, on the road side. These seats are higher than the others, and have no one directly behind you to cause trouble. Being on the side of the road removes the risk of people on the street banging on the windows or trying to dispose of their chip papers through said windows onto you. If these seats are taken, do not sit directly in front of them, as the people in them will have a massive height advantage on you, and this is risky. Instead sit one row in front of that, the mid-point of the bus and the best Sam could do for this journey. As he sat down he wondered if he had overthought this seating plan, but then remembered after several unpleasant occurrences during past journeys, that it was better to be safe than sorry.

As the last of the fortunate took their seats, the doors closed and the bus pulled away. Undeterred by the banging on the window of a dishevelled looking couple whose jog to the bus stop was not quite fast enough, and whose jog alongside the bus was proving unrewarding, the driver coldly headed up the street. Sam checked his phone. Nothing.

Looking out of the window, Sam saw how the night had gone for other people in the city. Although the faces were different, he felt like this was the same bunch he had seen on the way in. On that journey, he felt the faces held such a sense of optimism, of promise of everything about to be amazing. They were about to experience the best night of their lives, meet their one true partner, or cement their existing relationship into a thing of legend. Now Sam saw a mixture of people, a mixture of states, both emotional and physical. As the bus moved down the main streets the scenes unveiled like a human carousel before his eyes. A group of lads, all in near matching shirts, walked along the street with their hands in their pockets, undeterred by the time and looking for the next venue and the next beer. Two girls walked the opposite way, barefoot on the pavement, shoes in hand. One was laughing and waving at seemingly nothing, the other carefully looking where she was placing her vulnerable feet. A small group stood on the street corner, each one pointing in different directions as they planned their next move. Perhaps debating where the taxis were, or the clubs, or the fast food. A woman sat sobbing in a doorway, clutching her handbag tightly as people walked past. Sam hoped she was ok, before his attention was claimed by a whirlwind of noise and bravado as two men shouted at each other and pointed angrily as their respective girlfriends held them back from each other, as though they were walking dogs in the park that had taken a dislike and needed to be held back on their choke chains as they barked at each other to determine who was the alpha.

Sam watched the world through the glass of the bus window as it passed by. Or as he passed by. Same difference he thought. It felt like he was watching TV, life happening behind glass that Sam felt no part of, just an observer. He had enjoyed the night though, he always enjoyed being with Ellie. He still had a strange feeling, but she had assured him that everything was fine. He mustn't over think things. It was something he knew he struggled with, and he felt he could be happier if he just learnt to go with the flow. His thoughts drifted back to her smile, the way she walked. He wanted to tell her a million things to make her feel better. If those million things could just form one perfect sentence, that would be great.

He glanced at his phone once more, still nothing. It seemed Ellie was gone for the night. That was ok, well he would happily message her constantly, but he didn't want to be pushy or demanding. He also didn't really have much else to say, and he couldn't hold her through his phone. As the bus left the last of the main streets, Sam turned his glance to the other passengers. Although some looked contented, and a few were asleep, most seemed to share Sam's feeling that things maybe could continue if only there was some way. One chap had not yet given up on the night and was trying to strike up a flirty conversation with the girl on the opposite seat. She had angled her shoulder away from him and was staring at her phone, hoping he would get the signals of disinterest and either be quiet or turn his attention elsewhere. Sadly, he either did not pay any attention to learning women's body language signals, or he saw it as a challenge to overcome, as he could not be deterred in his less than eloquent vocal advances.

Sam watched over the drunk fellow, just in case, as the bus drifted into the night. There would be other chances, he thought, for all of us to get it perfectly right, the perfect date, the perfect night.

22

The summer breeze was cold, Louisa was unimpressed. Months of people complaining about how they wished it was summer, and now they wouldn't shut up about how much of a disappointment it was. Each time the cold gust hit her, she pictured the faces of the complainers, their dissatisfaction manifest.

"Serves you right… this is not a tropical country, don't wish your life away waiting for… this."

Neither the wind, nor the complainers answered. Typical. She turned her attention to her destination, something that she could affect. She was nearing the huge glass door of the gallery, and she began to look around to see if Jess was already here. The door should be imposing, but it wasn't. It just sat, a bit in the way, a bit over the top. Louisa had wanted to come here for some time, but had always been a little bit nervous about the whole thing. She didn't go to art galleries, that was what… 'other' people did. People who knew what they were talking about, people who might laugh at her and point if they found out all she could remember from art class in school was being shouted at for drawing thick borders around her pictures.

Jess was not here. Jess was often not quite on time. Louisa didn't mind too much, she was never incredibly late, and after first meeting her and thinking she was the perfect example of a woman, it was good to find a flaw. It made Louisa feel like there was hope. Turning her attention to who was here, a sense of not quite belonging began to develop somewhere deep inside. She felt like the other people in the foyer were looking at her and asking what she was doing here. It was all a bit disconcerting. She decided to move across the large open plan area to the gift shop and have a look at the trinkets on offer. Art books, understandable. Children's books, that made her feel a bit better. It was unlikely she knew less about art than children. Postcards, mugs… jewellery?

Jewellery was an odd choice for such an establishment. It must be art jewellery? That genre was new to Louisa. Handmade and local, and very, very, expensive. Ah. Art hipster jewellery. That made more sense. On close inspection, it didn't really look that nice. Was the price tag justified by its rustic authenticity? She wasn't even sure anymore. It all seemed like a massive con.

"Hey! Oooh presents!"

Jess had snuck up out of nowhere. Or Louisa was lost in thought about shops. It was difficult to tell. Louisa assumed the first option must be accurate.

"Oh hi! There's some weird stuff here, look at these."

Louisa pointed out the glass case containing the jewellery. Jess bent slightly to have a thorough examination. She looked intently at each item on the display. She returned to the first item and went through them again. She stood straight. She bent back down. Louisa began to feel like she was missing something.

"Right, ok. Two things."

Jess was leaning closer to the glass case as she continued her proclamation.

"One. I'm not sure, but I definitely couldn't make something like this, so I don't know if that makes me a bad person for thing number two."

Louisa's curiosity was piqued by this disclaimer.

"Two. I'm pretty sure this is all bollocks."

Jess's face remained still and serious. Louisa snorted a giggle of surprise.

"So, this is the arts and crafts version of a pale ale, isn't it? Are we supposed to pay more and accept lower quality because it's handmade and local? Shouldn't things that are for sale still be good? I mean, I know that's a matter of taste, but remember when you would buy cheap jewellery from chain shops? That's what this is like, but it's eight times the price!"

Louisa was pleased that her position on this had been validated.

"Yeah, I know what you mean."

It was an uninsightful response, but, it was a Sunday.

"Right, enough of this tat. Time for the main event! Where's all the arts!"

Jess began to wander off, Louisa assumed she knew where she was going, and began to follow.

"No, really, that was a serious question. Where do we go?"

Louisa was a teeny bit shocked, she had assumed that Jess would know about this kind of thing, that she had been before. She tried to think how to explain in diplomatic terms that she hadn't been before, but was saved by fate.

"Ah. Big door marked gallery. Probably start in there then I suppose. Don't mind me, I know exactly what I'm doing."

It was the first time Louisa had seen Jess looking a little embarrassed, the first time she had not immediately had all the answers. It was endearing, Louisa felt like giving her a hug. Probably not a good idea. Bit patronising.

The door to the gallery was huge. Several people wide, and not stopping until the ceiling demanded it too.

"Imposing, no? there must be some serious stuff behind here."

Jess placed both hands on the large steel bar of a handle and prepared herself for the excursion of opening such a monstrous block of thing.

"F… oh."

Jess pushed with all her might, and stumbled slightly as the door swung wide open, a slight whirring of motors replacing the expected creaking. Louisa was impressed, but then decided that she should have known it wouldn't be a difficult door to open, she had just been reassured by the children's books. This was all very complicated.

"I like the power assist on the doors, that's my favourite bit so far."

Jess was still holding the door handle as Louisa walked through, both of them looking for any sign of the motors or engines that powered them.

"Pamphlet?"

The voice made both of them jump. A member of staff, dressed in smart black shirt and trousers was stationed just inside the doorway. Startled, Louisa managed a polite "no thanks" and a smile. She noticed the ear piece, curly cord running down the staff girls' neck and vanishing behind her collar.

"Why does everyone wear ear pieces now? Are they all spies? Is there something going on I don't know about? Does everyone else know?"

Jess snapped Louisa out of her conspiracy by linking her arm with hers and dragging her into the gallery.

"So, this is art then. Proper art, like not people having a go in their bedroom, but proper on the wall we are people who've come to see it on purpose art art."

Jess seemed excited by the prospect of being here. Louisa knew that Jess had always expressed an interest in doing arty things, and she seemed to be disappointed when they didn't turn out to be as good as she thought they would. Louisa wondered if a part of Jess wished she could have been a professional artist, in a way though, she kind of was. Sort of.

"Well... I mean perhaps some of them make stuff in their bedrooms."

Louisa wanted to both reassure Jess's creative dreams and point out that it was actually quite likely. Or she hoped it was. She wasn't ready for a world where people couldn't aspire to things like this, where you had to already be super established with studios and things before you could be considered an artist worthy of display. This was a modern art gallery after all, it wasn't like the artists had all died long ago. Hopefully.

"Yeah maybe."

Jess seemed unsure. Louisa had little choice but to walk with her to the nearest wall. It contained a medium sized picture made out of some sort of thick paint splodged in different thicknesses and directions. Louisa wasn't sure what it was of.

"This is..."

Louisa tried to find some expressive words, but Jess beat her to it.

"Brown. This is very, very brown."

Jess moved over to another picture on this wall.

"This one is less brown, more grey."

Louisa couldn't help but agree.

"Yes. Nicely spotted. What does it mean?"

Jess scratched her cheek with her free hand.

"I'm… I don't… erm… art?"

"Yes. I agree with you there, it is most definitely art."

Louisa was reassured that it wasn't just her that felt a little bit lost. Was she supposed to know what these were pictures of? Was there a significance to the colours, were the two connected? They were on the same wall, was that deliberate? Or had someone just thought here was a nice space for them both. She felt a little bit insecure. At least Jess didn't seem to know either, that would have been horrible, if it was just her.

"Next!"

Jess turned sharply, almost pulling Louisa off her feet. Stumbling to regain her balance, and slightly flustered, she was unprepared for the next item in the gallery. A large sphere sat in the middle of the next area, out of which many coloured pipes protruded, in many directions. Each easily as long as Louisa, the pipes had cables attached to secure them to the ceiling. They wobbled slightly. Louisa felt it was a little bit weird. Some kind of space alien octopus hedgehog thing.

"Whoa. We've got an art right here. A big one!"

Jess seemed just as taken aback. She spoke in a hushed tone.

"What is this?"

Louisa spotted the reason for the sudden hush… there was a man on the other side of the hedgehoctopuss, chin in hand, deep in contemplation.

"Erm, yeah."

Louisa wanted to be more insightful, to feel like she belonged in here. It wasn't going to plan so far.

"Is it moving? Or is that just me?"

Jess leaned in a bit to check. Louisa opted to squint slightly, before confirming the suspicion.

"Yeah I can confirm movement."

Jess straightened, as if startled.

"Is it alive? Is it going to get us? What is it?"

The many coloured pipe arms of the hedgehoctopuss swayed slightly, possibly from the breeze of the air conditioning unit overhead. Louisa wasn't sure if it was supposed to be doing this, or if it was unintentional. Or if it was trying to escape being tied up and left for all to look upon in wonder, a freak show in a circus tent. And what of the gentleman on its other side? What was his story? He was still motionless. He was well dressed, perhaps a little overdressed. Louisa felt a little uncomfortable at the sight of him. If he could stand for so long looking at this… art… what was she missing? What did he know that she didn't? Jess offered a possible answer, still in a hushed tone:

"Maybe it has a face on the other side, and it's talking to him about the mysteries of the universe."

Louisa felt her eyes widen. It was a captivating idea.

"We must speak with it!"

This time it was Louisa who would do the dragging and pulling along the polished floor. She felt Jess's arm tighten in surprise at her sudden movement, but she had to know. She didn't expect a talking face, although that would be amazing, something from one of her cherished books perhaps, but the idea that there were sides to this creation and the reason she felt she didn't understand it was simply that they were at the back was too revelatory to ignore.

It seemed to take an age to walk around the arms of the beast, but at last, the other side came into view. An astronaut waiting for his orbit to reveal the far side of the moon, Louisa's excitement was palpable.

"Hmm."

Jess was the first of the intrepid adventurers to comment on their discovery.

"Well."

Louisa's additional comment was about as insightful.

"So. That's that then."

"Yeah… but what I don't get then, I mean what I extra don't get…"

Jess began backing away, pulling Louisa along with her, before she continued her sentence at a safe distance.

"So what is he looking at? What's he seeing that we don't?"

Now stood behind the man, who was still gazing motionlessly at the hedgehoctopuss, which was no different on this side, Louisa was thankful that Jess seemed to be as lost as her. Part of her wanted to ask the man what it was he was seeing; the other part was scared that he would report them to the art police for being dumb and have them thrown from the building.

"Maybe he is thinking about something else, his shopping list? What he's going to have for tea tonight? Perhaps… he's a crazy person… either way, let's try the next gallery."

Jess's words were as wise as ever, Louisa was more than happy to move to the next gallery room. This one was just a bit… weird.

A second door, same as the first, except for a giant number two emblazoned in its centre. This time prepared for its power assist, Louisa opened up this new and exciting area. Jess followed her in as she began to take in its contents. This gallery was much bigger, containing more art and more people. Another slick dressed staff member stood on the inside of the door, smiling too much for someone whose job appeared to be standing by a door. The centre of the room had wide shelf like displays, covered in many small arts. Louisa's eyes were caught by the movement of some kind of film being projected on the far side wall. It seemed to be repeating shaky images of a beach on old style looking film. A couple of people were stood in front of the projection, potentially hiding the important parts from her view. She contemplated moving around to get a better look, but her recent experience in the first room made her reconsider. She didn't want to discover there was no more to see, and it was just another thing she just didn't understand. She was glad she had come along with Jess, and that she was voicing similar concerns. If she had come along on her own, she may have felt quite upset about how she didn't understand it, and how everyone else here did, and how they must be judging her stupidity. She turned to see if Jess wanted to take her arm again, to discover she had vanished. Just when she felt the most comforted for her being around, typical. She scanned the room to see if she could find where her comfort blanket of friend had got to, finding her on the second sweep of the room. A small bank of TVs were set up against the corner of the wall, each in a different coloured cabinet mounting. Headphones painted in matching colours hung from each set, and Jess was firmly attached to the blue one.

"What's this? What've you found?"

Louisa felt asking a question to someone wearing full covering headphones was another example of her not quite knowing how to interact with people properly. Jess, ever the saviour of awkward social situations, responded anyway.

"Yeah, I thought this looked cool and interesting, but it's a bit weird, have a go… I'm going to try the next one."

She handed Louisa the headphones and moved to the red cabinet. Louisa placed the headphones on, and looked at the screen. She was greeted by what seemed to be disjointed images and weird rushing water type electronic sounds. Confused, she moved to the red cabinet as Jess moved to the green one. This one had a car image, and the sound of engines on a loop. Standing for a minute, Louisa wondered what on earth was going on in here. What was this supposed to mean? Was it just *'hey let's look at a car, aren't they nice? Brum brum'* or was there a deeper meaning that was again escaping her. She placed the headphones back in their holder. She had no desire to try the next cabinet. Feelings of intellectual inadequacy had returned, coupled with the wider feelings of general inadequacy that often reared their ugliness from deep inside Louisa's mind. As Jess was still absorbed in her cabinet, she turned her attention to the other people in this gallery.

A mix of ages, a mix of genders. A similarity of attire. The other art lookers seemed to know exactly what they were looking at. They all seemed well dressed, some quite expensively by the looks of things. Several had eccentricities in their appearance, which Louisa felt must be connected to their artiness. One had crazy coloured shoes, another a trilby with a large crow feather attached. Several women sporting shawls, one very colourful, one very expensively lacking in colour. Louisa wondered if she was simply in the wrong place. Was this the domain of some other class of people, all privy to the special knowledge of how this place worked? A part of her wanted to go home now. Back to her understandable flat, and her book.

"What did you think?"

Jess had emerged from the colour cabinets of screen and sound.

"Oh, I'm not sure, I mean I don't know."

Louisa was trying to not let her worries show in her voice.

"Yep. I tried all of them, didn't get a single one. Not one. What the hell was the car one supposed to be?"

Louisa was reassured by Jess's reaction, but part of her still felt that just made them both outsiders to the world, it didn't mean that Louisa fit in.

"Let's go and look at these shelves of objects next."

Jess was off again, her unshakable positivity was normally so infectious, but this time it wasn't working. Louisa felt like it wasn't her and Jess versus the world, it was the world versus them, and that was a much more daunting situation. Still, she followed her friend to this new area of discovery. She looked at the objects, not really getting why they were there, or what they were made of. Perhaps Jess would understand this more, with her history of attempts at making things. Maybe she should ask her? She didn't want to seem like she knew nothing at all about anything in here. It was getting a bit demoralising. Jess summoned Louisa over to her with a quick wave, and her usual smile.

"Hey Lou, look at this one, it's a mouse!"

Louisa smiled and nodded, it was indeed a mouse, and she had to admit it was quite sweet looking.

"Now these things…"

Jess pointed at various objects as she spoke:

"All these things, I get that they are all way better than I could make, by far yeah, but also… this is an art gallery… I expected them to be even better… like oh my god how were these even made, you know?"

Louisa was again reassured that Jess didn't seem to be overly impressed with this place. It was perhaps becoming evident that she was not having the best time.

"Lou, are you ok? You seem a little bit, off?"

Jess's smile had been replaced with a look of concern. Louisa wanted to tell her everything that had been bothering her, and how this trip was making it all a little bit worse. She wasn't sure if she could say it though, she wasn't sure if it would upset Jess and it would all spiral out of control somehow until Jess would stop wanting to be friends.

"There's a café here, it's meant to be alright? Shall we go get a coffee and some cake and you can tell me what's up?"

Jess wasn't waiting for an answer. She linked Louisa's arm again, and they were off in search of this land of cake and beans.

The café was humming with activity, much more than the gallery. The people in here were more diverse in their appearance, and much more animated. There was a second entrance from the street, and Louisa wondered if these people had even set foot inside the gallery, or if they had simply walked in to get a drink in order to say they had been inside. Did that make them posers?

Or considering how she felt right now, was it smart? Avoid the feeling dumb bit, and just sit with a drink and post to everyone that you spent the afternoon in the art gallery. As she drifted in her head wondering about all of this, a whirl of Jess acquired two coffees, two slices of what looked like quite nice cake, and a small table just out of the way enough to have a chat. Louisa was as impressed as ever by Jess's ability to sort anything out. As they both sat down, she decided she may as well tell her everything, and maybe she could work her fix it magic again.

"So what's up then Lou, you seemed to phase out a bit there?"

Jess stirred her coffee as her eyes moved between Louisa and her slice of cake.

"Do you ever?"

Nope, don't start like that, Louisa decided to change her angle of approach.

"Did you get anything in there? I mean, did you understand why it was there? What it meant?"

Louisa waited for the response, slightly afraid what would happen if Jess responded that she did.

"Hmm."

Jess leaned back in her chair in thought, before leaning forward and taking a sip of her coffee.

"Oh far too hot. I never leave it long enough to cool down. Anyway, hmm. If you mean do I get why it's there, I suppose it's because it's art, and this is a gallery. But if you're asking if I know *why* it's art, and *why* it's worthy of being here, then no… I have absolutely no idea."

Louisa felt a weight lift from her. That was the first step, and it was a big one.

"I'm so glad you said that, I was feeling really dumb… I couldn't figure out what it meant, and it made me feel I shouldn't really be here with you."

Jess looked both sympathetic and shocked at the same time. It was an impressive expression.

"Lou, I haven't got a clue what's going on in here. Large sphere thing with tentacles? Coloured TVs playing engines? Brown paint? I thought you would think less of me… I'm supposed to be arty! I watch all those programmes and I have absolutely no idea what any of it means. Not. One. Clue."

Louisa let out a stress relieving chuckle as she rested her head on her hand. She felt much better, it was still her and Jess in their little bubble, outside of the world but safe in the knowledge that they were in the same boat.

"Is that all that's bothering you? It feels a bit like it may be more? It's ok, you can tell me, or not – but do try the cake! It's quite nice!"

Jess had begun to tuck into her slice, ignoring the refined supplied fork, and opting for the traditional hand based application of cake to face. Louisa felt it may be worth telling her everything that was bothering her.

"Well, the thing is, I've been trying to get back into dating."

Jess almost dropped her cake, a look of intrigue spreading as fast as the crumbs fell.

"Oooooo juicy! TELL ME EVERYTHING!"

The reaction was not unexpected, but Louisa felt the expectation of juicy gossip stories of adventure would be sadly missing from the tale. She began to tell her story anyway, how Nia had suggested it all, and how she had agreed it was maybe worth a try. She went on to tell of the failed attempts, the misunderstandings, the rude pictures she had received. So many of them. How she had started messaging a guy who seemed nice, but after a week of messages back and forth he had vanished, never replied again, mid conversation. She told Jess how it made her feel like she wasn't good enough for a proper date, how all the guys just seemed to want nothing but casual sex, and how a large number of them seemed to already have wives or girlfriends as well. The cake offered excellent comfort as she let out her frustrations and anxieties. She went on to how she always felt like she didn't quite fit in, how today had just made that feeling well up, as she stood with people who looked different to her, who all seemed to know what everything meant, and how she never seemed to understand things the way other people did. Jess listened to everything she said. As she finished, feeling a little bit teary eyed, Jess reached across the table and clasped her hands around Louisa's.

"Now you listen to me, and you listen properly. You fit in. You fit in with me, always. These other people? Who cares about anyone else. I'm sure if you spoke to them, you would find you had things in common with some, and not with others. That's just being human. Not everyone fits with everyone, but when you do find people you fit with, you grab them, and you never let them go. And that's what I'm doing now."

Louisa felt a tear escape her attempt to hide it away in the corner of her eye.

"I came here today, thinking I would get a real rush from being in with the art, you know, I like to think I'm arty and that, but to be honest, it upset me a bit too… I'm not joking, I really don't know what the hell any of this stuff in here means. I'm so glad you came with me though, if you hadn't, if I was on my own, I would've felt really dumb. So I know what you mean."

Louisa felt a warmth emanate from Jess's hands as she spoke. It was helping, a lot. She was so relieved that she had said she felt the same, even echoing some of the things she felt herself. Louisa sat and let the warmth spread as Jess continued.

"As for the dating stuff, at first, when you said that, I was excited. But then what you said happened? That's horrible! And that it's been like that for so long? Screw that. You don't need that kind of negativity in your life. It's not worth it. Yes, I am overjoyed that I managed to find Steven. If I hadn't found him? I would still be me. It wouldn't be the end of the world. Only the end of the world is the end of the world, and at that point, well it wouldn't matter, would it? You are still you, you don't need anyone to be you. You certainly don't need any of those weirdos.

Put that nastiness away. Delete it all. Give it some time, figure out what if anything you want to do, and we will look at any options together, ok?"

Louisa was feeling incredibly relieved now, almost all the weight she had been carrying around felt like it was lifting. She knew she didn't want to carry on with the dating sites. They were just too upsetting. They seemed to follow rules she didn't understand, and didn't really want to understand.

"Right, the cake was nice, the coffee was ok, let's get out of here. Back to mine. We can watch some silly films, order a pizza, and take the piss out of Steven for something trivial. Proper girl's night."

Louisa liked the sound of that, very much. She wanted to give Jess a big hug to say thank you, but felt it was probably a bit much. She was still thinking that as Jess wrapped her arms around her as they got up to leave. She really was an expert in making things better. More than that though, she was genuine with it. Louisa was incredibly pleased she had taken that chance to go to the house warming party and try to make some friends. She felt she had made the best one ever.

Turning to leave, Louisa felt like she wanted a souvenir of this day. It had felt like a turning point. She had hoped it might bring her closer to Jess, but she had no idea how well it would turn out. She saw a small pile of the leaflet things the staff in the gallery had been waving around. Small, free, the perfect keepsake. She picked one up as she walked past, and casually looked inside as she followed Jess through the door and onto the street.

"For fuck's sake Jess!"

Jess turned, rather startled by Louisa's outburst.

"This thing tells you what the art means! It describes it all! What it's for, why it's the way it is! That's why everyone else knew what was going on, they had fucking instructions!"

Jess began to laugh hysterically as she took the brochure and began reading. Louisa couldn't believe it, all of that feeling lost, feeling everyone could magically interpret the art, it was all a con. They had just read what to think about it from a little free handout. Louisa felt a little anger at the staff, for not making it clear that that was what these things were, how important they were. Jess was walking down the street howling with laughter at each turn of a page.

"Right that's it."

Louisa aimed her anger at the universe.

"If there's ever a little instruction book again, you'd better make it more obvious."

23

Sam sat alone in the pub. He felt the chair opposite should still be swaying from Matt's departure. Sadly, the physics of a solid wood chair didn't allow for this, much to Sam's disapproval. It had been a good pub lunch. Nothing amazing, but a solid good. Sam also felt he had been productive, helping Matt with his problems. Not in an actual being able to make the problems go away sense, but in a good friend, listening, making some suggestions kind of way. The rain had pounded the walls and windows as they spoke, a water based manifestation of Matt's troubles. Sam thought he had heard thunder while Matt had been expressing the depth of the issues, but he wasn't sure if he had imagined it for dramatic effect. Either way, both had now passed. Sam was glad that Matt had called him to talk things through. It had made Sam feel useful, helpful even. It was a good feeling, a good diversion from feeling like he was not quite in control of his own situation.

Looking out of the window, the clouds were getting lighter. The angry dark grey was changing into a merely temperamental dark white, as though a toddler was slowly calming down after a nasty tantrum. Now looked like the right time to move. Gathering his things, Sam headed for the door. It wasn't a short walk to the bus stop, and he had foolishly believed the weather app on his phone, which still had a cheeky sun poking out from behind a fluffy white cloud. Perhaps the staff had all gone on holiday and left the same picture on by accident, or just thought it was a safe bet giving the fact it was the middle of summer. Or maybe, weather reporting was this centuries form of alchemy and witchcraft, divining knowledge from bits of straw and old bones, asking spirits and seeing what floated in the local river to determine what had favour. They were all about as accurate as the supercomputers that were supposedly used.

Rain still fell from above, not enough to be annoying in normal circumstances, but given Sam's wise choice of 'Hmm looks alright I won't need a coat' it was raising a sad frustration just in the back of his mind. As he reached the top of the street, and whilst slightly grumpy at the umbrella wielding pedestrian walking down the other way, there was an almighty crack in the sky. Even the buildings seemed to wince at the power of nature. Within a few seconds the great tap of the gods was turned to its fully open position and the entire ocean appeared to drop on the street and its inhabitants. People quickly chose allegiances against this outrageous downpour as it beat mercilessly upon them. Team huddle under any conceivable shelter was the first to act, seemingly teleporting everywhere they could hide such was their speed. Under awnings, bus stops, in shop doorways, even underneath advertising signs only a few inches thick. Team this is Britain and we just get on with it because don't you know the queen would and don't be so wet rugby players don't even wear helmets the cane never did me any harm continued walking along as though nothing was happening at all, seemingly willing the rain to not hit them because they didn't believe in it. Sam was a firm member of team erm it's raining much harder than it's supposed to be raining what do I do? Do I stand still and hope it doesn't see me or is that the advice for dinosaurs? Do I keep going and just get really wet? What happens to my clothes if they get really wet? Should I go and stand under the oh wait that's full of people already oh no I'm totally drenched I may as well have just sat in a bath oh bugger maybe I will just go full hysterics and sit on the floor splashing my fists in the puddles until someone makes it dry and gives me a lollipop.

The streets became rivers; Sam was becoming aquatic. Having decided to keep walking towards the bus stop, large drips of water were now falling from larger drips of water which were falling from Sam's face. Raising his hand up to try and stem the biblical flow, and thinking his decision making skills were as wanting as ever, he tried to dart into the doorway of a coffee shop. Filling the doorway with what felt like the personification of ‘ner ner na ner ner’ was a woman with an open umbrella. Just stood. Under an umbrella. In a doorway. Sheltering under shelter with some extra shelter whilst Sam was being sorely tested to see if he was any kind of wicked witch. Confusion, rage, and colourful language poured through Sam as the rain poured all around him, sky, water and emotion all becoming one flowing entity, seemingly crystalizing into a single word, released under his breath.

“But…”

Baffled and annoyed, Sam moved on to the next doorway. Full. And the next. Full. A glimmer of hope as some space appeared in the doorway of a building Sam wasn’t sure if he’d ever seen before, possibly some sort of office he thought as he squeezed in. His mystery doorway was near the end of the street, allowing Sam to see across to the city’s central square. Often a source of stories and adventure, today the expanse of flat concrete slabs was being attacked by the heavy rain. The impact splashes seemed to bounce back up towards the sky, as though the water had enjoyed falling so much it wanted another turn. A loud knocking caught Sam by surprise, and slightly startled, he turned around to see a man in semi smart clothes on the other side of the door to the mystery building knocking on the glass and shooing Sam away. As Sam took a few steps to the side of his hiding place, the man opened the door and suggested in no uncertain terms that this was not a place to loiter. He then looked at the weather, cursed, and walked off down the street. Still baffled by the experience, Sam watched as he strode away looking like he was still cursing. An older woman walking up the street caught Sam’s eye line as she neared his now apparently inappropriate hideout. With a tone of slight glee at the drama of the weather she pronounced “Wasn’t like this earlier was it!” And before Sam could decide if he was supposed to respond to this statement she added “Easing off though now.” It wasn’t.

Looking back towards the square, still full of bouncing water frolicking on the slabs having far too much fun to show any signs of relenting, Sam contemplated how or if he should answer. He turned back towards the woman to see only her back as she continued walking up the street. Open mouthed and confused as to what just happened, Sam wasn't sure if he had been rude not to answer, missed an opportunity to chat with someone new who may know the secrets of the universe, or pleased that someone that would be weird enough to ramble odd phrases to strangers as they walked past had gone away. The only certain things were that the rain was not easing at all, standing here was not getting him any closer to his bus, and he was a bit concerned that if the old story about things happening in threes was true, staying here meant another odd encounter was imminent. Taking a deep breath, he left the relative shelter of the doorway.

His first step ended in a sudden jolt as he nearly collided with a teenage boy who seemingly appeared out of nowhere. A raised hand to protect from any potential collision, and the customary "Sorry" from Sam were met with a quick glance and a nod from the boy. Wearing a full football kit, He appeared totally dry, complete with immaculate sculpted hair. With several strides that seemed too large for his shorter frame, he was gone. Sam began his journey again. His confusion not relenting, he glanced up the street to see If he could spot an explanation for this latest strange occurrence. As the rain hit him, he could only summon a single word.

"How...?"

The shortest distance between two points is a straight line, which would mean to get to the bus stop Sam should cross the road at this point. Turning to face his destiny, Sam was taken aback by the Venetian quality of the scene in front of him. Ever present tarmac had disappeared, in its place a fast flowing off-brown river of unknown depth and ferocity. Contemplating what to do in this unexpected situation was leading to more wetness from the incessant rain storm. Nothing for it but to try and jump over the worst of it. Sam's legs were long, it would be fine. Probably. With a deep breath and slight fear that the continuing weirdness around him would result in a shark or whale suddenly emerging from the depths below, Sam leapt into the road.

A large splash erupted as Sam almost but not quite made it across the middle of the tarmac river. Looking down, he couldn't tell If the splash had hit him and made his state worse, or if his clothes had just reached the point of not being able to be more wet anyway. An attempt at cursing the situation resulted in a strange "maaaa" noise emanating from deep within, encapsulating the frustration at how sodden he was and the strangeness of the people and the watery world around him. He resumed heading towards the square, flicking his hands and feet as he walked as though it would solve any wetness they were experiencing, whilst hopes of a dry bus home fleeted through his mind.

The tram lines that skirted the square had become fast moving mini canals, perfect for tiny ships to take much needed supplies to mouse factories. The square itself was approximately eighteen times wider than usual thanks to the ocean that was falling on Sam with each step. He began to feel sorry for all the fish who must be losing their homes out in the Atlantic as all the water in the entire world seemed to be falling directly onto him. Five steps into the trek across this open plane of concrete made it seem like a very bad idea. Sam started to look around for more shelter, preferably shelter he could fit in. The wooden buildings of the summer market offered no hope, all closed off as if they had prior warning from the local witchdoctor. The al fresco pub seemed almost laughable in this situation, as did the few men casually leaning against the bar, sheltering under the tiniest of awnings, each with one hand over their pint glasses.

Sam took several steps towards the main entrance to the market, thinking in desperation that the sign that hung overhead may be just what he was looking for. Sadly, the sign turned out to be only about an inch thick. As shallow and lacking of depth as most of the commercially driven enterprises that resided here. Beyond sighing, Sam let out a small chuckle as he turned back to finish the swim across the square.

The shops that lined the bus side of the square stood proudly declaring their opportunity for shelter. A pillared walkway graced the entire line of them, seeming majestic in the current circumstances. Although already full of people, Sam was confident he could squeeze himself in somewhere, receiving some much needed respite from nature's assault. The sight of possible shelter grew steadily bigger as each weighted and thoroughly soaked step squished onwards. The people who inhabited this promised land were of two clans. The first, perfectly dry and stationary, huddled in groups to watch the storm. Sam was slightly embarrassed to be part of the entertainment, he expected they would be commentating on him:

"Ooo look at the state of that one!"

"Can you believe that idiot? Walking across the square in this weather?!"

Too far away, and with too much noise from the bouncing rain, Sam could only grow grumpy and self conscious with what he perceived they would be saying.

The second clan was nomadic. Wandering up and down the street under the loving embrace of the covered walkway. It was this clan that Sam hoped to join. A couple of squelching steps later, and Sam was safe. Or so he thought. The walkway was only the width of a few people, and with the two clans competing for space it was packed almost solid. The nomadic clan were pushing and jostling their way past the voyeuristic clan. Standing still and taking up a lot of the limited space, the voyeur clan seemed less in awe of nature, and more enjoying the suffering of others. Eyes wide and shaking with chuckles, if they had had the opportunity Sam felt they would have released alligators onto the square to add to the enjoyment of the scene.

Leaving them to their fun, and occasionally being bumped into by nomads, Sam tried to assess his situation. His shirt had taken on properties he didn't know it was capable of, feeling like his arms were wrapped in a thin yet tight wet second skin. His jeans felt much heavier than normal, although the dark colour made it difficult to tell the damage. They too clung onto his skin as though he had just got out of the shower, wrapped a towel around himself and then realised the towel had also been in the shower with him the whole time. How were the backs of his knees wet? He had given up on his hair, which felt like it was stuck to the sides of his head as though someone had just thrown seaweed at him. He checked his pockets, in case they had filled with water and destroyed his phone. The damp screen sprang to life, thankfully. A chuckle of frustrated misery escaped from him, signalling that he had had just about enough of this sort of thing.

Assessment complete, situation saturated. Bus stop not too far away. Operation get the hell out of this oceanic nightmare commence. Time to join the nomads. Squeezing his way through the tightly packed walkway was slow, but relatively dry progress. And then Sam saw it. A second unexpected river cut a black path in front of him, severing his sheltered escape route in two as though a triumphant fantasy villain had conjured its existence just to thwart him, whilst cackling maniacally from the back of a dragon. Pouring from an alleyway between old stone shop bearing buildings, Sam felt the thick, black, and fast moving water could only be described as a torrent of flotsam and wrongness. Appalled and intrigued in equal measure, Sam watched the water spew out from its alley borne mouth. All of the filth, muck, and horror that resided in the shadowy world of city centre alleys was being carried kicking and screaming into the light, the rain water forming an angry mob of villagers casting out the vampires and demons from their usually hidden dark holes.

Cigarette butts, crisp and sandwich wrappers of unknown vintage, strange lumps of indescribable… stuff… all bobbing along on the worryingly dark water. The rain was still hitting hard on the slabs of the square, and this new river was joining in the fun, spreading like an oil slick across the standing water. Sam did not want whatever this was on his boots. He contemplated going back into the rain to try and walk around it, but as he looked back to see where the filth river dissipated all he could see was it spreading, flowing, merging with the wider ocean on the square. As he looked in horrific wonder at this latest besmirchment of nature, his eyes instinctively darted to fresh movement. A cigarette packet was floating out of the foul darkness of the alley. It drifted down the river, and off, out to sea. Explorers, finally free of their putrid home, off to seek their fortune across the vast ocean that spread across the city centre, cheering their liberation from the darkness… finally. Half of Sam's mind was cheering them on on their brave adventure. The other half was huddled in a corner, weeping, softy murmuring *"what the hell is going on."*

He was probably better off where he was, relatively speaking. A sigh of resignation as to what must happen next could be heard by any passing nomad as he tried to reason an escape.

Taking a step back, and tensing his legs like he had any idea what he was doing, Sam was ready. He leapt high into the sky, majestic, an Olympic athlete. Or so he hoped. No sand, no adoration, and no circular piece of metal awaited his awkward and off balance attempt at avoiding the torrent. A loud splash rang out as his foot hit the edge of the wrongness, and he quickly jumped again in the hope that if he was fast enough, the first foot fall wouldn't count. A couple more of these not really happening missteps later, and he was safe on the other side. Not wanting to check to see if any of the horror had attached itself to him, following the logic that if he didn't see it, it wasn't there, Sam continued his journey to the bus stop. One more corner, and a hundred or so more yards to go. No more shelter, back out into the rain. Saddened to be feeling the too familiar smack of water again, Sam just wanted to go home. Blue and inviting, the bus stood like a saviour. He quickened his pace to avoid the heartbreak of the prophesied vehicular rescuer driving off without him when he was so close.

One final push, one dripping bus card, and one more sigh, and Sam was on board. Free at last of the rain. The faces of the fellow escapers seemed to share his pain. The inside of the bus was humid, dank, and wet. As Sam made his way to a free seat, he felt a new kind of displeasure at the thought that the water in here was not from rain penetrating the roof or tightly sealed windows, it had all dripped and flowed from the passengers. Shuddering from a combination of that thought, and the cold he now felt from his own sodden mess of clothes, he sat down, making a squelching sound that did not help the shudder abate. As the bus began to move, Sam sat in a growing puddle. His clothes seemed wetter than if he had just been sat in a bath, his shirt sleeves clinging onto him like an over affectionate aunt at a seventh birthday party. He thought that at least some of the water must be leaving him as he shifted about uncomfortably on the increasingly wet seat. Happy to have finished the ordeal, Sam put his head in his hands as he contemplated that all he wanted to do when he got home was have a hot shower to wash away the rain.

24

"What?"

Louisa looked up from her desk. The office was about as buzzing as it ever was, like a fly in its death throes on a window ledge of some more important department. Half a dozen people in semi matching grey clothing were going about business as usual, or how to check the internet with an 'I'm working really hard that report will be done by close of office' expression. The photocopier in the corner seemed to be the only thing in the room pleased to be here, joyfully spitting out duplicates of 'probably important that we have these filed somewhere' bits of paper while its light danced back and forth on the original document like an over excited puppy.

"Have you got anyone to bring to drinks on Friday? You know? Yeah?"

Leanne sat opposite Louisa as always, on the sprawling mess of a desk that was technically job shared by the whole office. No one seemed to have adapted to the 'you can work anywhere, it's freedom of movement' spiel that the consultant brought in last year had rambled on about. Energising work flow was much less important a motivating factor to get through the day than the throwback tribal turf ownership of 'but I've always sat here'.

"Oh right."

Louisa wasn't sure she had agreed she was going to the after works drinks thing, let alone how she could conjure up an excuse for not bringing a date. What she really wanted to do was complain about how she was constantly expected to bring someone, what did it matter? She had vowed to never go to a work do again, but Leanne was insistent that this was different. It was not a proper work thing, just some people who happened to work in the same company going out. It was mostly going to be the marketing department anyway, so not the usual crowd that frequented the dreaded things. Maybe that made it better? Louisa knew that they shouldn't have the money to throw around like the normal lot did. Maybe that would make it less awkward? But then is considering something *less awkward than usual* a good excuse for going?

"Yeah, maybe."

The response wasn't accurate in any way, but felt like the right thing to say. It was only after she said it that Louisa realised she meant to reply to the question of if she was going, not the question about taking someone. She hoped that was clear. Leanne's eyes revealed a slightly too enthusiastic interest in Louisa's circumstances. The rest of Leanne's demeanour revealed the same over enthusiasm for everyone else's circumstances. Her over extended glue on nails were never far away from either the latest copy of a tabloid magazine or her candy pink smartphone, you know, just in case.

"Oo tell me everything about him! I'm so glad you've found someone, you've been so miserable on your own."

Leanne started to twirl her hair as she leaned in to hear all the gory details, of which there were none.

"Oh, no, I don't mean… I mean…"

Louisa was taken aback both by how Leanne had misunderstood her last statement and also managed to amplify it whilst simultaneously being quite mean about her personal circumstances in such an offhand manner.

"Secret, is it? Oh he's not married is he? Hmm…"

Leanne leaned back in her chair, a slight look of displeasure on her face.

"Trouble that, not worth it. Unless, you know!"

With a wink, the displease vanished from Leanne's face, replaced by a coy smile.

"Leanne! No! I just meant I might be coming along, not that there's a date, I don't have a date!"

Louisa was still reeling from the remarks about how sad she seemed because she was single to even begin to process the current reflection of martial values. Then it hit her; *'Why does everyone assume if I don't tell them I'm dating someone I must be having an affair with someone that's married? What's going on?'* She tried to rally herself to properly respond.

"I don't know where you get these ideas from."

A typically less powerful rebuttal than Louisa had wanted it to be. And she felt she maybe did know a little bit where some of it came from, as she glanced at the magazine by Leanne's hand, its cover emblazoned with a celebrity Louisa didn't recognize in a meagre excuse for a swimsuit, complete with arrows pointing to any and all possible flaws with her appearance. She gathered herself for another go at a rebuttal.

"What did you mean about me being miserable? I'm not miserable!"

Louisa wasn't sure how she felt, other than annoyed and slightly concerned that while she had been struggling with the online dating disasters, it had become noticeable to others. Still she had taken Jess's advice, and binned the lot of it. She had been feeling better about it all since then, so why did Leanne think she was still miserable?

"Oh love, you need a fella! Someone to take care of you and take you out places."

Leanne had an expression Louisa could only perceive as 'attempt to look sympathetic whilst not really being that interested in case more sympathy was required than was willing to be given'.

Louisa understood now. Leanne wasn't talking about her; she was projecting herself and her own hopes, dreams and misery onto her. Leanne had been single for almost a year, since the last boyfriend had forgotten to get enough surprise gifts to warrant the attention required for a relationship. Louisa had not seen being single as a problem that needed to be fixed, and had only been trying to date since people had talked her into it. Louisa was determined that this conversation was not going to descend into an attack on her personal circumstances in some veiled attempt at self flagellation.

"Are you bringing anyone then?"

"Well…"

Leanne looked up at the ceiling as if ticking off some floating list of suitors visible only to her.

"Nah, I mean, I could, but then what if there was someone better there? I would be stuck! Could miss a chance!"

"But…"

Louisa considered questioning the logic of the last statement but thought better of it.

"Well I suppose I can see your point?"

She couldn't. It seemed an awful way to think. But she wanted out of this conversation. Agreeing would maybe achieve this quickly.

"Exactly! The grass is always greener!"

Leanne looked pleased with herself, her logic validated, she rose from her chair in a victorious and slightly proud manner usually reserved for someone that had just won some kind of award ceremony. She turned and began to walk towards the door.

"Coffee?"

Leanne shouted back as she walked through the door, and before any answer could be yelled back, she was gone. Louisa lowered her gaze to the keyboard on her cluttered desk.

"Right. I will show her, I'm not miserable. I'm fine. I don't need someone to go with me, I don't need anyone's permission or blessing, I will go to this stupid thing, and I will have an amazing time because *I* choose to."

The keyboard did not respond to Louisa's slightly angry tone, it did however, make all the right letters appear in all the right places in the invite acceptance email that was appearing on the screen above.

25

Sam felt a bit better. Sitting on the sofa, softly holding a mug while the vapours caressed his face, his love affair with this particular cup of tea was as satisfying a thing as he could remember. Well, all he could remember at this point was the walls of his room and how to play the next episode of the TV drama everyone said was so amazing. It wasn't amazing. It was derivative and badly acted with female characters that wore outfits that would get them called into HR for a meeting if this was a real work place.

Sam had really not enjoyed being ill. It had been incredibly un fun. Aches, pains, fever, and not in an overdramatic way, in an actual sweating out your whole body I can see ghosts all around me did I actually die kind of way. Still, Sam was pleased that he had recovered enough to be slightly annoyed. That felt like real progress after the virus had knocked him completely on his ass for the past couple of weeks. Four days waiting to see a doctor who told him "you don't look too well, do you" swiftly followed by "there's nothing we can do, this thing has been going around" had sent Sam into a temperature induced hole of not being able to care anymore until today. Sam definitely felt better, and slightly annoyed.

"Does everyone feel like this when they start to recover, is it a typical British reaction?"

The thought of other cultures having different reactions danced through his mind as he breathed in the steam from the mug and took a long sip.

"No, people are just people. There's no such thing as a stereotyped response to sickness, just some people will be grumpy, wherever they are from."

The conclusion made Sam feel a little bit connected to the wider world, people from different backgrounds and countries, brought together by being slightly annoyed at still feeling like crap after being ill for what felt like an eternity. He then immediately felt guilty about all the people around the world that didn't have access to drugs, clean water, hospitals… feeling a little grumpy suddenly felt like a bit of a luxury.

Time to begin re-joining the world. Time to start to reconnect and prepare to become one of those people that goes to the outside places and does the grown up things. Well perhaps not the grown up things, they were usually not very fun. Time to do the washing. Well not quite that time yet. Time to check messages. Picking up his phone, Sam saw a nice well-wishing message from Jess that had come through whilst he was having his tea based affair. Smiling at the thought, he responded with mostly symbols of faces and random other emoticons. Close enough to actual words. He was sure she understood the deep meaning to his reply.

"Hmm."

Still no reply from Ellie. That was odd. Actually, that was really quite odd. Ellie always had her nose attached to her phone screen. Illness had made the passage of time go a bit wonky, but Sam was sure he hadn't heard from Ellie in some time. Checking the message history, he had sent several messages in the past week with no reply from her. He started to feel a bit concerned that perhaps she had also succumbed to this devil plague and was trapped in her flat, unable to text, staring at her screen unable to command twitches in her fingers to coordinate into the tales of adventure in the bus queue or a link to a website showing ten things you wouldn't believe a cat did whilst in space. You wouldn't believe number seven.

"Hey Ells, how're you? I hope you've not caught this bug!"

The progress bar on Sam's message rapidly filled to 98% and then sat for a good long while before remembering to actually send his message. Still slightly concerned for her wellbeing, and more concerned that he hadn't been more aware of her lack of communication, Sam set the phone down on his lap and waited. Ellie's usual instant response was not forthcoming. Maybe she had caught the bug. Sam moved the phone to the sofa beside him and started the next episode of the TV drama. As the characters moved about the screen at varying levels of rage at each other, in various stages of unnecessary undress, Sam alternated between sipping his tea and glancing at his phone for a response.

The next day brought enough feelings of recovery to face the horror that it was time to go back to work. Gathering all relevant objects, keys, attire, and doctor's notes, Sam headed for the outside world. His door opened with ease, despite Sam preferring to imagine it spilling cobwebs onto the floor and giving an almighty creak as though years had passed since any mortal had tried to pass through this sacred portal. With the relief of a released prisoner and the fear of an escaped puppy, Sam headed down the street to the bus stop where a good number of smartly dressed men and women waited. The ones who had arrived early enough to get a spot in the lean-to shelter casually flicked the screens of their phones and adjusted their shoulder bags whilst the ones who had arrived later clutched their coats and bags to them against the relatively stiff breeze that rushed across the street. Sam joined the end of the queue, clutching his bag and wondering if the wind felt this cold to everyone or if it was a remnant of his death plague.

As the bus turned around the corner everyone began to get themselves together for its arrival. Sam looked at the driver. A tallish man, he wasn't looking at Sam. Or anyone else. Or the stop. The bus sailed past the confused and arm wavey queue with the driver looking firmly out of the opposite side window as if to say *"Well I didn't see any of them, no need to worry about stopping and risking running late and ruining my schedule."* As the metal conveyor of crushed hopes continued on up the road without any of them, Sam heard several loud sighs and muttered expletives emanate from the smartly dressed ones around him. The general tone sounded a lot like *"But… we queued and everything… in a straight line even though its windy… but…"*

"Well that's great. Off sick for two weeks and then late for work. I'm sure my manager will be well impressed."

Sam was intensely displeased that he had struggled to get here, battled, and for nothing.

Settling in to his spot on the pavement, he took out his phone and commenced wasting the time until the next bus was scheduled to arrive and play with everyone's nerves and emotions. There was still no message from Ellie, and he was beginning to feel a bit confused. He could do with something uplifting to help him get through the day before he could escape back to the sofa and tea. Arranging something couplely might be nice too, after the death plague had kept him from the house party she had been so keen on attending. Several minutes of random internet searches later, a bus arrived and actually stopped and everything. Slipping his phone into his pocket whilst retrieving his travel card, Sam gathered himself for the journey. As he stepped onto the bus he felt a vibration from his thigh. "Oo this must be Ells" he thought as he beeped his card and looked for a seat with a renewed sense of excitement. After sitting down with great care, taking a minute to decide if his head was spinning from still being ill, or that he just needed to get used to being back on a bus again, he reached for the phone.

"Oh hi! I've been really busy! I've got some good news though – I will tell you later!"

It was nice to finally get a message back, although Sam wasn't sure if the tone was weird, or if he was just still a bit out of it. At least she hadn't said she was ill though, so that was good.

"Great, I've got some good news too – speak later :)"

Sam wasn't sure why there needed to be any waiting, Ellie was usually so keen to message away all of the time. But, it was nice to have something to look forward to. Something to help get through what he expected to be a bit of a difficult day.

The wind howled the entire day. Sam lurched through his work routine to the best of his ability as the windows rattled as though something was trying to get in, or perhaps out, of this place.

Perhaps he had become telekinetic? A super power bonus from the virus? Maybe the rattles were him, trying to steady himself as he tried to focus. He couldn't wait to get back home. Where it was comfortable, and there was tea. And he could lay down and text the night away with Ellie. He missed her, her flamboyant energy. Not long now, almost time for home. Then not long till he could arrange to see her again.

At last. Sam was home. On the sofa, mug of tea steaming away next to him. It was time. He raised his phone and sent his message. He was excited to hear Ellie's news. Perhaps she had something planned for them both? Sam pondered while he waited for the reply. After what felt like an eternity, a buzz.

"Oh hi! Yes so fantastic news! I have a boyfriend! :) :)"

Sam stared at the screen. He continued to stare at the screen. That was weird, did she mean she was finally going to tell her friends about the two of them? Had it at long last become official? Another buzz.

"I met him at that house party I was telling you about, it was magical! We just clicked straight away! Everything was so easy :)"

Sam's insides imploded. It felt like someone had reached inside of him and pulled all his insides out through his eyes. He was speechless, breathless, mindless. A pain began to emanate from somewhere inside his chest. Another buzz.

"So what was your news?"

"I got better."

Sam's fingers moved without being told to. He didn't understand what to do. A boyfriend? He was her boyfriend? They were a happy couple? In love? Against the world together. Sam's mind was collapsing. His body felt heavy, and warm. His skin tingled. He might be slightly shaking, he couldn't quite tell. Buzz.

"Oh that's good, you had a virus didn't you."

How? What? Sam couldn't fathom what was happening. Was she now onto small talk, after casually destroying his soul? His fingers began moving.

"What do you mean you have a boyfriend? What about us? I thought I was your boyfriend? What?"

Sam was struggling. Drowning.

"Oh I thought you knew that we were just friends. I told you I wasn't sure about dating again."

Sam read and re read Ellie's text. A thousand thoughts spun through his mind. A thousand demons eating away at his mind. A million fragments falling. He tried to think, to what had been said, what had happened. Yes, he remembered her saying that, once, on their first date. They had been seeing each other for months – hadn't they got past that? He thought they had got past that? He was giving her the time and space… He was being supportive and nice… he wasn't pressuring her to make a fuss with her friends until she was ready… but they were still together? How did she? All the time they had spent together? All the nights? How was that not?

"Ellie we were a couple, what are you talking about???"

Sam was lost, tumbling, falling. Buzz.

"Oh hunni we spoke about how I needed some time to heal and move on from my last boyfriend, I thought you would be happy for me when I told you I had managed to."

Falling faster, deeper, further. Typing. Difficult, spelling all wrong. Several attempts.

"I thought I was helping you move on, we were moving on together?"

Buzz.

"I never meant to hurt you."

The words guaranteed to hurt the worst. Buzz.

"I think I should probably leave you to it for a bit, but let's get a coffee or something and I can tell you all about it? Let me know when you're free :)"

No more buzz. Sam's soul collapsed in a heap somewhere deep underneath his flat. Somewhere dark and cold. He didn't know what to do. He wanted to scream. He opened up his social media accounts, and flicked through his friends to find and open Ellie's page. Maybe it was a joke? Maybe there was something on there saying it was some kind of badly thought out prank? If not he could post something, let everyone know what had happened? Maybe then they would agree she was supposed to be with him, he was the boyfriend.

Her profile page sparked to life. He had not checked anything while he was ill, it seemed so pointless. Atop her page was an announcement of coupledom. Ellie and some bloke with close cropped hair. It was not a picture of her and Sam. The despair and rage rose from deep inside as he looked at the huge number of likes, smiley faces, and love heart emoji that had been posted in support from her friends.

"I'm so happy for you!"

"Yay! You finally found someone!"

"you've been single so long, so pleased for you both!"

Reading the posts made Sam feel sick. A deep, painful, might actually throw up an organ or two feeling. He wanted to post something – a declaration that he was here, he had been here… she wasn't single…

It dawned on him that none of these people knew him. He had respected Ellie's wish for space, he had never met any of her friends. They obviously hadn't been told. Ellie had never told them about him. If he posted he would look like an insane stalker, claiming some crazy perverted crush from afar, they would think he was a freak, a weirdo. He wasn't sure if it was accidental, or… was it on purpose? Ellie could sweep him away like nothing, all of her friends would side with her against the weirdo who posted random things. There was no point. He closed the profile page, and turned off his phone. No more buzz. Never again. Heavy eyes, wet face. He placed his phone on the table, a headstone for his subterranean soul. Buried, gone. Darkness.

Cold.
Nothing.
Broken.

26

"Come on then you fuckers!"

Louisa was ready. Ready to prove that she belonged here, in the outside world, with people. She was not a recluse. These people wanted to have a party night out on the town, and she could fit in with them. She didn't need their permission, she didn't need to bring a date. She was here. Herself. And that was enough. One note though, next time she went out somewhere, she was going to meet someone first. Or start at Jess's flat. She was a little bit tired of walking into venues on her own, trying to find people in places she hadn't been to before.

No. Actually no. She was fine with that. She was fine walking in by herself, she didn't need anyone to hold her hand. She opened the door and stepped through. She was ready.

She entered a small room, deliberate in its plainness. A large desk ran almost the entire length of the room, a single staff member stood impatiently behind its cream coloured hulk. Moving towards this person, she realised she was unsure what she was supposed to do… ask something in particular? Use a code word perhaps? But she didn't know a code word… this place was trying to be an old time speakeasy, hidden and secret. Maybe she wasn't cool enough after all.

No. She was perfectly able to be here. She would just ask.

"Through the door marked 'Staff Only'."

The desk person answered her question before she spoke it. Still looking impatient, and a little annoyed. So much for the magic of secretive bars. Louisa pushed open the suggested door and walked through. She found herself in a bathroom. Moderately decorated, but with far too much red. This was a little exciting, a bit different, and, dare she say, she found it a little bit cool. There was a hand sign on the wall, next to the sink. The hidden door was not quite closed properly, which was both a little disappointing as it ruined some of the surprise, and a bit of a relief, as she knew that she wouldn't look foolish pushing on the wall. It required quite a firm push, swinging back slowly to reveal the true venue.

Stepping through, Louisa felt a twinge of disappointment. The first area was full of garden furniture. LED fairy lights wove between sections of trellis attached to the walls, which were flaking their whitewash in an attempt to look a bit rustic. Potted plants dotted the ends of the tables. A small hedge lined one of the walls.

"Why go to all the trouble of making a secret speakeasy, to then have *another* rustic quirky bar? Shouldn't it be decorated to look like an underground secret dive? That's what speakeasies were, and we are actually a little bit underground? Why would there be a rustic garden through a bathroom?"

Louisa's thoughts danced through her mind in a confused ballet. So much effort, to then look a little bit like everywhere else. Another new venue trying to look rustic and old for the sake of modern fashion. What did it say about a town when all the venues were trying to look so run down? Was the entire city trying to look like it was falling apart at the seams? A well suited greeter shocked Louisa from her thoughts. He smiled as he gestured she should follow him deeper into the venue as the cable between his radio and earpiece ruffled his waistcoat.

"Seriously what's with all the earpieces?"

Louisa panicked that she had said that out loud. She would never know. The greeter didn't say a word. Moving past the garden, a larger room beckoned. Dark hard wood floors, panelled walls. A large bar ran the length of the far wall. Many bottles of all shapes and sizes stretched its length, reaching almost to the ceiling. Coloured lights illuminated them all, declaring their presence and magnificence, as well as the knowledge and skill of the bar staff to manage and maintain such a vast array of booze. There was no garden furniture in this section, dark wood tables and chairs were the order of the day. Several plush leather booths dominated the side wall. No pot plants. Not special enough. Cherry trees lined the remaining walls, in full pink blossom.

"Oh for fuck's sake."

Louisa was growing slightly weary of the pretentiousness of these places. She wished someone would ask her to go to a proper pub, just a pub, with its own history and stories. Not some brand new fake old confused mess of ironic rustic chic. If she had turned up to her house at university with a fake plastic tree, her housemates would have laughed at her before referring her to the course counsellor to discuss her madness. This was a bar. Enclosed, slightly underground. Why would there be cherry trees. Cherry trees were nice, sure. Why not have some actual cherry trees though, in an actual rustic garden, actually outside. Why not use the inside place for inside things? Louisa found it a bit depressing, a reminder that summer was going to be gone soon, and she was not outside making the most of it.

"Hey Lous, over here!"

Leanne's voice cut through Louisa's internal rant like an object cutting through a softer floatier object. Slightly dazed by the plastic plant rage, Louisa moved towards the source of the noise. She didn't like 'Lous' as a shorthand name. It sounded like lose, or toilets. Neither of which she particularly wanted to be associated with. She never really liked her name, it was a bit to long for everyone to apparently use properly, and it never shortened to anything nice.

"Hi Leanne, how's it going?"

"Yeah it's a good night so far, great place isn't it? So quirky, special!"

"Sure!"

Louisa didn't know how else to respond. The slight wobble deep inside. Every so slight. *'why does no one else see things the way I do… what's wrong with me…'* Ignore it. People have different tastes, that's fine, who was she to say others couldn't enjoy these authentic places. No time for introspection now, Leanne was beckoning her ever closer.

"This is Josh, and this is Harry. They are from marketing! Josh, Harry, this is the girl I've been telling you about!"

Leanne's enthusiastic introduction, followed by the warm smiles and handshakes from the marketing duo left Louisa feeling like she needed to know pretty soon what exactly Leanne had told them about her.

"Hi yes, don't believe anything she's said about me!"

'Seriously don't' Louisa kept the last bit to herself. Others could learn from this. The keeping things to themselves.

"I thought there was going to be more people out?"

Louisa directed her question at Leanne, and she struggled to disguise the sudden wave of panic accompanying it. She had counted. There were two women and two men. She did not like the look of this at all. Leanne was busy flicking her hair and giggling like a teenager in the general direction of Harry. Josh stepped in to answer for her.

"Oh yes, the others will be wandering in at some point. We had a teambuilding session earlier, ended in a meal for some of them. We decided we would rather take the chance to meet the two of you first, you know, the spirit of inter-departmental cooperation."

Josh's words contained many triggers for Louisa. The slightly creepy tone of trying to get here early to have first go at the ladies, the mention of 'teambuilding days'. The use of 'inter departmental cooperation' outside of an easily ignored workplace email. This may be a long night. But, she would show them. She would prove that she belonged out here in the world. And then she would go home again. Read her book. Victory.

"So you girls are from admin, aren't you?"

It was small talk. Uninspired, but a usual start.

"Yeah, that's right. So how's marketing?"

Equally uninspired response, but the best Louisa could manage at the moment. It was normal enough. She had to keep it going. She could do it. She refused their offer for a drink, and instead directed one of the smartly dressed spy wannabe staff to fetch her a glass of wine.

They continued the dance of words, back and forth, nothing really being said. Leanne interjected every now and then, a cackling laugh spilling across for the smallest of reasons. Louisa was struggling to keep her attention focused. At each opportunity her mind wandered off. Sometimes far away, sometimes across the room to the other people in here. At the next table, a woman in a flowing summer dress sat with a guy in grey trousers and a tan short sleeve shirt. She sat facing away from Louisa, he sat rigid. He had the looks of a male model, very tanned. Perfect hair. No facial expressions. Every time Louisa glanced over, nothing. She hadn't seen him move once. She wondered if he was actually in his sixties and botoxed to within an inch of his life… or maybe the girl was crazy and it was actually a mannequin… or some kind of android… Louisa wondered if she could get an android… she could programme it to have more of a personality than Josh from marketing. No, she thought that wasn't fair. He had a personality, and he was trying his best to small talk her to death. It was just that she didn't really get his personality, it wasn't connecting with her.

Across the room, a group of young girls sat quietly. They seemed to be chatting, but Louisa felt that many girls in a place like this together would normally be making way more noise. They seemed to be enjoying themselves, there were smiles and occasional raised glasses. One of the girls had decorations on her face, along with glitter and little number 21's. She seemed happy, but not loud. There was always a quiet one at a party, or so Louisa had been told whenever someone tried pointing out that it was her. Maybe this was what happened when all the quiet ones made friends with each other? A whole group of quiet ones, celebrating, quietly. It actually seemed quite appealing the more she thought about it.

Louisa was drifting. She realised she needed to pay more

attention to the people she was out with. She tried to try harder. The others were talking about films she hadn't seen, and celebrities she didn't know about. It was tough. She suspected they wouldn't know about the books she read, and none of them seemed to be paying any attention to the other people in the bar. She wasn't quite sure what to do. It was around this point, that an answer to her question appeared.

"Hello everyone!"

A quite loud man had appeared out of nowhere, with a group of people in tow. He was welcomed with almost cheers by Josh and Harry. This must be the rest of the marketing team. Louisa scanned them all, making quick decisions why she didn't like the look of any of them. There were four men and three women. At least the genders were pretty evenly split. The men all wore identikit thin legged suits, with thinner ties. Louisa couldn't decide if this made them look like an old jazz band. Maybe a ska band. No sign of brass instruments though. The girls all wore tight jeans and blouses. Louisa shifted awkwardly in her dress. She wondered why she always got the dress code wrong, why she was always out of place. She saw the girls look her over, judging eyes roaming free. Why did she always look different to everyone else? Even when she wasn't trying to? She felt separate enough from the world without having to have it so obvious.

"Well hello, I'm enchanted to meet you."

For the second time in quick succession, a man's voice dragged her out of her thoughts. Louisa looked at the source, it seemed familiar…

"My name is Dean, and I must say it's a pleasure to meet such a gorgeous specimen."

Oh. It was Dean. Louisa remembered him from Jess's housewarming. He had seemed such a confused chap back then. He didn't seem to have improved.

"Hi Dean, how've you been?"

Dean took a small bow, taking Louisa's hand.

"Why how nice of you to ask, I've been splendid. Such a lovely young lady. And what may I call you?"

Louisa took her hand back.

"Dean, we've met before. At Jess's party. It's Louisa."

Dean shifted his stance, a quizzical expression scanned Louisa from top to toe.

"I'm sure I would remember such a fine lady."

"Well, apparently not so much!"

Louisa couldn't help but chuckle at Deans' attempt to be whatever it was he was attempting to be. She had begun to recall their previous meeting, how she couldn't quite get a handle on what he was talking about. She had better do something to make sure that didn't happen again. She looked around to see if any of the other new arrivals were trying to join in the conversation. Sadly, they were not. Leanne was holding court with a lot of the guys, trying to test them en masse for new partner material perhaps. The girls had formed a small tight group with Harry and one of the new guys, busy gesticulating at each other. It was just Louisa and Dean for now.

Well, maybe it was an opportunity. Dean didn't seem to be quite like the others, so maybe she could use this as an opportunity to find out what was going on there. Louisa had no idea how to do that.

"So, you had a team building day? Was it awful? I hate those things!"

Louisa began to try.

"We did! It was great fun! We went bowling, and my team thrashed one of the teams from finance."

Dean stood tall, proud of his victory on the battlefield. Louisa shuddered. Work do's. She had vowed never again. She was told this wasn't really a work do. The fact that the people here just belonged to a different department did not seem to count.

"Has your department been yet? You should go!"

Dean's enthusiasm was met with winces and shudders.

"Yeah, we went last year, it was awful."

Louisa had not enjoyed the experience one bit.

"It started like a school sports lesson, all lined up and being chosen by the managers for their teams one by one. I'm not very good at bowling, so I got picked last."

"Oh I would pick you first for my team, without question!"

Louisa chose to ignore Dean's comment and continue with her story.

"So I wasn't doing very well. I suggested I stopped and just watched, but one of the guys from sales decided he should teach me."

"Well that's nice, and did you learn how to do it and save the day?"

Louisa glared away Dean's latest comment.

"Well somehow teaching me bowling required his hand to be on my ass, so no. I still couldn't do it. Like I said. And when our team lost, they all had a go at me for making them lose. So it was not very team buildy."

Louisa was still a bit angry about that day. She wished she had sworn at them all, and punched that creep from sales.

"Well that's a shame, perhaps you weren't trying hard enough. If you like I can show you some pointers sometime?"

Dean smiled as he spoke, sipping his ale. Louisa wondered if he had heard anything she had said. Maybe he just thought he could try the hand on ass teaching technique. She needed to change the topic.

"What do you think of this place?"

Dean looked around, before responding energetically.

"Oh it's wonderful, isn't it? The cherry blossom, it reminds me of my travels. Do you travel Louisa? Oh, you must, it fills the soul!"

Louisa had two flashes in her mind. The first, a recollection of Dean's travel from the last time they spoke. The second, the realisation why she got a strange feeling at seeing all the blossoming cherry trees. She looked around again, seeing a picture of a geisha on the wall. This place was trying to make out it was in the middle of the Japanese cherry blossom festival. The Hanami.

"Oh that's it! Hanami! That's what all the cherry trees are about!"

Louisa's excitement seemed a bit lost on Dean.

"The what?"

"Each spring, across Japan, everyone has parties to celebrate the cherry trees coming in to blossom. I think that's what they are trying to do here, although it's a bit weird don't you think?"

Louisa felt a sense of relief, that she had figured something out, and something about a foreign land, and with a travel fan right here.

"That sounds lovely, how nice that it's been recreated here then. Have you been to Japan?"

Dean seemed a little nervous in his question. Louisa was more interested in why he didn't find it weird.

"It's strange enough to have all these fake trees indoors, but then to be pretending to celebrate another country's festival, at the wrong time of year, it would be like going over there and finding an all year round Christmas party bar complete with tree and stockings?"

Dean seemed baffled by Louisa's excited comments. She felt let down that he wasn't seeing it the way she was. She started to drift again. Thinking about it, Japan being the crazy exciting strange place it was, they probably did have an all year round Christmas bar somewhere. And Louisa loved Christmas. Maybe it would be awesome.

She tried talking to Dean. She really tried. He kept asking her if she would like to go away some place. She didn't get it. They were here now, they could talk now. Why did he keep trying to make plans for them at some other time? It didn't make any sense. She waited for an opportunity to escape. Her wine ran out, and she went to get a refill. After acquiring said swirling glass of comfort, she returned to the group at a different angle. Proud of her subtle way of shifting who to talk to. She joined the small group of girls and guys that seemed to be keeping to themselves. She introduced herself, and they responded. They quickly returned to talking amongst themselves. Louisa tried to join in, but they just talked over her. Talk of who in the office was stupid, who was the worst at their job, the least attractive. Louisa decided the answer to these questions could be found within this group. She decided to try again.

Moving round the group, she found Harry. Leanne had abandoned him and seemed awfully close to Josh. Her testing strategy seemed to be paying off at least. Harry smiled as he asked how she was getting on with everyone. Louisa politely bent the truth. It was the right thing to do if she wanted to continue her plan to prove she was no outsider, that she belonged out with her peers, out in the world. They chatted for a while, the same small talk again. Louisa was trying, it was very trying.

"Is that a smart watch?"

Harry's attention switched to Louisa's wrist as she removed a pesky hair from her eye.

"Err yeah it is, it was a present from my family."

Louisa had forgotten she had it, but she was a bit pleased someone had noticed. She thought it was cool, like science fiction.

"I don't see the point. I mean, don't you have to charge it every day? I don't want to have to charge a watch every day."

Louisa was totally thrown by the comment. This was a sci-fi watch present from her parents, it was cool.

"I charge it every two days actually."

Louisa was a bit hurt, and wanted to point out Harry's mistake.

"Well, I don't want to have to charge a watch every two days then. Same difference. I never have to charge a watch, and anyway, my phone tells me the time when I need to know, what's the point?"

Harry drank from his beer, happy that he had proved his

superiority and wisdom over foolish little girl Louisa. He had not.

"Well it wasn't bought for you, why should I be bothered by what you don't like about my watch? If you don't want one, don't get one, fine. But why have a go at me for something I have that you wouldn't like if it was yours? It's not yours, it's irrelevant what you think!"

Louisa was incensed. What a total asshole. How dare he. She turned her back on him and walked over to Leanne, to voice her displeasure. Her extreme displeasure. Leanne was busy with Josh. It took a couple of attempts to get her attention.

"Hi Lou Lou, how're you?"

Leanne burst into laughter at her drunken rhyme. She gathered herself enough to continue.

"You met Josh didn't you, he's lovely! There's plenty of other lovely men here too, we are all going to go on to the club soon, it's going to get messy!"

Giggles, and suggestive gestures from Leanne further annoyed Louisa. She moved away, returning to a free edge of table to collect her thoughts. She could hear some of the guys chatting behind her.

"Watch that one in the dress, she's got a nice ass but she's a bit of a bitch."

Harry's voice cut through the crowd, and deep into Louisa. She nearly dropped her glass. Hurt was quickly replaced by anger. Anger with rage. She drank the last of her overpriced wine, and smacked the glass down onto the table as if to chastise the venue itself. She walked over and grabbed Leanne by the shoulder, spinning her round to face her.

"Enjoy the rest of the night, I'm off."

Louisa didn't even wait for a response from the bemused face sported by Leanne. She was already on her way. Past the fake plastic. and the trees. Through the pointless bathroom wall that was now resting fully open. Stupid. Past the bouncers. Past the queue of idiots waiting to go in. Out into the night. She thudded up the street, each step a kick at the world.

"Enough!"

She screamed under her breath.

She had tried. She had tried to come out into the world. Tried to join the people out here, the ones that everyone said were normal, right. The ones that said she was wrong. The ones she was supposed to be with, supposed to be. She had proved she could do it. She had proved she could go into the world if she wanted. She had discovered that she just didn't want to. It was horrible, they were horrible. If they wanted to call her weird, they could. If they wanted to call her lonely, or miserable, they were wrong. She was happy as she was, with her books, with Jess and Steven. She never wanted to be like them. She was not interested in it at all. Not. One. Bit. She felt stronger, validated. She had not been missing out, she had been enjoying her time in her own way, her own rules. She would continue. And anyone that disagreed with the way she did things, or any of those horrible excuses for people in that bar… She stormed through the city like a vengeful spirit tearing this world apart as it fought its way back to its own dimension… Anyone that didn't like the way she was, who she was… they could…

Fuck.

Right.

Off.

27

The darkness filled every space. Creeping around corners, seeping across the floor. Pouring through the crack in the doorway. Sam could hear the noise it made as it embraced him. A close but distant buzz in his ears, seeming to come from everywhere around him. He pulled at the covers, trying to make his bed more comfortable. Sadly, the discomfort was not in the mattress and pillows but inside him. A ticking in his mind, a churning of pointless thoughts. That day in school, had he really said that? What must they all think of him. The girl at uni, what did she mean when she said that? Had he missed an opportunity? He turned angrily onto his other side, as if trying to throw the thoughts off his body. Peace. Darkness. Did his shirt look ok the last time he saw her? What had he done wrong, where was the time he messed it all up? Why had she done this? Why wasn't he good enough… was it the shirt? Did it look stupid? Did he always look stupid?

Shapes began to emerge out of the darkness. The edges of furniture, the figure of some kind of demon by the wall that was in no way actually Sam's coat hanging from the hook on the back of the door. Swirling magical objects darted around as his eyes adjusted to the dark. If he wasn't careful, the dark would give way to the beginning of a new day. It felt like that must be any minute now. He had been lying here sleeplessly for about seven years. He had tried breathing deeply. So deeply he had to take an extra quick breath between each long inhale and exhale. 'That can't be right' he thought as he gave up on that plan to gain unconsciousness.

He tried counting sheep. A classic, he thought, worth a go at this point. He gave up on that after he realised he was more concerned with where the sheep were going and what they had done to require being counted. He tried just counting, but that seemed ridiculous. He felt embarrassed in case any psychics happened to be reading his mind at that moment and wondered why he was so ridiculous. He wondered about psychics for a while. If they couldn't exist, why were there so many stories about them? Simply a desire to know what other people thought echoing throughout time, a classic power fantasy of 'I know something you don't know' coupled with 'you can't hide from me, or lie to me' and 'I will clearly understand your motives and what you mean at all times.' Sam began to see the appeal of such an ability. He had no real ambitions of power, but understanding what people meant, their intentions, and their not being able to lie, that was very appealing indeed. That would have helped a lot.

He heard a distant rumble drift through the window he had left open. The nights here were very quiet, especially this late. The rumble got closer, menacing. Sam realised it was a large vehicle. The spirits and shadows danced trying to provide an otherworldly explanation. Somehow, it was worse than that. It was the last late bus from town, rumbling down the main street a few hundred yards away. It must have been a Saturday, and Sam had almost forgotten. Everything was drifting into an aching oneness of trying to get through the day. Each day. Every day.

Staring at the shapes on the wall Sam's thoughts drifted to the bus. Who was on it? The same people he saw the last time he was on one? The older couples, red faced and loud… The young guys clutching their take outs and the young girls clutching their phones. Why were the young girls and guys not clutching each other? The older couples seemed to be a dying race. Had they all had fun? Were they sat there, blissfully content on their journey home from an amazing night to their warm beds or were they full of remorse, of 'I should have said' and 'I should have tried more' or even 'I can't believe I just…'

For a moment, Sam was sat there with them, contemplating all of these possibilities and chances, an infinite amount of outcomes to an infinite amount of adventures. The rumble faded as the bus disappeared towards its next stop. Everything passes. Its journey continued, slowly emptying its cargo of souls, one or two at a time, until it was empty of all but the smells and rubbish left behind, and the strange energy, the crackle in the air, the promise of fun. For once Sam felt sorry for the bus. He imagined himself sitting on it all alone, looking at the steamy windows and discarded take out boxes. The odd glitter smears and hair gel stains. The smell of perfume and chicken. Hollow of the people, empty of the souls as they disembarked into the darkness. Used and empty, the bus too vanished into the nothing.

The monochrome edges and black clumps of the unknown gave up no secrets in the quest for sleep. Sam's bedroom looked alien yet familiar. Out of place. It was as though he had stumbled into a replica, a model that he should never have seen. The effect of no sleep had left him feeling disjointed and separate. He should not be here, this was a time that didn't exist, a void that was skipped over in favour of a new beginning.

His thoughts drifted back again to Ellie. He hated when they did, but couldn't stop either. It was in these sleepless moments that her ghost had the most strength. He couldn't remember ever being hurt as much as this. The sudden cut off had blindsided him. But he was beginning to feel like it wasn't a one sided incident. Yes, it had hurt, and yes it was bad, but what hurt him the most was knowing that he put himself in the position. He had assumed, he had guessed, he had hoped that it was something bigger. He was ready for something bigger in his life. Ready for that special someone, the deep commitment, the life of building and dreaming together. He had finally found the one. Except he hadn't. Not in any way. He had found someone, and for a while it was good. In places. There had always been doubt. Examining it with hindsight, perhaps she had always voiced a lack of commitment, a concern of nothing serious. The fact that some of it was good, and the outdated notion that it was guys that lacked commitment and women always wanted it had itched in the back of Sam's mind. Like a prankster spirit whispering in his ear, he had filled in the blanks of the relationship with his own ideas and impressions. He had thought his desire was enough to carry both of them. He had listened to the voices; they had convinced him. He had convinced himself that it was enough, that it would work, she would see the sense of it and agree. His love was enough for both of them, she would understand. If he gave her time. Only in his mind.

The ghost slowly drifted in front of Sam, a shadow in a sea of half light. Each night since the breakup he could sense it. He could still sense the presence. A mixture of past experiences, the familiarity of her being nearby. It was beginning to fade, slowly. Time was passing. Sadness twinged somewhere in his chest as he relived some of the most powerful moments they had shared. He was starting to believe that she hadn't meant him any harm, she was doing what she was doing, and he was going along trying to push it to be more. Perhaps some of the pain had come from inside himself, from the fact that he wanted more than she did, and perhaps him pushing for more was what had made her want to find someone who felt more like she did. Maybe if he hadn't pushed and hoped, it would have drifted together on its own. Maybe. Unlikely, he thought. That was the itch in his mind that had got him into this mess. He was happy, she was happy. She had her secret casual supportive fling, and he had his one true love. Different people in different places crossing paths. He was still in disbelief about how he had got it so wrong. He wanted to feel like she was to blame, that it was orchestrated. He didn't though. It was thoughtless. He wanted to reach out and touch the ghost, once more, to feel that togetherness.

Strips of blue began to cut into the darkness. The shadows began retreating into the corners, lurking, waiting. As the monochrome shifted slowly to colour, Sam felt ghosts fade. His desire projected in an ethereal form echoed his misinterpretation of the real relationship he had shared with Ellie. Shadows and ghosts, chased away. As the sun continued to rise, Sam finally fell asleep.

The That'n'that

28

The nights were really starting to draw in. Louisa's window view was already dimming. Her eyes were drawn to the light of her phone as it protested for her attention. Cars passed nervously in the street below, as if the change in lighting was some new form of witchcraft they couldn't have possibly foreseen or prepared for. Some opted for incredibly bright headlights, casting deep shadows on the walls of buildings whilst reflecting brightly off glass and metal. Others opted for no lights, determined not to give into the changing season. Louisa could see the twisted logic, the fear of the dark, the loss of the summer with its promises of warm sunny hugs from above and holidays of endless possibility... but refusing to accept the reality around you, to try and deny the world even if it put you in danger of crashing... that was just dumb. She closed her eyes, to contemplate. The world spins, time moves. Enjoy its dance... she took comfort that its journey continues, and that she could see herself as part of that journey, spinning through space, every day new and full of promise. And this day, this was her day. A Saturday, free from work. Free from expectations of others. Free from having to dress appropriately and act correctly for the outside world. Free from having to conform to anything. She had allowed a deep sense of relaxed joy to well up inside her all day, from doing what she pleased, when she pleased. And now, as the hue of dusk embraced the sky, she was ready for the best bit... a Saturday night in. Warm. Comfortable. Ready to snuggle up in warm blankets against the darkness of the outside. Safe in the knowledge that she didn't have to go anywhere, didn't have to feel the cold. Not today.

Her attention snapped back to the wider world as a familiar chime sprang from the sofa. She moved to pick up her phone and see what had caused such an invasion of her moment.

"Hey hun, how's you? :)"

Jess's ever friendly voice came through even in text form. Louisa couldn't help but smile as she clicked to respond.

"Hey! Fine thanks! Saturday! :) Hope you're having a good evening!"

"So short notice and that, but trying to arrange an impromptu night out! Inviting the select few and most awesomest of people! What say you?? :)"

Jess's positivity was infectious even through a phone screen. Louisa pondered the invite. Nights out with Jess and Steven were fun, and she hadn't been out for what felt like an age. But this was her Saturday, she had planned it out from her cold desk at work all week. Should she change her plans? It would mean getting ready… very ready compared to her current state. It would mean putting away the snacks she had gotten ready, and that was a very hard thing to do indeed. This was proving to be tricky.

"Sounds fun – kinda got some plans already though : /"

Louisa felt that was a true statement, she had planned her evening, and she felt that the addition of the wonky smiley face highlighted her state of uncertainty, whilst conveying that she didn't want to disappoint Jess, or be left out of future invitations. What a versatile little symbol. A slight concern fluttered in the corner of her mind: *"that is what that smiley means isn't it? That's what everyone thinks it means?"*

"Aww hun no worries! The notice was perhaps a bit too short! How about we plan properly for a night out soon? All in advance and everything! :) :)"

Jess seemed to understand wonky smiley. This pleased Louisa greatly. She liked the idea of a night out, but that required proper preparation. Getting her mind ready to deal with the randomness that could be encountered, choosing the correct look and outfit, then finding different correct looks and outfits, before the inevitable realisation that she really wasn't bothered about looking correct and picking something she just liked instead. And, most importantly, being able to drift away at work thinking about it, being able to properly look forward to it. Yes. She had made the correct decision.

"That sounds good!! Next time!! Hope you have a good time :) :) :)"

Louisa opted to raise the stakes on the smiley faces, upping the number from Jess's last message in an attempt to show excitement about the future prospect. A bold move, perhaps it was too many… she wondered what emotion too many smiley faces would represent? Over happy perhaps? A bit mad? Deranged? Was three too many? Why was this important? She still suffered some nerves when Jess was involved, even after all this time. She had become such a good friend, and Louisa was still a little concerned that Jess might one day figure out that she wasn't cool enough to sit at her table.

"Next time!! :) :) :) :)"

Wow. Four smiley faces. Louisa laughed at the sight, Jess had taken the challenge and raised the bar. The world wasn't ready for so many smiley faces. Especially such a large smiley face to word ratio in one message. It couldn't be topped. Placing her phone back in its nest on the sofa cushion, Louisa returned to her plan. Flick a few switches, retrieve a few items. Cupboards opened and closed with satisfying clunks. This was it. The jumper was on. The kettle was boiling. The tea bag was waiting. It was Saturday night, and Louisa had been looking forward to it all week.

29

Sam looked in the mirror. He wished he had not. He pulled at his clothes, his hair. All a mess. Maybe if he rolled around on the floor for a bit he would look less ridiculous. He wasn't sure about this at all. Time had passed, but he still felt the pain from what had happened. It had formed into a nervous clench of uncertainty somewhere deep inside. Uncertain how to be… what to say… Pulling his phone from its home in his jeans pocket, he checked for oracle style advice. All it displayed was the time, in large, unhelpful, colourless numbers.

If he was going to get there on time, he was going to have to go now. Well, if he was going to get there a bit late but hopefully not too late to cause offence, he should probably have left a few minutes ago.

"Oh Fuck it."

Sam fell into the sofa, and turned on the TV.

30

Sam awoke from a deep sleep. Still groggy, he balled up his hand and rubbed his eye as he let out a yawn. His vision was blurry as he struggled to open his eyes. He heard a soft murmur, and her face came slowly into focus. Tish was still asleep, her face resting gently on her hands, a few inches from his own. She had a half smile as she breathed softly, her hair looked golden in the first light of the day, swept back from her face except for a few loose strands which danced in her breath. Sam reached out his hand and gently collected the stray strands. He smiled as he stroked her face, and she let slip a small moan as his hand brushed her ear and continued across and into the rest of her hair. He felt each strand of sun as it ran through his fingers. He felt that he had never been so happy.

A flashing light bounced into view, brighter than the glow emanating from the curtains. Again it flashed, harsh and unwelcome. Once more, and this time it's was accompanied by a shrill shouting robot noise. The golden glow seemed to shimmer and fade, the room began to spin, Sam tried to tighten his grip on Tish, but with each second he could feel less in his fingers. Darkness began seeping into the corners of Sam's vision, encroaching, crawling, slithering in… replacing the warm gold with a cold grey black horror. Eyes blinked, cracked, and the gold was gone. The room was arranged differently. There was a greyish glow from the curtains and a numb realisation that this was the familiar layout of Sam's solitary bedroom. His arm lay across an empty bed, looking feeble. A bright point of light with accompanying beeping noise mocked him from the side of the bed.

"You dick, phone. Total. Dick."

31

With a loud crack the door swung open. A blast of air hit Sam, sparking a panicked dance in his hair. Taking a deep breath, trying to quell the strands of hair that were trying to run for their lives at the sight of the outside world, Sam stepped out. It was a day, unremarkable, like any other really. The world was still spinning; Sam's head was still spinning. If only he could get the two to spin in the same direction maybe everything would work out ok. As he began walking up the street he fought the usual feeling of *'did I lock the door?'* that had become more of a routine than an actual panic about physically locking the door. He couldn't remember how many times he had stumbled out of his flat for the Sunday shop since everything had gone wrong. He had felt disjointed, disconnected, like he was watching someone else acting the role of a normal person doing normal things. Drifting somewhere else, in a dimension of confusion and aches. Sam wasn't sure if he had ever experienced anything quite like it. But then it had gone on for so long, he wasn't quite sure if he had ever experienced anything else at all.

Today though. Today felt a bit different. The wind was cold, that wasn't fun. But it wasn't that. As he walked down the familiar street, he began to notice that things felt a bit more usual. He felt a bit more confident in his steps. A bit more… there. He had really felt himself falling after Ellie. Falling both for her, and then falling away from her after. He had been falling for a long time. He had felt like he was falling away from himself. So keen to make a relationship work, he had begun to adapt himself. Consciously at first, trying to fit in with what she might want him to be. What he thought a couple should be. What everyone else's couples seemed to be. He held back on some of the music he usually listened to. Softened some of the clothes he wore. Tried some different films and books that she recommended, without really pushing for her to do the same on his recommendations. At first it was no bad thing, it was interesting. New. He was learning to see from a different perspective, he had found some new things he really liked that he wouldn't have otherwise been looking for. But it went too far. He started to lose himself. Little by little he had begun to feel less and less in control and more and more at the mercy of his efforts to be what he thought she wanted. But she didn't want. He kept looking for a way to make himself that ideal partner, to show her he was the right choice, he was right there... ready for her. Nothing he could have done would have made her want. She just wasn't looking for anything. At first, that had hurt so much. With time, it became clearer that it was not as simple as it being her fault. She had never said she felt the same. She had kept him separate from her life, and he let her plunge into his. In the dark of the night, he often wondered if he should have seen it coming, if he should have just recognised it for what it was, and made a decision to either enjoy it while it lasted or simply walk away. But as much as he wanted to be, he was not a time traveller. There was no point in analysing past choices. It wasn't getting him anywhere. From the moment he saw her, he had wanted to be with her. He had wanted it so much. He thought that he wanted it enough for both of them. Clearly, he was wrong. And now she was gone.

The void he felt inside himself had begun to crave other things. Rather than longing for her, it was now beginning to long for himself. The old him, the him that he had tried to suppress to make the couple work better. It was time to go back and watch some of his old films. Listen to old music. Look for clothes in the style he wanted to wear, regardless of what others may think. Time to rebuild and take stock. Time to remember that he had to be himself before he could be anything else.

As a sharp pain shot through his toe he remembered it was also time to pay attention to where he was going and maybe not drift off in thought while going to the shops. Stumbling, he avoided falling flat on his face. He did not avoid flailing about in a most ungraceful manner.

32

Cold. Cold cold cold COLD. Louisa was not impressed. She liked the autumn colours, the Halloween magic, the run up to Christmas… these were all exciting and familiar, happy times. But the cold that came with it, no. It was fine when you were prepared. Wrapped up toasty, mug of hot chocolate by the fire. But when you had gone out to do the shopping, misjudged the outside temperature, and forgotten to put the heating on so your flat was like a fridge when you expected it to save you from your less than adequate coat choices… NO. She moved as quickly as a human ice pop could. Away with the shopping. On with the heating. On with the kettle. She had timed it so that she would have enough time to get back, cook, and get ready to go to Jess's 'Spectacular new venue adventure!' But now that would have to wait a little bit. Louisa could feel the cold attacking her very DNA, attempting to pull it apart and transform her into some kind of ice being. She needed to take a little break to readdress the situation. Confirm to her DNA that she intended to stay as a warm blooded creature. The sound of bubbles, the loud click. Hot water into mug. Tea would be, as always, the solution. Taking her steaming salvation with her, she flopped onto the sofa. Not enough. She reached and pulled the throw over herself, burrowing as deep in as she could. Better. She would have to remain in this nest for a bit, to properly chase away the ice and give the heating time to kick in. An idea formed somewhere deep in the back of her mind, and began to wander cautiously to the front, demanding her full attention.

"Hmm."

This was a perfect opportunity to watch the first episode of that series she had read about. Everywhere said it was good, but she was unconvinced. Looking at the clock and making a few calculations she decided she would have just enough time to watch the first episode with her best judging face, drink her tea, warm up, and then cook, get ready, go party. She wouldn't even be that late. No more than a missed bus late. Perfectly acceptable.

Leaving glass view screens of the bus behind, Sam headed for the bar, pretty sure he knew where it was. Jess had told him it had replaced a bar they had always been unsure of going into, seeming brash and off putting with overly friendly bouncers and harsh spinning disco lights escaping the door and windows, infecting the street and any passers-by with neon radiation. The too loud music would creep out of the door like a mist rolling in from an angry sea, threating to envelop any who wandered too close. Who knew what angry spirits and monsters may lay within. Best to stay away. It was funny how Sam would sometimes have such an adverse reaction to a place. Often, but not always, Jess would agree with Sam on these psychic warnings. She assured him that it was better now, it had in fact been several years since those heady neon times. Sam was appalled at how time had escaped from his clutches. Apparently, it wasn't only them that had been put off by its previous incarnation. It had been sold, destroyed, and remade several times in the image of a more welcoming establishment. Now it was time for a new judgement to be passed on its worthiness.

The wind was bitter as Sam placed his hands into is pockets for protection against its attack. The streets were full of people heading out for another evening of searching in bars and bottles for the missing elements that would make them feel better. Or pass the time, or simply just for something to do. A movement on the other side of the road caught Sam's eye, and he glanced over to see a young woman walking along the pavement in the opposite direction. She was shivering; arms wrapped tightly around her, striding along as if she wanted to run to escape the cold but couldn't because of the choices of footwear she had made.

Sam felt a wave of sympathy and confusion as he watched her awkward stride. She was obviously suffering as the wind's iced hands groped her exposed skin, so why had she chosen to dress like that in this weather? A short skirt, low cut top and exposed midriff – Sam felt cold in the embrace of several layers of fabric. Was she trying to look sexy at the expense of how she felt? She looked pained rather than alluring. Was she willing to struggle to look how she wanted? That may be commendable, or, worse, did she feel she had to dress like that to fit in as a young woman on a night out? Was it the pressure of peer and glossy paper pressing on her ears, whispering that she had to, or no one would like her, she wouldn't be happy, and she wouldn't find 'the one' that everyone had been programmed to look for in some bizarre quasi-religious quest for fulfilment at the hands of others?

A piercing slightly disgusted eye blade of anger shot across the street hitting Sam clean in the face. The woman appeared to not appreciate Sam's prolonged glance. Not privy to the inner workings of his mind, she appeared to believe Sam's intentions were to muse on her body rather than musing on the complex modern social structures of the world. She wasn't really wrong either. Sam was musing on her body, reducing her appearance to a puzzle to be solved in some weird male patronising horror. It was exactly what Sam was trying to avoid. He realised he deserved that angry stare. Perhaps she had just forgotten her coat. Perhaps it was simply none of his business. It was definitely none of his business. Returning his gaze to the more standard target of his own feet, Sam returned his thoughts to the evening ahead of him.

Turning onto the main square, workmen blended in with the drifting souls. Panels of wood were being moved from large stacks, slowly pulled upright and attached to each other to create the centre piece of the winter, the outdoor bars and small market fair that always managed to both fail to impress and satisfy the desire to 'be outside' and make the most of it all. Differing from the summer market mostly by name, it was being erected similarly late into the season. The sounds of hammers and drills mixed into a rhythm that could be mistaken for some kind of newly hip music favoured only by the most slickly bearded of society.

A contingent of teenagers sat around in the doorways of closed shops, blaring music on their phones whilst splitting their time between watching the workman and throwing insults and objects at each other. As Sam moved past he could see some of them were asleep, wrapped in their hooded tops, metal wallet chains glistening as the artificial lights of the street caught their attention. Looking peaceful and at home on the street it was hard to tell if they were passed out drunk already, or if they were just hiding from the cold… tired out from a hard day of raging against the world.

A loud bell chime stole Sam's attention, a passing tram, angry at men in unseasonal short sleeved shirts deciding at the last minute that they had the right of way on the street. If they could face the winter in a summer shirt, they were surely manly enough for a tram to bounce off them if it so dared to encroach on their power walk across the street. Letting both disgruntled parties pass by, Sam crossed and headed up the hill towards the bar. A busker sat atop an amp, playing drum and bass on a keyboard whilst nodding along to his creations. Sam felt it was a nice change from the sound of acoustic guitar rendition of a popular love songs, but it soon became apparent this fellow was just pressing random buttons and waiting for the cash to flow. He turned his attention back towards his destination. Trees lined the hill, leading Sam's eyes up towards the more historic buildings. It was a nice part of the city, and the lack of neon bleeding out of the venue was a pleasant change. Or was it more boring? As Sam neared the bar, he felt a part of him missed the zany over the top brashness of its old incarnation. There was such a thing as too pleasant. It had a danger of becoming bland.

Sam nodded good evening to the bouncer as he stepped through the entrance to the bar. He realised he didn't know what it was called anymore, it had had several names over the last few years, another example of ever changing coolness and hipster chic. An entire building trying to keep up with the current trends and expectations, as if it had been on a panicked shopping spree after reading the latest edition of pub vogue magazine and thinking the other buildings would look down on it for being so last season. Sam looked around at his new surroundings. It was trying to be cool, so trying. Was it a bar? Was it a pub? It was very clean, very fresh. There was wood panelling everywhere, too clean to be rustic and welcoming, too organised to look friendly. Orange lights glowed from behind cast iron logos. Was that supposed to be cool? They looked a bit like a workman had dropped the iron frames onto lamps, squashing them under the unnecessary weight.

In the centre of the room there was a single island bar. Circular, with more scrubbed wood accented with more glowing lights. Several staff with immaculately groomed hair and beards were gesturing wildly at the huge stainless steel vat that sat in the centre of their island, it's multiple nozzles all promising various fine brewed ales. Racks of bottles of all shapes and sizes rested to the side of the vat, complete with a small table with bowls of fruit, knives, shakers and measuring devices ready for the call to be combined in any manner of ways, under any manner of crazy name.

Mirrors hung on nearly every other surface. On the walls, on supporting pillars, on pillars that seemed unneeded, other than to house more mirrors. They were either designed to make the whole place seem bigger, or to seem more crowded. They did confuse Sam a little on whether this was a small bar with a lot of people in it, or if the fact that everyone was dressed so similarly hid that half of them were in fact reflections. Guys in jeans, some with t-shirts, some in smart shirts. Plaid, plain or flowery. Girls in mid length dresses, matte colours, some pastel, some black or navy blue. Again, some floral. What was with this floral subculture that had sprung up? What did it mean? Was this the height of modern subculture – having flowers printed on your clothes… The rebellion.

No music. The only sounds were the hum of chatter and

the production line machines of the bar. Sam found it all a little unsettling. He wasn't sure how anyone could feel at home without music. Music could tell you that you belonged in a place, or, sometimes more importantly, that you were of a similar mind and taste to the other people in the place. If you struck up a conversation, everyone would have things in common. As he looked for the people he was meeting in this social factory he started noticing the other souls haunting this new yet old building. A couple of girls with perfect posture gesticulated wildly at each other over glasses of wine, as if they were swatting flies away from their drinks and each other. A group of guys in plaid shirts stood staring blankly at each other, taking it in turns to sip from their pint glasses whilst checking their phones. An older couple sat at a table on the edge of the venue, looking like they were trying to enjoy the night as best they could. Perhaps they had been coming here for years as the walls changed around them. Two girls at the bar turned to welcome two newly arrived guys with smiles and hugs, but as they awkwardly leaned towards each other, their eye lines shifted to meet their own reflections in the mirrors, as though they were more interested in themselves than each other. A guy leaned against the bar, deeply conversing with one of the well-groomed barmen. In front of him were several small empty glasses, and several more filled with various shades of beer. It was Matt. *"Trying to get drunk on free samples again you git"* thought Sam as he made his way through the pastels and flowers to his friend.

"Morning."

Sam used his usual greeting as he tapped Matt on the arm to announce his presence.

"Is it?"

Replied Matt, his usual response to Sam's not that funny anymore opener.

"You ready for a night on the town?"

Matt's Jazz hands punctuated his faux excited tone. Sam wasn't clear if Matt was looking forward to this evening's scheduled shenanigans or being sarcastic. It was a thin and blurry line with Matt, knowing what could be enjoyed properly, and what was to be enjoyed ironically.

"I guess?"

Sam guessed.

"How's the beer here?"

"The here beer? These beers here… Here be beer… It may take a few more of these free tries, but I'm pretty sure they are just like all the others everywhere else. I shall keep you informed."

Matt pointed at another couple of taps and gave a quizzical glance to the barman. A second immaculate server appeared in front of Sam with a quick "Yes mate" as he prepared himself for Sam's order.

"Lemonade, no ice please."

"Do you want a slice with that?"

The barman seemed tired.

"No thanks, neat."

Sam replied, in his standard it's funny because that's how you order whisky but this is a soft drink way that even he wasn't sure was funny anymore. Sam hadn't felt this self-conscious about his jokes in a long, long time. Perhaps he was getting old and unfunny. Perhaps it was the aftershocks of the mind quake that had been the breakup with Ellie. He had felt so shaken to his core that he had started questioning every aspect of himself. Lost confidence in his humour, in his place in the social world.

"No problem mate."

The barman's shoulders visibly dropped.

"That's the easiest order I've had all night, appreciate it."

He took a glass from the washer, placed the nozzle of the hose on the lip and sighed as he pressed the button as though the flow of sugared water represented his will to continue in his chosen profession draining out of him.

"So Sam, you ever going to drink real drinks?"

Matt was casually leaning on the bar next to Sam, his final selection of real ale next to him as he tossed a peanut into his mouth and chewed awaiting the reply.

"Wasn't aware lemonade was fictional."

Sam handed over some coins to the barman and took a sip from his glass.

"Or do you mean I should drink something that has the word 'real' in its title, and is currently the hip thing to drink?"

"Ha! You wouldn't know hip if you knew what it was mate. Also no one says hip anymore."

"So you're saying it's not the hip thing to say? Ironic. Or is it? Always struggled with irony. Is that ironic? Or is it ironic that I'm confused about how to use irony in a discussion about irony?"

Sam wasn't even sure where him trying to be funny ended and where he had genuinely confused himself began.

"I think it's moronic you're looking for, try a mirror. Plenty about. We will pass some more while we try and find the others. Just look out for the fella with the fake drink."

Matt threw the last peanut into his half smile and headed off into the crowds. Sam looked at his glass and started off after Matt. *"Well you are see through."* He mused a punchline related to mirrors that was neither accurate or had any kind of lead up statement. He panicked that his concept of humour had deserted him forever as a woman pushed past him to take a spot at the bar.

"Hey Bar dude, I will have a Cosmopolitan, but instead of Cointreau can you use Grand Marnier? I'm sure you've got some tucked away. Small dash of grenadine around the lip of the glass, small dash mind, with a lime twist… French you know? And can you hurry up I've been waiting aaaages."

Sam had to stop himself from laughing. He looked down at the floor for a few seconds to gather himself whilst mumbling to the gods of pubs.

"I'm going to order a lot more lemonade."

Sam expertly danced through the crowd of people, making no

contact and not risking his drink in any way. Well that was not true at all, he bumped and squeezed his way on a lacklustre path, losing drink and having to nod and say sorry more times than he liked but less than was required to be a disaster. There weren't even that many people here, how Sam managed to be this clumsy in a public place baffled him. He felt that he usually moved with such grace. He thought perhaps tonight was just going to be one of those nights as he caught a glimpse of Matt shaking hands with Steven at a table nearby.

"Hello Sam."

Steven boomed as if they hadn't seen each other in many moons. It had been a while. Jess added a softer but no less enthusiastic greeting. Sam felt grateful to receive such a warm welcome.

"Hello, hello and hello!"

Sam gave a small wave to both parties with his free hand.

"How are you both and what is going on?"

"We are both good thanks, just been watching the local wildlife."

Jess half pointed with her wine glass at the next table. It was occupied by a small group of women, who were doing the same hand waving over wine glasses that Sam had seen earlier.

"Two of those creatures seem annoyed that they are wearing very similar dark blue dresses."

Sam clocked the two as he sat down opposite Jess, and they indeed seemed to be very pointy towards each other, perhaps trying to decide who was in the wrong.

"Oo see in some cultures that would be fine, flattering even. In the culture that inhabits these watering holes, I'm guessing not so much."

"Yes indeed. I think it's escalating into a battle of who is the dominant alpha in this social pairing, who gets to decide in future what the dress order should be."

Jess seemed to be treating the girl's conversation as if it was an episode of a wildlife documentary TV show.

"Well in this habitat…"

Sam quickly played along, taking the role of documentary co presenter.

"We can clearly state that appearance is most important. The surroundings, although bland, are deliberate in their appearance. They conform to the idea of the trend of the moment, and therefore to be a proper inhabitant of this locale you must also conform to these social norms."

Sam raised his hand to his chin and frowned as if in deep academic thought, as Jess continued the examination.

"Yes indeed, indeed. What's more, to stray from the norms, or to appear to be copying another, is to show great disrespect to both the habitat and the inhabitants. It may lead to not only your own loss of the chance to find a reproductive partner, but, by association, the loss of such opportunity for your immediate social group."

Jess seemed pleased Sam was here to play along with her. He had seen her try to play with Steven, but he would often just look at her with a face that read '*so this is what people meant when they said you were quirky but charming.*'

Matt took the last chair at the table, next to Sam and opposite Steven. He didn't join in with the nature observations of the girl table, instead choosing to focus on a more common target for his inquisition.

"So Steve, how's the typing going?"

Matt sat open legged, leaning back with his locally micro brewed real ale in one hand whilst his other arm swept backwards over the wooden chair.

"I'm not a typist, Matthew, I'm…"

"I know, big man is a computer programmer, touched a nerve there did I? Apologies and that. You do, however, in fact, type in order to programme, so still valid as a question, yeah?"

Matt seemed quite pleased with himself as he took a sip of his drink.

"I'm a software developer, and you know that's quite different to computer programmer. Why do you always poke fun at my job?"

"To be honest, it's you I poke fun at, not your job. Also, genuinely not sure of the difference between computer programmer and software developer. They both type though, so I'm claiming it as a win."

Sam felt that Matt's confidence in his response hid his distrust of Steven's job. Sam knew he really didn't understand what exactly it was Steven did, and didn't understand the insistence that programmers and developers were different. Sam was also sure they weren't. Although he felt he was easily smart enough to know about this, he hadn't actually asked for an explanation because Steven would see it as an excuse to lambast his lack of knowledge for the rest of their friendship. So Sam and Matt would sit, poking fun at Steven to cover the fact that after knowing him for so long, they were both too embarrassed to admit they weren't really sure what it was that he did.

"Whatever Matthew. There's just no reasoning with you."

Steven gave up on the direction of the conversation. Although he often seemed annoyed by Matt's jokes at his expense, Sam also recognised that he didn't seem to feel threatened or belittled in any way, and was happy to just let it go and try and move on with the evening.

"What do you think of this place? I'm quite enjoying it. It's nice to have somewhere a bit upmarket isn't it? Makes a nice change when they put the effort in."

"Err yes… no? it's a pub? Not sure what difference it makes what it looks like, they serve the drink, I drink the drink, it's an evening out."

Matt stumbled in response, forcing Sam to hold in a burst of laughter. Not very good at forcing anything, Sam failed. The strange snort spread quickly to Jess. Matt did not seem amused.

Sam knew what Matt would think of the place, he didn't need to say it out loud. Matt would think that the bar was trying a bit too hard, and therefore it was rubbish.

"I do however, like the new trend of being able to sample drinks before you buy. If you get a different barman each time, you can get quite a lot of beer that way as the night goes on."

Matt had collected his response, and sat proudly upon its completion.

"You know that's not the point, right? You're supposed to be sampling the flavour and making an informed decision on the right drink for you."

"Steven."

"Matthew."

"It's a beer. It's not complicated. You drink it because it has alcohol in it. You put it into your face and you feel better."

Sam and Jess both watched the dual before them go back and forth like a verbal tennis match. Both participants wore expressions of confusion at the ridiculous argument of the other.

"You know that makes you sound like an alcoholic, right? It's actually quite nice to develop a taste for these things you know, have a favourite, look forward to it?"

Steven shifted his tone, as though he was talking to a child, trying to explain the complexity and joy of adult life to a six year old that just wanted to finger paint on the walls. Sam thought Matt would probably enjoy that quite a lot. But he would grow tired of using his fingers and end up using his face just to see what it was like. And Sam would too. He should remember to tell Matt this later, could be a fun afternoon in there somewhere.

"I do look forward to it. I do have a favourite. My favourite is beer. And sometimes, especially in the summer, cider. In. To. My. Face."

Matt shifted forward in his chair and took a large swig of his beer, followed by a huge sigh.

"Ah… tasty, tasty beer. That may make me sound like an alchy, but, it's very important to remember the key fact in the matter."

"What would that be?"

Steven seemed interested to hear Matt's take on it.

"That it was your suggestion, and everything you say, by its very nature, is wrong."

Matt returned to his lounging position, looking like a he had just hit a power shot off the baseline to win the set.

33

Wow. That was good. Way better than she had thought. Her judging face had faded away in the first ten minutes, replaced with an expression Louisa considered must look intrigued and impressed. But the cliff hanger! She had to know what happened, who in their right mind would end an episode like that. What was the opposite of closure? Opener? She looked at the clock. There was still time. She turned back to the screen, it's next episode countdown was in full swing, counting down to the revelation she needed to know… there was still time, she could just find out what happened, cook, get ready, go out. She would only miss some pub talk and a drink. She would just have more money to have drinks later. Yes. Genius idea. Also, she would be able to tell them all how amazing this series was, recommend they all watch it. Even better, if they had watched it she could discuss its amazingness! The countdown reached zero and the next episode began. This was going to be good.

The evening moved on, the hum of the bar grew louder as the beer and wine flowed into the inhabitants. The four spoke and laughed, reminisced of times gone by, reminded each other of forgotten embarrassments, relaxed into each others company. The world around them was occasionally punctuated by a raucous belly laugh, with a stable hum of chatter that defined the place as being successful in its intent to bring people out of wherever they were and in to this place. Some of the groups of people that had been here when Sam arrived had begun to disappear, moving on to their next watering hole for the night like a band of migrating beasts on the ancient plains. The group of girls that formed the subject matter to Sam and Jess's documentary had also picked up and left for new pastures in a flurry of handbags and high heels, pointy gestures replaced with the pained squeak of chairs pushed along the probably one hundred percent natural locally sourced hardwood floor, the results of their discussions lost to Sam and Jess for all of time. Sam had watched them leave with a smile on his face hoping they had resolved their pointiness ready for the fun and excitement of the rest of their night out. As he turned back to Jess, he was surprised to see her smile had vanished, replaced with an expression off fidgety awkwardness. She was rolling the stem of her wine glass between her hands, as though she was trying to light a fire on the table, perhaps trying to burn away a sense of guilt for something. Sam had no idea what had transpired in the few seconds he had looked away.

"Look, Sam…"

Jess shifted in her seat as her tone joined her expression in awkward almost guilty seriousness.

"I'm… well… sorry about Ellie."

Sam lost the smile.

"Oh… well… these things happen I suppose…"

It was Sam's turn to shift both in position and tone, both becoming more awkward and thoroughly less comfortable.

"It's just, I don't know, wasn't meant to be I guess."

He didn't really want to talk about it, and was a bit confused why he was having to. It didn't really have anything to do with Jess, after all.

"I didn't know she was like that, would do that. I encouraged you and it's my fault you got hurt."

Jess was talking into her wine class, staring into its swirling contents as though trying to sail away on the tiny red waves. Sam thought back to the first time he had meet Ellie, feeling a wince of loss as he relived the warm rush of adrenaline when he had first caught sight of her walking past.

"I thought I had pulled her on my own, what with me being such an awesome stud and all."

Jess let out a small giggle, possibly at the idea of Sam being some kind of dating maestro. Sam's attempt to quip his way out of a difficult conversation was only going to take him so far, and he was concerned that Jess may think she had anything to do with what happened.

"Seriously though, I really liked her, and I would have tried to make it work anyway I could. It's just that she didn't want to try like that, she never saw us the same way I did."

Sam wanted to be diplomatic, he had wrestled for many hours with why Ellie had done what she had done, and why she was so comfortable doing it, like it was totally normal. The internal struggle became his whole existence for a while, and he didn't want to go back through it. He was only just beginning to climb out of that pit. To him, it was all her fault, unambiguous and terrible, a great wrong to his name and dishonour to his house that must be rectified. To her, it had been a throwaway comment and a happy proclamation of her new adventure. The way it ended had devastated Sam. He felt he shouldn't have gone in so blindly, so open. He caught himself, teetering on the edge of thinking about it all over again, how it must be his fault, he went wrong somewhere, he wasn't good enough…

"Deep breath"

Sam nearly fell. Twice. That dark cliff in his mind was smaller than it had been, but it was still there. Still dangerous. He didn't want to feel like this anymore. He certainly didn't want Jessica to feel any of it was her fault. It had taken him a long time to climb out of that pit to the point where he felt comfortable to be back out in the world and attempting to joke around, but he still wasn't comfortable talking about it. Or thinking about it too much. Or remembering it. He had let himself fall for something that wasn't there, he had let the idea of finding the perfect woman cloud his judgment, and he had paid the price for it. At night, alone in the dark, the inner voice would still call from the bottom of that internal pit, punish him with the idea that if he had stepped back from the situation, or asked different questions, or made demands, maybe it would have gone differently… He would've seen it wasn't what he thought it was, he wouldn't have gotten it all so wrong. Perhaps worse, in the darkest nights, he could hear it softly calling… from deep, deep down, that if he could go back to the start, and try again, he could do better… Convince her this time that he was the right one for her… She would realise it this time.

That was what made him most uncomfortable. She clearly didn't want him that way, and it made him feel wrong inside that he had never quite accepted that. He didn't want anything to do with her anymore. He wanted that whole experience to disappear into that pit so he could seal it up and throw it all away. He would be more careful next time. Cautious. Time had passed, Sam was ready to try and leave it all behind and move on.

"It's not your fault. I liked her. A lot. I think you saw that, right away. And you tried to help me out. You always try and help me out… that's part of what makes you such a good friend."

Jess was still looking guilty as Sam tried to express himself in the middle of a quieting pub.

"Sometimes, things just happen, they just do. I'm not going to say I'm happy about what happened with Ellie, but none of that has anything to do with you. And I think I learned some important lessons, somewhere, when I find them…"

"Well I've learned my lesson, not to try and stick my nose where it doesn't belong… I used to think I was good at matchmaking, and seeing who would be good with who, but maybe…"

Sam quickly cut Jess off:

"Whoa there! Nope! Never stop! You are always welcome in my business!"

Sam stopped and considered what he had just said.

"Wait, no… that sounded wrong!"

Jess was already laughing. Sam was relieved to see her smile.

"I just mean… look, Jess, you are the most positive, helpful person I have ever known. You are always trying to help everyone, fix everything. Sometimes… sometimes things can't be fixed… but please, never stop trying. I don't even want to think about what kind of hideous hell scape I would live in if you weren't always trying to make everything better."

Jess had stopped rolling her glass. The laughter had stopped, but the smile remained. Sam hoped he was helping. Ellie had caused enough pain, and it was time for all of it to go away. All of it. Banished to the past.

"What are you two on about?"

Matt leaned over the table, physically sticking his nose into the conversation.

"Are you whining on about that Ellie again? Come on. That was never going to work. Leave it yeah? Plenty of other things in the stuff."

"Oh you knew it wasn't going to work? Say anything about it did you? Oh wise man?"

Jess stared, awaiting Matt's explanation.

"I didn't need to say anything. It was obvious. Sam and Ellie? Sam n' Ellie… Salmonellie… Salmonella… Yeah, that's no good is it? Puke that out. I mean really Sam. Mate. Really."

34

Okay. Louisa looked at her empty mug. And the clock. The credits were rolling on another episode. She had only watched a few. No one even knew how many a few even was, they couldn't be mad. And she shouldn't be worried that she was so late. She had to get up now anyway. Hungry. Yes. Cook and get ready, go out to the pub.

"Oh."

New plan. Too late for the pub. Crap. She was looking forward to that. Oh well, she couldn't travel back in time and arrive earlier. Time to work with what was left. Kitchen. She wondered what it would be like to be a time traveller, all the things you could see, do.

"Focus!"

Kitchen. Food. Crap. Not really enough time to cook what she had planned too. If Nia was here, instead of away spending the weekend with her partner, again, she could:

A) Have kept her on track, ensure that she hadn't sat in front of the TV and actually cooked at a sensible time.

B) Both hear Louisa's complaints about it all, and potentially be blamed in some ridiculous and fallacious way.

These kinds of things were never Nia's fault. Louisa found this most unfair. Right. Sandwich. They were quick. And counted as a meal. Excellent. Louisa opened the cupboard to start the preparations. Empty. Frustrated, she reached for the shopping bag she left the newly acquired bread in. What was the point in spending time unpacking things if she didn't actually do it.

Crap.

The bag was empty.

Crap.

OK so she had forgotten to buy bread. It wasn't the end of the world, only the end of the sandwich world.

"Ok. Think."

Louisa continued to consult the walls of the kitchen. They offered little advice. Pasta. Pasta is quick, kind of. That would do. She hurriedly gathered the ingredients, spilling only what could be considered a small percentage of them. She was getting flustered. But she was also getting there.

"Right."

Things in pan, sorted. She could still meet them as they went to the club, that would be fun. She could say hello, maybe dance, all good. She reached for her phone to send an apologetic text to Jess. She had sent one earlier saying she thought she might be late, but hopefully not too late. She suspected Jess had realised that by now that those hopes were maybe a little bit optimistic. The phone beeped and whirred as Jess responded with an assurance of there being no problem, and the accustomed smiley face. Louisa felt instantly calmer. Right, sorted. It was all going to be ok. There was just enough time to have a little look online about what people were saying about the series. Did they agree with her? Were they comically wrong? She had to be careful not to spoil the next few episodes.

Careful internet negotiation. Smiles at shared joy at how good the story was. Surely enough time had passed now for the pasta to be ready? Louisa turned her attention to the pan. Still no bubbles? This seemed odd. She prodded at the contents with her food prodding spoon. This didn't seem right. She checked the hob settings.

Crap.

Ok, it would probably cook faster if she turned the hob on. The kitchen walls bore witness to a series of expletives. They did not reply. Louisa gathered herself. The clock ticked too loudly for its own good.

"Smug clock with its ticking. Tick off!"

Louisa was flustered. And frustrated. Flustrated. How had it gotten to be so late? She only had two things to do today, get the shopping, go out and have fun outside with good friends. So far, she had evidence building that she was failing at both. She needed to calm down. Maybe if she started the next episode, she could watch a bit while her food cooked, and finish it while she ate? She decided this was an excellent plan. This would totally fix everything, and she still had time.

The club loomed into view, a site of pilgrimage only in the hours of darkness. The touch of sunlight would seal the portal to this realm shut, access to sites and sounds restricted until the deep night fell once more upon its threshold. No one remained in the pub, all had now moved on to the next stage of their journey through the playground of the night. This place was the chosen destiny for this night. Jess and Steven walked straight in, Sam couldn't help but stop and stare. The large oak doors he had seen closed and menacing on his way through town to work over the last few weeks were swept open, beckoning Sam inside to see what mysteries were lurking in the dark just waiting to be discovered. Two large men stood guard, one at each side of the door, their fine black suits as sharp as any knight's sword. The vibrancy of the street fell away against this gateway. Darkness emanated from the entranceway, punctuated by the rhythmic thud of music played too loudly with more bass than any artist had originally intended. Sam moved closer, beginning to feel the bass in his chest as though it was trying to force him to turn back. Only the strong pilgrims could brave this portal.

Movement caught the corner of his eye and he turned to see a small group of girls huddled in the corner just inside the door. The dresses they were wearing were angular and slashed, revealing a lot of the occupants. Sam guessed the girls were around twenty, probably new students. Part of him was shocked at what counted as fashionable evening wear for a twenty year old, and part of him was sad he wasn't twenty anymore. Both parts were sad that he had immediately judged their fashion sense like he had any idea about anything. That was a sign he was definitely not twenty anymore. Not that being twenty again would have given him a chance to befriend girls like this, in fact he was just as capable now as he was then at getting turned down and looked at like he was an outrageous weirdo, a mystery as to why he had even dared to speak to women. What he saw in their faces though, was optimism and a sense of having fun on a night out that had escaped Sam since Ellie. He longed not for the girls, but for their ability to be just enjoying standing around in a club doorway.

"This place is a bit weird isn't it?"

Matt had appeared beside Sam, and was looking like Sam felt… a little unsure if he was in the right place.

"I only came here because you said it was a good idea!"

Sam's half-truth was unconvincing. He wasn't sure if he had wanted to come to the club, he was happy sitting in the pub. He was worried though, that if he went home now he would go back to sitting around on his own thinking about how things had turned out. He felt he was close to moving away from that, so close, so why not stay out and see where it could all take him…

"Didn't say it was now a bad idea, just a bit… weird… Did I get old? I don't recognise the music at all. I'm not old… weird…"

Matt strode off towards the inner door of the club, pulling it open to release a large amount of colours all at once alongside a vast increase of volume and intensity of bass. Matt looked back at Sam wide eyed and grimacing as he let the door slowly swing back into place. The colours and sound retreated back into their realm as the door inched closer to its frame.

"I'm not sure I'm in the mood for dance pop r'n'b bass dropping madness tonight."

Matt's eyes and fingers were gesturing as if he was sifting through a bag he had just found on a street corner, simultaneously horrified by the contents yet driven by his curiosity to see what may be hidden inside.

"Hmm yes… I think I agree with you there."

Sam crossed his arms for a second before raising his hand to his chin in the group's well established mock thoughtful pose.

"But… I'm afraid… I must know what is behind this door. For purely scientific reasons, of course."

"Oh… OF COURSE!"

Matt raised his hands to the sky in mock revelation.

"Science is a noble pursuit which knows no bounds, and therefore it is our duty to further its cause."

Pointing with both hands towards the door, and with a ridiculous accent Sam couldn't even begin to fathom, Matt added:

"You first, your professerness, for the benefit of us all, and on behalf of all of mankind, we salute your sacrifice!"

The fingers on Sam's hand inched towards the door handle, seemingly in slow motion compared to the speed of the train hurtling through his mind.

"What am I doing here?"

"I don't belong here."

"Everyone will look at me like I'm an imposter."

"I don't like this music."

"I don't look like they do, they will all laugh at me for being in the wrong place."

"Why on earth did I say we should go in when Matt was ready to give up?"

"Too late to change your mind now, Matt is already making fun of me, and Jess and Steven are in here somewhere. Can't just run away."

"Can I just run away?"

Sam's fingers took hold on the handle. He could feel the bass vibrating the metal as he began to pull the door towards him. A sharp blast of air hit Sam's face a second before the edge of door hit his shoulder almost pushing him over and leaving him slightly stunned.

"Sorry mate!"

A bald man in his forties shouted towards Sam slightly less loudly than his Hawaiian style shirt did as he wandered towards the street without looking back.

"Err…"

All the retort and commentary Sam could muster as he stood still holding the door.

"Oh that was classic, wish I'd caught that on camera chap – any chance you can shut the door and do it again? You, know, for the sake of the internet and all the people of the world that need to see?"

Matt was giggling and clearly enjoying himself too much at Sam's expense. Two girls walked in through the door that Sam was still holding open, without even looking in his direction. A young couple then walked out, gazing at each other as they vanished into street. Now unable to hold in the laughter, Matt also walked through the door.

"I think you've found a new career opportunity."

"Err…"

Sam let go of the door, almost forgetting to walk through himself.

35

The club seemed to pulsate to the rhythm pumping out of the huge speakers that bookended the medium sized dancefloor. Slightly raised at the end of the rectangular room, the dancefloor was filled to bursting with revellers out to forget themselves and enjoy intoxicated motion to the beat. Sam scanned for Jess and Steven as Matt headed towards the bar, which clung to the middle of the long side of the club like a besieged fort in the middle of a particularly heavy attack. The front lines of the attack on fort bar were compressed together into a mass wave of compressed shouting, while those further back stood looking bored yet eager for their chance to fling themselves at the forts' walls. Opposite, a large group of men stood nodding gently along with the music, the contents of their pint glasses swishing along with their too cool to dance motions. Weaving through them to try and find a better vantage point to spot Jess and Steven, Sam was disconcerted to note that each of these fellows was at least twice his size. Feeling more than a little intimidated, and concerned what may happen if his shouts of "excuse me" were not a good enough explanation for his presence in this forest of giants, Sam contorted his way through. Only one of the giants looked at Sam, a blank stare of indifference as he took a step about one inch to his left, not really helping the journey.

"I really hope I don't have to go back that way."

Sam muttered to himself as he finally escaped the forest of giants and reached the destination he was hoping for, the edge of the raised dancefloor.

"Sofas?"

Sam asked the club to explain itself. The one thing he was not expecting to see from this position was a row of sofas lining the back of the dancefloor, complete with end tables and shaded lamps. Aside from one overly familiar couple and a collection of assorted handbags and coats, the sofas sat there as though some removal firm had hit end of shift and clocked off halfway through a job. No sign of Jess and Steven amongst the dancing mass. A wide and diverse range of people were consumed by the exceptionally loud music pounding out of the ever present sound system. From the late teens to the late forties and everywhere in between, Sam felt strangely comforted by the idea of all of these different people with different backgrounds and lives all getting along together thanks to a shared desire to move to the music. Although Sam did wish they had slightly better taste in music.

Perhaps Matt had had better luck, although Sam now couldn't see him either. From his vantage point he could see more of the bar area, and he thought it was time to try and head back to the entranceway now that he'd lost everyone he was with. Carefully moving off the somewhat dark steps to the dancefloor, Sam contemplated his path. There was no way he was going back through the forest of giants. He looked to the other side of the throng of people, searching for a Sam sized opening. As he saw a promising lead and began to move toward it, a sharp yelp pierced the music, causing Sam to spin around and check what horrors may be occurring behind him. He was just in time to see a young man finishing his less than graceful trip up the dark stairs to the dancefloor, his drink leading the way as it flowed eagerly from his glass. As the young man collected himself, cursing loudly, with an expression of embarrassment and hopefulness that no one had seen the incident, a second young man began pointing and laughing loudly, before slapping him hard on the back. Sometimes it was useful to lose sight of your friends for a while.

Moving through the Sam sized hole in the crowd had revealed a new and unexpected obstacle in the quest. A circle of club dwellers surrounded three couples that were dancing as if they were in a music video montage. Sam was as equally impressed as he was surprised by their gyrations. He stopped to join the circle of onlookers, focusing on the nearest couple. They were moving in a way that suggested no one was watching, with expressions of glee that everyone was watching. The girl, wearing a skin tight short black dress with silver hoop earrings and matching necklace and bracelets was alternating dropping to a squat position and standing straight up arching her back towards her dancing partner, brushing his face with her ponytail. He was trying to keep pace with her, enjoying her move in circle motions against him whilst he kept his hands placed on her highly energetic hips. Sam knew this was supposed to be highly erotic, but he was honestly more impressed by the girl's balance and strength to be able to move like that, especially in jet black high heels. Her partner impressed Sam much less, with the same dark jeans and pale plaid shirt identikit man about town outfit, his dance moves now appeared to consist of letting her push against him whilst holding on with an expression of tough man glee smeared across his face. As the girl dropped down to a particularly low stance, her partner dropped with her, almost leaning over her, and began trying to gyrate himself. It was at this point Sam decided the situation of him stood there watching had crossed a line into getting a bit weird and he shimmied around the circle of revellers with his usual smiles, nods, and well intentioned familiar *'excuse me'* until he found his way safely out the other side and back to the entrance way.

The oak doored dimensional gateway was now serving as a discussion area, the lack of speakers lowering the volume of the music enough for several groups to have congregated, laughing, smiling, slapping each other on the arms with looks of hysterical shock, pointing at each other, and taking selfies. The assault on the bar was relentless. There was no way Sam was going to join the fray for the sake of more lemonade. As his eyes continued to scan the area, it seemed he was not the only one to conclude the bar was a forlorn hope.

"There you are you weirdo!"

Matt's jibe greeting seemed less playful than normal, as though an attempt at comedy was masking a deeper frustration at the situation.

"I thought I lost you too then. Did you get a drink? I take it you didn't find Jess and Steven."

Sam was very pleased to have found Matt again. Although fascinating and interesting to watch, Sam didn't feel all that comfortable in this place. And he was pretty sure you weren't supposed to just stand and watch.

"I queued for my entire life, but didn't get any closer to the bar. Creatures evolved around me as I was waiting. They grew from insects, became sentient, found science, laughed at me for just standing there, and ascended into the next plain of existence while I waited for any sign of a barman willing to serve someone that wasn't in a tight dress."

Matt's eyes darted around the club, as though he was sizing up the place, ready for judgement.

"What do you think of it in here?"

He plunged his hands into the pockets of his jeans as he spoke in a badly faked relaxed yet slightly defensive manner.

"There's lots of different kinds of people, and lots of ages, I was quite surprised. I've seen some weird things though. But it's nice to see lots of different people all having fun together."

Sam copied Matt's stance, as if in solidarity. It also looked both comfortable and comforting.

"Diversity and that."

Matt nodded in approval as his words competed with a particularly intense bass drop.

"I really don't like the music though, it's not really my thing. Everyone seems to be enjoying it but I don't quite get it. I don't understand what they see in it. I'm not sure I would come here again unless I was in the right mood. It doesn't feel right for me."

Sam's posture closed in as he spoke, as though he was protecting himself from his surroundings.

"So…"

Matt pulled his hands from his pockets and crossed his arms, staring at Sam for a good few seconds before raising his right hand to his chin, the well known group posture of wisdom.

"What you're saying is everyone is coming together, from different places, to be one mass of fun and enjoyment, and you think that's awesome, but you don't want to be a part of it because you judge them all to be wrong about their taste? They have all come together as a mass of humanity, leaving cares and woes behind to be here in this place. But not you, you know that they are wrong. Mate that makes you an ass hat – you do know that right? The forever outsider, alone, disconnected, and somewhat of a dick yeah?"

Sam was startled by the comment. He felt like he had lost his balance, blindsided by the cross examination of what he thought was a fairly ok statement. His mind began plummeting like a lift with a snapped cable. Was Matt right? He often felt disconnected, an outsider to the majority. Was it his own fault? Was he stopping himself from enjoying the moment, and then judging others to be wrong for him not allowing himself to become a part of the things around him? How had he looked at everyone dancing together and not included himself in that diverse crowd? Why had he automatically classed himself as an outsider?

"Earth to Sam!"

Matt poked Sam in the arm several times, checking for signs of life.

"You've drifted off into Sam world, come back towards the light!"

"Err I was just thinking about what you just said"

Startled for the second time, Sam pulled himself out of his mental quagmire and refocused on Matt.

"Yeah? What about it?"

Matt returned to his professor pose.

"Surprised at the level of depth and insight I bring to the table?"

Sam mimicked Matt's pose, stroked his chin a few times for dramatic effect, and replied:

"You didn't say '*and that*' at the end. I like it when you do, it adds gravitas to the statement. Kinda spoken punctuation. Not sure I can take what you say seriously when you don't."

Matt seemed unimpressed with Sam's attempt to throw his insight away in the form of a counter attack. Sam hoped it worked. He was still reeling from it. It was too much to deal with right now. He didn't need more examples of how wrong he was to think about.

"You two! What are you doing? Why are you on the wrong floor?"

Steven's boom was welcome relief for Sam.

"What do you mean wrong floor? Where have you two been? It's mental in here!"

Matt frowned at Steven as he demanded answers. Sam felt at last something was starting to make some sense.

"I mean, dear Matt, that this is the pop floor. The point of this evening was to go to the other floor. You know, the one with the music we recognise. Upstairs. We thought you'd got lost or something."

Sam looked at Matt. Matt looked at Sam. They both looked across to the dance floor. They spoke as one:

"Oh…"

Sam felt better about feeling out of place. Matt laughed, recounting the story of Sam's complaints and his insightful yet cutting response to Steven. Sam felt a little less better as Steven listened intently to Matt's tale.

"Hmm."

Steven crossed his arms as he considered his response. Matt's smiling face eagerly awaited the forthcoming wisdom.

"You're both right. This floor is fine, but it's not any of our first choices for music. There's nothing wrong with that. Sam, stop being so judgey. If you don't feel at home here, that's ok. But these people do, they are enjoying it. Matt, stop trying to destroy Sam's mind. You know it's fragile. No one's taste is better, it's just different. That's why the club has two floors. Now come on."

Steven turned and headed for a nondescript dark staircase that had gone unnoticed against the brash colours all around. Sam and Matt sheepishly followed Steven, heads lowered as they absorbed the words of Steven's parent voice.

This was it. This was the stuff. Each of Sam's steps up the stairs took him nearer to a feeling of belonging. As each stair passed underfoot, the music of downstairs faded away a little more, replaced with a heavier sound. As Sam reached the half way point on the stairs he felt the corners of his mouth rise uncontrollably into a smile as the sound of guitars and drums became louder. Jess was already at the top, spinning around, beckoning Sam and Matt to follow her into this exciting land of sounds.

"This is alright!"

Matt yelled as he pushed past Sam to get a better look around. Sam tried to respond, but the combination of Matt's back and the loud guitars put a quick end to the effort. Instead he moved to join him, standing at the top of the stairs, admiring the new sights. The dancefloor was much more defined in in this area, and although there were less people up here, there was just as much enjoyment to be seen. A woman with long pigtails danced and spun on her own in the centre of the floor, blissfully lost in the music. The soles of her baseball shoes flashed brilliant white whenever she raised her feet, as though the pure energy of dance itself was sparking from her motion. Another flash of light drew Sam's attention to a man whose white shirt looked almost radioactive as he jerkily danced in front of the DJ booth. Sam thought there must be one of those black light things somewhere, or something. It was an impressive sight to behold, turning the normal run of the mill white shirted male about town into a magical glowing being. As the DJ began the next song with a hail of guitar riffs, Sam decided that he could get used to this place.

"Bar! Do you want your normal fakeness?"

Matt pointed to Sam with one hand, and the uncrowded bar with the other. He looked extremely excited by the lack of siege on this floor's drinks, keen to strike quickly in case the situation changed.

"Yeah Cheers!"

Sam responded as Matt moved, pulled magnetically towards all of the drinks. Jess beckoned again, this time from a small yet high table in the middle of the room. Sam raised his hand in recognition and began to move towards her. The area between the bar and the dancefloor contained a large sofa area to the side, and several of the small but very tall tables in the centre. Sam pondered that these tables were genius for a club, as they allowed people to both stand up, dance a little bit, and have somewhere of a relevant height to place their drinks.

"Isn't this great!"

Jess's ever present smile received an extra magical glow thanks to the lighting. Even Steven's standard stoic yet relaxed look was tinged with sparkles from the buttons on his shirt.

"I like it. I very like it."

Sam found his head had begun to move in time with the music, ever so slightly. He didn't mind that he needed to shout to be heard, or strain to hear Jess and Steven's comments of what he and Matt had missed on their adventure downstairs. It was worth it. Sam felt much more comfortable up here. The thud of the bass in his chest was somehow welcoming in here, instead of slightly aggressive push he had felt downstairs.

Matt returned, glasses in hand. He passed Sam a weirdly squishy plastic glass, containing a slightly luminescent liquid. Sam found this very exciting. It tasted strongly of chemical lemons. Under normal circumstances, this would be a sub par beverage, rating quite low on Sam's city wide soft drink ranking system. However, the lights were causing it to glow as though it was some kind of magical potion. This was easily the best lemonade ever.

Matt's beer by contrast seemed exceptionally dark, perhaps the lighting affected different shades of normal colour in different ways? Sam had never wanted to know about lights and lighting to such an extent. This was fascinating. He turned to look around for more examples of this witchcraft. Jess's tall glass of ice cubes and alcohol was shining brightly. Steven's beer was as dark as Matt's. Sam found this all very exciting.

A woman raised her hands high into the air and screamed at the top of her lungs as a new song poured out of the sound system. Her whole side of the room shifted to the dancefloor in one fluid motion, called to action by the battle cry. Flashes of light erupted through the movement, as the lights caught earrings, shoes, handbags… and then Sam saw the brightest of shiny things. A woman stood chatting at the end of the sofa. Her thin dress seemed to be being x-rayed by the magic lights. Her white underwear was glowing as though radioactive, for all to see. Sam panicked, wondering if this was an unintended side effect of not knowing how clothes would react in these conditions. Did she know? She must know? Would her friends tell her if she didn't realise? How could she not realise? She could surely see herself? She seemed happy enough, laughing with her friends. Perhaps she did know… Sam thought back to the skimpy outfits in the main entrance way… maybe she was being clever with her appearance, not being revealing until she got in here and then… He really wanted to ask her if this was her sexy plan or a terrible mistake. He felt that was not a conversation he could manage without seeming incredibly weird and inappropriate. An image of the scantily clad cold woman from his journey in flashed into his mind. It was a good job Sam had been warned about inquisitiveness and the fate of felines. Sometimes it was best not to overthink these things, to just think *'huh'* and move on.

"Finished! Time for dancing! Come on boys!"

Jess placed her glass in the centre of the table victoriously. All traces of luminescence were conquered and gone. Grabbing

Steven's arm, she pulled him in the direction of the dancefloor. Matt looked at Sam, motionless.

"I must move to the music. It is the way of things. It cannot be fought. It is life itself!"

Half a beer in hand, he turned and followed Jess and Steven. Sam downed his lemonade, as if that was a thing people did. Smiling at Matt's decree, he felt his traditional nerves about having to move in public. There was little option, it was time to go to the dancefloor.

The music really was much more to Sam's taste than the downstairs realm. More people joined them on the dancefloor with each song, drawn in by the guitars and drums. Sam didn't feel so separate anymore. These people must be in some way similar. One less thing to worry about. Much more important now to worry about whether or not his attempts at dancing were making him look stupid. Matt still had a third of his beer as he moved back and forth to the music. Steven was stood almost still, the occasional hand motion and contorted facial expression defining his style. Jess moved freely, bouncing back and forth as her hands swam around her. They all looked much more comfortable than Sam. He tried his best shoulder moves, forward and back in time with the drums. He tried moving his feet, clunkily. He wasn't really sure what to do with his arms, what do you do with your arms! He drifted off into thought about why he cared so much when no one else seemed to, considering that this was his default position for his entire life, it wasn't just in this moment. He looked around for some inspiration for both new moves and how not to be bothered by what others thought, seeing only carefree moves interspersed with flashes of magical glow.

The crowd seemed to move as one, guided by the drums and guitars. Like the waves of a sea, they all bobbed with the sonic tide. Closer inspection revealed sub groups to the dance mass. Friends in small circles like his own, couples close together. Lone men moving around the small shoals of women like hungry sharks, blocked out by synchronised movements from the women. Any gaps in these small female groups would seal like a roman shield wall, preventing entry to the hungry predators. Two women and a man danced around a glowing handbag next to Sam and his friends, hair swaying and thrashing around to the tide. One of the women was moving with a serpentine style, her arms moving in front of her in a series of slow and mesmerising waves. She seemed to glow with some sort of mystic energy, some new form of the lights effect even though her clothes were dark. Each step she took seemed to writhe through her whole body, and Sam watched as it did. As he followed her long hair move in time with the latest motion, he caught her eyes. A slight panic that he had been caught doing something he shouldn't be doing was quickly squashed by her half smile. She turned away, leaving Sam both embarrassed and relieved. She turned back as the chorus kicked in, smiling again as her eyes cast across Sam.

Sam looked away, a bit shocked. What happened? Was that a thing? Had he had a thing? He better look back. Should he? Inside his mind, all the usual suspects appeared, and joyfully set up their chairs and tables for the imminent debate over what was indeed going on, what he should do about it, how nothing and everything was here for the taking… But didn't he remember that he was himself? And he should remember that at all times he was rubbish at everything. A majority of the internal opinions voted for him to look back at the woman despite the shouts of disapproval from the others. He tried his best subtle dancing in that direction anyway so it's a coincidence that he can see her moves… she was looking the other way. It was ok. No wait, it was not ok? Sam realised he had worried so much about why this girl had looked at him like that that he had forgotten to get an opinion as to whether it was something he wanted to happen again or not. He turned slightly, to be facing somewhere between Jess and this mystery serpentine woman. This way, he would not be staring at her, but he could still kinda see. Impressed with his sly plan to keep an eye on things, he began to mull the situation over.

Movement and rhythm, the pulse of the bass and the sway of the body. Matt's beer had vanished, and he was bouncing up and down oblivious to everything other than the sound. Steven held Jess as she swayed slowly back and forth, their eyes locked as they both sang along with the music. Sam felt more at peace than he had in some time. He was less concerned with how he looked, with how he felt about anything that had happened in the past. That was all gone. The music was old, he had heard it before. Memories flooded back of those times, dancing in university clubs to these songs, with friends long departed… He could be there now, younger and more optimistic… History had a way of dulling the bad and intensifying the good. These songs had been with him during both, but all that mattered now was the fact that he got through all of those times, he was here, now, the bad would fade, the joy would last forever.

Sam fell from his sonic bliss as he felt a hot wet smear across his back. He turned, to see two very drunk men drenched in sweat. Their style of dancing consisted of high knee lift walking around with matching air punches, as though they were boxing invisible enemies. They seemed unaware of the effect of their energetic dance on Sam's shirt, and he had no desire to try and explain it to people who seemed quite content in throwing fists at nothing. Best for Sam to just move around the floor a little bit, out of harm's way, and return to his own less sweaty from of dance. It was not uncommon for Sam to move away from others in this fashion. He wondered if this was an effect of not drinking alcohol, the fact that no one else seemed as concerned as him about such matters. He found a spot away from any potential disruption and returned to his shoulder based dance moves. The song had not even reached the next chorus before he saw a swish of dark material in the corner of his eye. Annoyed to be distracted again, he decided to give a meaningful look of annoyance in the general direction of the swish.

Dark material, long hair. For a second, he thought he saw Tish. The moves, a rhythmic writhing that started at the hips and flowed through slow waving arms, just like the clubs at uni. The lights were flashing with the chorus… the girl turned, it *was* Tish… No, wait, it was the serpentine woman from earlier… with the half smile and eye contact… why was she here? Sam had moved from both his group of friends and hers to the opposite side of the dancefloor. She swayed closer as the music swelled, causing Sam to miss the beat with his shoulder dance. Just as quickly, she moved away, turned away, and continued with her snakes.

"Oh crap what was that!?"

Sam' s internal debate team awoke excitedly from their slumber. They began submitting their arguments for the deliberation of the court.

"Was that on purpose?"

"She looked right at me when she moved!"

"Was that flirting? How do you flirt when dancing?"

"How do I not know this!?"

Sam tried to remember what he had read about social interactions. This could be flirty. She was really attractive. Was the fact she was attractive colouring his opinion on whether or not she was flirting? He could work this out if it was happening to someone else. He could tell in an instant when people were flirting with other people. It was so obvious. When it involved him? No idea. Maybe if she went away and flirt danced with someone else he could observe and then he could figure out…

"That's ridiculous!"

Sam panicked that he had exclaimed out loud how his trail of logic had led him off another social cliff. It was ok, the music was loud. And Serpentine woman had gone again.

"Oh."

Sam decided it was indeed not ok that serpentine woman had gone again. He looked around the dancefloor for her. He hoped she was not in fact taking his advice and demonstrating flirt dancing with someone else. They might be better at working out what it was than him.

"Wait, now I'm straining to look around for this girl, is that weird? What would I do if I saw her anyway?"

At the exact moment he contemplated what he would do, he saw her. She had rejoined her friends. They were not as far away as he thought they were, perhaps they had repositioned to avoid the sweaty air punch dudes too. Sam felt a tinge of disappointment. Maybe it wasn't flirting after all, just a coincidence. He returned to his world of music. Movement and rhythm, it was enough to be happy.

36

Well. Credits rolled. That had been an excellent series. Louisa had sat in her nest and let herself get swept away. She hadn't been so drawn into a TV show for some time. The TV returned to its home screen, casting bright light across the room. Stretching, she caught a glimpse of the clock. Yeah, it was well into Sunday morning now. There was very little chance she could make it anywhere. In fact everywhere was probably shut by now. Reaching for her phone, she checked for any messages from Jess. There was nothing there. She hoped she hadn't upset her by staying in. She hadn't meant to stay in, it just kind of was late all of a sudden. Too late.

A feeling of sadness crept up on her. Not just the usual sadness of a good series or book finishing, it was more than that. She contemplated that this was another thing she had enjoyed on her own, a story someone had written, while her friends were out writing their own stories. People out in the world, her alone in here. She wondered what had happened in the pub, if the club was any good. Usually so content to sit in her own world, she realised she felt like she had missed out. She began to feel a little upset. This was the feeling that had driven her to try all the new things this year. Some of them had gone very badly, but some were alright. Jess and Steven were fantastic. She knew they would have had a good night, they always did. Jess would make sure of it.

Picking up the various mugs, glasses and bowl that had accompanied her through her show, Louisa prepared to go to bed. She would send Jess a text in the morning, apologising. She would promise to be there next time. She had to be. She had come too far, been through too much to go back to how she was before she befriended Jess. There was still time to grow, to fight against the loneliness. But she had to get a better grip on time itself, manage it better. Placing the pots into the sink for tomorrow, she gathered her thoughts and flicked off the lights. She didn't want any more opportunities to slip away into the darkness.

Songs continued, time moved. Sam tried to lose himself to the healing power of distorted guitars. Some songs were better at this power than others. The crowd agreed, as every now and then a song would arrive that would clear the dancefloor almost entirely of its occupants, only for them to be replaced by a different crowd, hands and voices raised in pleasure as it blasted out at them. It was like a tide of taste, when one group turned their noses up and retreated to the bar, another wave took their place. Sam remained, a constant rock against the sea, he had not felt this good in a long time. He was going to enjoy every second he could, and he knew it wouldn't be long before the evening was done, and he would have to face the cold outside world once again.

A dark swish, catching Sam by surprise, serpentine woman was back. She was right in front of him. Sam froze. She was facing away from him, close enough for him to reach out and touch without even straightening his arm. She moved with the music, arms held high above her. Sam felt an urge to hold her, to place his hands on her hips like the couple he had seen downstairs, to feel her sway… But she was facing the other way… she might have just got carried away with the music and wandered over here, not realising how close she had gotten to him. There was no way he was just going to grab a stranger, that was incredibly inappropriate.

"What do I do?"

"Should I ask her what to do?"

"She's not looking, how will she know I want to speak to her?"

"Maybe I should touch her shoulder to let her know I want to talk?"

"If she wanted to talk, she would be talking, I can't assume it's ok to touch her in any way."

Sam realised she had been dancing here for a whole chorus now, much longer than the last time she was this close. Was this significant? Sam's internal panic was dancing more than he was. His mind kept changing on his course of action as the debate raged inside. A crescendo built in his mind along with the music, she was so… he didn't know… the song ended. Properly ended, without a new song taking its place. A drunken cheer rose up from the crowd celebrating the end of the night. Serpentine woman began to walk away. Sam felt a wince of loss as she moved, but perhaps he had been right that it was coincidence. After several steps, she looked back over her shoulder, gave Sam the same half smile he had seen earlier, and shrugged before she disappeared into the crowd at the bar.

"Bollocks."

Sam had no other words. His debate team disappeared in shame and embarrassment.

"Hey Sam, how fun was that!"

Jess and Steven had snuck up from the other direction. Slightly sweaty, but full of smiles, they both glowed from the experience as well as the lights.

"Wooooooo!"

Matt was much more sweaty. But then he did like to bounce.

"Yeah that was pretty awesome!"

Sam did his best to keep eye contact with his friends while looking for the serpentine woman. Perhaps he could go after her?

"I think we should think about going, before the crush of everyone trying to leave."

Jess was perfectly sensible. Except that she was completely wrong. Sam needed another chance to…

"Yeah good plan."

Matt tapped Sam on the shoulder and began to head for the stairs. Jess and Steven quickly followed.

"Yeah, no but…"

Sam started to walk, his head on a swivel. Would it be weird to try and find her now and ask her if she had wanted to do something? Numbers or something?

The stairs were filling up, people that were not the woman Sam was looking for. Quite rude of them all he thought. Quite rude. Before he knew where he was, they were all outside.

"That was a fantastic night guys, we should make this a thing!"

Jess was beaming, still glowing even without the lights.

"I'm up for that!"

Matt was rubbing his arms as steam seemed to be rising from his head. The cold air hitting his energetically sweaty forehead was having a spectacular effect. The sight made them all chuckle.

"You alright mate? Look like you've forgotten something?"

Matt tried to redirect the laughter, or perhaps he was genuinely concerned. Sam had decided he couldn't ever work out what anyone meant ever in his entire life. And he was still glancing at the oak doors, maybe if she came out now he could?

"No, I'm fine, oh… I mean yes, all good!"

"Ok doofus, see you soon!"

Matt waved as he turned and commenced the journey to his bus.

"Do you feel better? I'm so glad you came out."

Jess touched Sam's arm to really hammer home the support. Sam couldn't help but feel the warmth of the gesture.

"Yeah, thanks, I think this was just what I needed. You guys are the best!"

Sam tapped Jess and Steven on the shoulder, in an attempt to repay the support. He felt it worked. Probably.

"Ok well take care, and we will see you soon."

"Night Sam."

Steven's farewell was shorter than Jess's, but it didn't lack any of the sentiment. Sam was grateful to have friends like these. He waved as they turned and began walking up the street towards their flat.

Sam stood. The cold was beginning to pierce. He missed his coat. His proper coat. It was time to start wearing it again. Time to be himself again. Time to accept what had happened, and to move forward. He watched as people moved up and down the street. Another Saturday night complete. Some had reached their dreams tonight, some had found new dreams to chase. Some, like him, were trying to start again. The city moved onwards, only forwards. Sam let out a sigh of relief and turned. He had better get moving if he was going to catch the last bus. Looking at the club, he smiled. He was amazed at his own ability to misunderstand and mess up the simplest of things. But it was who he was, and he didn't want to be anyone else. And it would definitely be weird if he went back in to look for the serpentine woman. He laughed at himself as he started walking for the bus.

37

It was a Sunday night. The kind where Sam was filled with a see saw of emotion, tipping between the satisfaction of a fun weekend and the dread of having to go back to work in the morning. He had felt inspired by the previous night's adventure, the sense that the world was still there even after Ellie. Feeling a bit more whole, and a bit more alive, he had decided maybe it was time to start looking at getting properly back out into the world. He felt like he had spent more time worrying, dwelling, wallowing in the pit of Ellie than he had spent with her. No more. After several hours of internal debate, he had opened up his laptop and logged back in to his old dating profile. At first, it had been awful. After a while, it had become truly dreadful. Nothing much had changed in the months since he had last decided this was, if not a good idea, then perhaps not the worst idea. The profiles that greeted him all seemed to be the same ones he had seen before, if slightly more aggressive in their wording. There were a few interesting looking women, but Sam couldn't decide which one he should message. Or what to even say. They all looked more confident than he felt, more well rounded. Profiles full of all the adventurous things they got up too, places they had been. At first, Sam had found it intimidating. Then he wondered how everyone managed to do all of these things. It dawned on him that perhaps they weren't completely truthful in their stories of greatness. Sam wondered how he could ever try and chat to someone who he suspected of being dishonest before any interaction at all. Maybe it was just him? Maybe he was just convinced now that everyone was too good to be true.

Sam needed a break from those pages filled with false hopes and falser people. If they even were people, they could be robots for all he knew. He wasn't ready to face that part of the world. He felt he may never be ready for it. He clicked open another browser tab and opened up some social media sites instead. The kind of media sites that allow you to avoid being directly social. Pictures and quotes sprang to life on the screen, all of them mildly interesting at best. Scrolling down the feed, Sam wondered if there was any point to even looking at sites like this anymore, he really wasn't concerned with how a person he hadn't seen since school was managing to eat all that hamburger without a care in the world.

"Oh hang on."

From the bottom of the feed sprang a post that caught Sam's wandering attention. It was a post about the club night they had been at last night. Jess had clicked that she liked the clubs' page, allowing Sam to see for himself. With a smile, thinking about the things he had seen, Sam clicked the link to open the clubs' page. Greeted by typical marketing spin, and some extremely flattering pictures of the venue, Sam scrolled to see if there were any photos that commemorated their adventure. More importantly, were there any photos of him on there. That was a sudden worry he wasn't expecting to have. A few photos showed revellers enjoying themselves. Sam didn't see anything too crazy, nor did he see himself or his friends. In fact, looking closer at the half dozen or so photos, Sam wasn't sure if he saw anyone over the age of twenty two. He also saw a lot more women than men, and he saw quite a lot of each of those women. The person in charge of this selection of photos seemed to have been given a very specific explanation of their task and how to portray the event. Sam felt a little sad about this, as one of the things that had stuck in his memory about the night was how diverse the crowd was, and the breadth of ages all enjoying the venue together. Why couldn't the page project that image? Surely that was more appealing to a wider audience than a half dozen shots of young women in skimpy outfits. Surely that wasn't all that mattered anymore in this so called society.

Further down the page sat the list of attendees. Sam scanned the list to see if this better represented the crowd he remembered. It seemed to, although it was a little hard to tell. Social media profile pictures were even more random than dating site pictures. Sam's own profile picture was of a night time view of a cartoon castle circled by various monsters. He felt it encapsulated his being quite well. One profile did manage to stick out from the bunch.

"Is that..."

Sam muttered as if asking the screen to respond. He thought he recognised the picture as the serpentine woman that he had expertly failed to dance with/chat to/marry. He clicked the picture, and the woman's profile appeared. With a larger picture available Sam was sure it was the same woman. He felt a rush of adrenaline, as the universe had seemingly given him a second chance. He clicked on the message button, and wrote a quick line saying hello and that he was the guy from the other night and clicked send. As soon as his fingered raised from the send button a massive wave of dread hit his entire being.

"Oh what did I just do..."

Sam raised both hands to his face in an attempt to hide from the world. After looking at dating sites, remembering how he would look at profiles and send messages... He had forgotten he was not on that kind of site anymore. For a moment, it had blurred with the memory of how a simple message had secured his first date with Ellie, how it had overcome his nerves and inability to communicate in person. But this was different. Very different. He had not spoken to this woman before. He had just sent a message to a stranger. A slightly flirty one as well.

To a stranger.

Panic began to fill his mind, and he desperately searched for an un-send message button that did not and had not ever existed. Even if it was the person he thought it was, this was not a dating site. Sam wouldn't even have known this page existed if Jess hadn't liked it, and his curiosity had led him to scroll down the page to the 'interested in going' section. She may not even realise that when she clicked she was going to the event her profile could be seen this way. Sam's profile was not listed on this page, and even it was, he had a cartoon picture and not a face. This woman may assume he had deliberately used social media to track her down and message her, an unsolicited message appearing in her inbox out of nowhere.

"No no no…"

Sam was getting concerned now that a brief act of not thinking could be interpreted as a deliberate act of very not good thinking. But there was nothing he could do, he couldn't take it back. He wondered if he should send another message explaining what had happened and that he wasn't a creepy stalker. He realised that although that sounded sensible in his head, nothing would make him seem more like a creepy stalker than sending multiple messages to this woman explaining why he was not.

"You idiot. Stupid. Stupid. Idiot! Fuck!"

Sam had succeeded in destroying his mood. He had begun so positively, ready to move forward. He was impressed that he could manage to make the disappointment he had felt in himself for missing an opportunity in the club last night worse. And if the serpentine woman had thought he was weird in his behaviour in person, she would certainly think he was weird and terrible now. He was angry that his actions may cause harm. He couldn't believe he could be so stupid. Everything he had done. For months. Stupid. He thought he had decided that he was better now, ready to move forward in constructive ways. That was supposed to be the outcome of the night out, not this. Now he may have upset some poor stranger with his utter misunderstanding of how to function in the world like a sensible normal person. Virtually slamming the computer shut, Sam decided he had had enough of digital communication and its misinterpretations, unclear protocols, unvoiced explanations and far too easy missteps. Upset that he might have upset the serpentine woman with his ill thought through and somewhat inappropriate message, wondering if all of his attempts to communicate were equally wrong, it was time to go to bed and give up for the day, if not forever.

38

"Argh!"

The door slammed shut with a most satisfying crash.

"You back then Lou?"

Nia's grasp on the obvious was… accurate.

"Yeah, sorry about that!"

Louisa was only sorry that she had been heard trying to let out her stress at that place. Those people. Stupid job. Stupid. Fighting with her coat, forcing it into its place on the stand, kicking off her shoes. She attempted to gather herself. Take a breath. She was home now. Done in that place for another week. She walked into the main room to see how Nia was, and to see if she needed to apologise again. Nia seemed quite alright, gathering items and stuffing them into her now trademark overnight bag.

"I take it you did decide to go over there again then?"

Louisa was getting a bit worried with how much time Nia was spending with her partner. It was almost every weekend now. She was happy for her, that wasn't the issue. The issue was sooner or later she may start awkward conversations about not paying as much towards the bills because she wasn't here. Or worse yet, announcing that she was moving out altogether, leaving Louisa alone to hunt for a stranger to fill her place. Whilst having to pay double in the meantime. This was not a happy place for Louisa's head to dwell. Bills. Money. Literally all of her problems revolved around them.

"Yeah, decided this afternoon, got a really nice invite for a meal and stuff so yeah… you don't mind do you?"

Nia was rummaging through the cupboard, removing foods and placing them in her bag. Louisa felt she could at least leave the snacks.

"No, no problem, hope you enjoy it!"

Louisa moved over to her place on the sofa. Her true home, her safe comfortable place. She felt a crunch as she sat. Reaching for the cause of such an occurrence she discovered several envelopes had been left in her safe space. Not friendly envelopes either. Bills.

"You alright babe? You seem more flustered than usual?"

Nia flopped into her chair, taking a break from her packing.

"Yeah, just work… it's been horrible lately."

"Boo. That's no good. What's up with it now? Still loads to do? Oh yeah, bills… I just put them there out of the way, we can sort it on Sunday night when I get back if that's cool?"

Louisa cast the bills to their new home of floorland. Castaway from the light of her sofa, to think about what they had done.

"Yeah sure. Sunday is cool. Work, yeah. Same shit. Extra people shit though."

Nia looked appalled by Louisa's comments.

"People shit?"

Louisa smiled, perhaps the first of the day.

"Not actual shit. People being shitty."

Nia laughed before gathering a more serious face.

"Tell me about the shitty people. What caused their stinkyness?"

"They want me to go out with them tomorrow night."

Nia raised her hands to her face in shock.

"The bastards!"

Louisa smiled again. She wasn't sure if she wanted to go through all of it again, and definitely didn't want to let out everything she felt about it.

"Yeah… it's not that, it's that they aren't very nice people, you know, the ones from the other team I tried to go out with before and came home early due to their shitness."

Nia looked like she was searching her memory. It was a while ago, and Louisa wasn't sure how much of an impact her life stories had on Nia at the best of times.

"Oh yes, the ones who said the nasty things? Yes. Shits. Don't go out with them."

Louisa was reassured that Nia at least partially remembered.

She contemplated going through it all, to let it out of her system, but Nia had gotten back out of her chair.

"Right, ride is here, time to go!"

"Oh… right… well have fun! Say hello from me!"

"Thanks! You too! If you go out with them lot try not to let them be nasty!"

Nia collected her bag and was gone. Louisa pondered her last comment. Why would Nia think that she would go out with them after saying… oh it didn't matter. Nia had her own stuff to deal with, and she was clearly having a good time at the moment. No need to try and sit and lecture her in everything so that she could give a more supportive response on her way out.

Louisa continued to sit on the sofa. The bills sat on the floor. Everything was still. She only went to that stupid job to pay these bills. And she only had these bills so she could live closer to work. The whole thing was stupid. She felt a vibration from jacket pocket run through her, causing her to jump in surprise. She reached in and retrieved the culprit. Her phone flashed with the new message. It was from Leanne, asking again about Saturday night. Louisa felt she had been quite clear that she had almost less than zero interest in spending time with those people. Her mind shuddered as she remembered the horror, the fakeness, the aggressive pushiness of those people. Honestly, she still wasn't sure why after all this time she was still being asked to go to the *'let's drink until we are blind and have no clue what we even did or with whom'* events that bunch of so called people had become known for. She wondered why she even had the name in her phone at all. As she typed her best polite but firm 'thanks but no thanks' reply, she remembered she kept everyone's number in her phone. Even the ones she didn't want to speak to. That way, if they called or messaged she could see it was someone she wanted to ignore. If she deleted them, she wouldn't realise who it was, and may answer by mistake. Finishing the message, she contemplated that this plan was not working. She never answered calls from numbers she didn't recognise.

As she placed her phone carefully down on the chair several feet away with a flick of her wrist, it dawned on her that most of that crowd were male. Perhaps she was being asked to make up the gender numbers, or worse, to be offered as a target. Fresh meat to the altar of *"you won't believe what they got up to on Saturday!"*

Nope. A thousand times nope.

There was no way she was going to go out with those people. It was making her shudder just thinking about it.

From its resting place, her phone lit up again. Louisa rolled her eyes. Annoyance and displeasure combined with a sense that this device was somewhere between a kitten and a small child in its demand for attention. She pondered how both of those things would be more rewarding to actually pay attention to as the unstoppable urge to check it drove her across the room.

"Hey hun! How's You? You know we talked about giving more notice? Well tomorrow is kinda the anniversary of me and the Steven moving here! Free tomorrow? Anniversary house party! :)"

A whole year?!

Louisa had to read Jess's message a couple of times to let it sink in. Had it really been a whole year since she had taken that chance to meet some new people and get out of her quiet rut of life on the sofa? It was a lot to think about. A lot had happened. But also, not much. It was hard to tell. Louisa had tried. She had learned a lot about herself, but it was mostly stuff she had learned she didn't want to do again. Befriending Jess was the best thing that had happened in a long time. Much longer than a year. Her mind drifted back through time. Everything had seemed so empty before. Sitting back down on the sofa it dawned on her that it was beginning to feel that way again. She was falling back into a steady routine of staying in, safe. Alone. But it was starting to feel worse. Since the restructure, she never saw Steven at work anymore. Only those others. And now the sofa didn't seem so welcoming. She had some great times out in the world, Jess had helped her find more of herself than she would ever be able to express. Now her sofa was feeling less like a cosy place to rest, and more like a prison cell, somewhere she had to sit and wait out her time until she could go back into the world. She knew what she had to do, without question or hesitation. Well, some hesitation.

"Hi! Wow! A whole year! I will be there! But if it's a big party with lots of people like last time I might hide in the corner for a bit! :)"

Louisa was determined not to miss out this time. She had felt a real sense of loss after getting too caught up to go out last time. This was too important to mess up. This was a chance to have her own adventures, tell her own stories. Not rely on the TV or books to tell her one. She had managed it last year, she had started a new journey at that party. There was no reason she couldn't do it again this year. Even if the thought of a lot of people was a bit scary. She had to make herself try.

"Cool! I may have slightly oversold it! I'm not inviting loads of people – too much weirdness last year and Steven quite rightly vetoed most of them! It will just be a couple of select friends! Quality not quantity! :)"

Jess's message was perhaps the sweetest thing Louisa had seen all week. Including that list of best cats in flower pots. Louisa felt a sense of accomplishment at being included in such a select list.

"Awesome! I will be there! Send me all the details :)"

Louisa was excited. All the stress and horror from the day fell away as she texted back and forth with Jess. Her weekend on the sofa was cancelled. Jess's last house party had changed her life. She was excited to tell her that. She was excited that it could happen again.

39

"Hi hun! Come on in!"

Jess motioned for Louisa to enter as she swung open the large wooden door to her flat. Louisa felt a gust of air pull her through the entrance as the door continued its swing, as though the flat itself was insisting on her entry.

"Hey, I made it this time! Nice to see you."

Louisa smiled and gave Jess a hug, happy to feel Jess's positive energy again. It felt like an age had passed.

"Hello Lou!"

Steven's shout of welcome boomed from the depths of the flat, out of sight, no doubt fiddling with beer or seating or something practical for a social gathering that didn't involve close proximity to the actual people involved.

Jess swept through the corridor towards the living room area, pausing briefly to gesture for Louisa to throw her coat in the general direction of the bedroom. Obliging, slightly clumsily, Louisa dashed to catch up to her friend. The living room hadn't changed since the last time she was here, which was strangely comforting. It felt like a second home, a place of safety. The whole place sparkled with Jess and Steven's energy, as though it was a brick and plaster manifestation of one of their warm hugs. Jess was already sat on the sofa, looking like she had been sat comfortably for hours. Steven waved from the kitchen area, taking brief pause from the assortment of drinks he was proudly arranging.

"So how have you been? Properly, haven't seen you for a few weeks?"

Jess inquired as Louisa allowed herself to flop onto the opposite end of the sofa, an explorer planting a permanent flag in a new land to call it home. Sofas. The best place to be.

"Yeah, alright thanks, been doing work and home and stuff…

you know, the usual."

Louisa wanted to keep everything happy and jovial, not let on that she had been struggling a bit lately. She was happy to be here with her best friends, she didn't want to drag anything down.

"That's good, we've been a bit worried that you may become a recluse, and not in the good adventuring doing things you enjoy away from the horrible people of the world who think everything is stupid way, but in a kinda retreating hiding sort of way."

Jess cut straight through Louisa's attempt to ignore everything. Perhaps she was a mind reader? Louisa wished she could be so perceptive of others, it was added to the list of things about Jess that Louisa continued to hope would in some way rub off onto her.

"Well…"

Before she could continue, a large glass appeared in front of her, contents swilling around at speed.

"Wine for the first guest, the house red as is preferred."

Steven smiled as his offering swished. Louisa reached for the glass, thanking Steven as he let go slightly too early. The wine sloshed to the top of the glass as it tipped, testing Louisa's reactions along with her ability to widen her eyes in panic. Both her hands grabbed, the glass's descent halted. Disaster averted. Breathing could return.

"Oh sorry! Nice catch!"

Steven looked slightly embarrassed. To drop wine was bad enough, to drop it onto a guest was an unthinkable act. Jess laughed as Steven retreated back to the kitchen.

"Nice catch indeed!"

Louisa didn't move or blink until the wine stopped spinning. The circular motion wound time backwards, revealing a memory from the year before.

"Whoa… I just remembered this nearly happened here last year, at your housewarming party! And I promised myself I would only drink white wine in people's houses in future… in case it ever happened again!"

"Ooo that's weird… mystical reoccurrences…"

It was Jess's turn to be wide eyed as she waggled her fingers, suggesting some kind of magic was at work.

"Although, I'm not sure I like the idea of my guests feeling they can't drink what they prefer out of some kind of fear of what might happen. If wine spills, who cares really? It's not the end of the world. Only the end of the world is the end of the world, and at that point, it also wouldn't matter… so don't worry about it!"

Louisa contemplated Jess's words. She was right, as she often was. Cutting through the issue to its logical core. She remembered Jess giving the same advice in the Art Gallery, setting her mind at rest at one of its least restful times. That had been such a momentous day for Louisa, it seemed fitting to hear the advice again tonight, on this anniversary, a time to contemplate how much had happened in a year. Although, it did make her wonder how far she had left to go. Why did she worry about things so much? She just didn't want to cause problems or upset, or have her presence somewhere cause difficulty for others. Did she worry too much? Or was that just what everyone thought? Worried she had been thinking too long, she felt she should say something:

"Don't worry, I am happy with whatever, I just remembered thinking that white wine may be less hazardous to the environment."

Jess gave a quizzical look as she thought about what Louisa had just said.

"So… I thought I told you not to worry, how did you manage to end up telling me not to worry… I'm supposed to be reassuring you…"

"Oh sorry!"

Jess slapped her forehead.

"Lou don't be sorry, be happy! You don't have to apologise for everything, especially not for trying to change your own habits to try and protect others! And certainly not for us, ya doof."

Louisa laughed, resisting the urge to say sorry.

"So, a whole year. It seems to have gone by so fast. Is time speeding up?"

Steven sat carefully in the chair opposite the sofa, leaving it unclear if his statement was meant to start a new conversation, or if it was just a proclamation of fact. A bottle of beer in one hand, a glass in the other, he seemed keen to not give drinks the opportunity to escape again. Louisa watched him sit, and as he began to pour the beer, she wondered why he had opted to do that here after spending so much time in the kitchen fiddling about. Or for that matter, why he was bothering with a glass at all. He always did things in the most complex way, under the excuse of it being the 'correct' way. He seemed to enjoy going to great lengths, getting a beer from the fridge expanding into some kind of elongated yet satisfying ritual.

"Yes, a whole year. It's been an interesting one."

Jess decided it was the start of a new conversation.

"Here's to a year in this home, and to the new friend it brought with it."

Louisa blushed at Jess's toast. She thought back over the last year. It had high points, it had low points. It had been an amazing experience either way. Before last year's party, Louisa had felt she was adrift… lost in the flow of work and home, unsure how to change and fit in with the wider world. Unsure what she was doing wrong to not be included in the happy and adventurous lives of the people she saw around her. The party had been her shot at changing, and she had jumped at it. She knew she would never be able to express how important Jess had become to her, how her insight and support had started to bring her out of herself. There had been lows though, such lows. Trying to fathom the world was upsetting, trying to change to fit in with more people, painful. And pointless. Louisa had discovered that the world she thought she was missing out on was not real. The other people she had met, or tried to talk to online, she didn't ever want to be like them. She didn't want to change that much, to that extent. It was too drastic. Too alien. And that was fine, cathartic even. Peaceful. It was getting too peaceful though. She was beginning to feel adrift again. Beginning to feel again that she was missing out, but now she wasn't even sure what she was missing. She saw how happy Jess and Seven were, how well they suited each other. She knew how she felt about being with Jess, how she knew she didn't have to change for them to be friends. Was that all there was though? Happy and safe with a couple of close friends, or having to transplant alien personalities to continue to meet new people, to have more places to go? Were those the only options? Perhaps she was just getting greedy.

"I must say this is a much better way to celebrate than last year. A small amount of good people is preferable to a large amount of… well…"

Steven struggled with a polite way to end the sentence. Jess did not.

"Asshats. Yes, over keen on the whole let's get lots of people to come aspect last year. Turned out having a large number didn't make it an automatic good experience! Oh, present company excluded, obviously!"

"What do you mean? I thought everyone had a really nice time? I saw everyone getting along and things, did I miss something?"

Louisa was genuinely surprised, she searched her memory for evidence of asshattery, all she could remember was feeling that everyone else was getting along a lot better than she was.

"Oh! Yes that's right! I don't think you were there when Steven…"

"Yes well lets never mind that shall we."

Steven cut Jess off mid sentence, which only sparked Louisa's confused curiosity more. What had she missed!? She knew it. She knew she was missing things!

"Let's just say…"

Jess gave a comforting glance to Steven as she spoke.

"Let's just say there were some people there, well, some guys, who were using the opportunity to try and make new female friends of a somewhat intimate nature, and they were not concerned how they acted in their endeavour, or how they tried to make themselves seem better by belittling others."

Louisa's shock emanated across the room with the force of a category two expletive storm.

"WHAT?! How did I miss all that! Who? What! That sounds horrible!"

Louisa again searched her memory, scanning for signs of asshat. Jess laughed, even Steven let loose a small chuckle.

"You were speaking to one of them, I thought he was having an effect for a while, until I saw you had cut his advances down like a combine harvester. His expression was so funny! You must remember that!"

"WHAT! WHO!"

Louisa demanded Jess explain herself. She had no recollection of any such thing. Surely she would remember such a thing?

"You know, oh what was his name, beardy hairy man... waistcoat... Oh! Dean! Yes, that's it, from one of the departments at work somewhere. He was trying his best pick up lines on you, but you cut him down like a reaper!"

Louisa searched. She remembered talking to Dean, how she thought the things he was saying were weird and random. Was that flirting?

"Was he? Did I? Eww! I thought we were just talking, and it was a bit of a random conversation to be honest. I remember him saying I should travel more, like him."

Jess burst out laughing.

"Not like him, with him! He was trying to get you to fly away on a romantic get away! You didn't realise? Hun that's hilarious! How could you not! That's fantastic!"

Was it fantastic? Louisa's mind was full of questions. And slight horror. Was Jess right? Was that what was happening... it made more sense with the foreign travel thing, it had seemed random. But how could she have missed it? And had she cut him down? This was a terrible turn of events, had she hurt someone's feelings without even realising? Did that mean she did that all the time? Or if she had missed flirting, did she do that all the time too? But also, eww, she did not regret missing flirting with Dean. Eww.

"I had no idea… really? Wow. Crazy. Oh wait, I saw him again."

Now it was Jess's turn to be shocked.

"What? After that? You mean…"

"No, not like that."

Louisa rapidly cut off any chance of further misinterpretation.

"I mean on a work night out, I went out with the marketing team, and he was there. He said some of the same things to me again, he didn't remember who I was."

Jess was forced to cover her mouth to stop from squeaking. Steven had no such issue.

"You went out with the guys from marketing? They've got a reputation for… well, yes."

"THIS IS AMAZING."

Jess had managed to prevent the squeak, she couldn't prevent the excitement from bubbling out.

"Hun you didn't, did you?"

"Didn't what? It was a horrible evening, they were all so…"

Louisa checked her internal thesaurus for the correct word to describe it.

"Eww."

"I don't really see you getting along with that group."

It was perhaps the most insightful thing Steven had said to Louisa.

"Yeah, I thought it was worth trying it you know, going out, drinks in the city, that's what we are supposed to do, right? But yeah, they weren't very nice, and I kinda stormed out."

"Lou! That's fantastic! Oh I wish I could have seen that! Can we set it up so you can do it again and we can watch!?"

Jess was beaming, laughing as she spoke.

"I hope you cut them all down the way you cut Dean down, oooh a mass reaping of asshats… AMAZING!"

"You know we go out to the city from time to time, actually quite a lot, it's not that far really. You should come with us more, don't go with marketing, I'm not surprised you didn't get on with them."

Steven seemed genuinely concerned. Louisa wondered if there were more stories there, things he was keeping to himself. She wanted to know, but wasn't really sure she could handle any more revelations right now.

"Yeah hun, stick with us. Them lot have the depth of a spoon, it's all appearance and maximum conquests with them. I mean, that's fine, if that's what you want to do, but I think you're more like us, and less like that."

Jess was still giggling, and occasionally shuddering at the thought of it all.

"Yeah, I'm happy to stick with you guys. I will make sure I don't miss your next night out! I wanted to come last time, but yeah… stuff."

Louisa was still reeling from it all. She felt she had been missing out, and now she felt she had proof. A vindication of a sadness that she had felt for a long time, that there was more to the world than she was getting to see, but also a fear, that the world she was missing may be even more unpleasant than she had thought. It was a little unsettling to think she could read a situation so wrong, but then she was happy to have missed out on the worst of it. Better to think things were weird than sleazy. The world was harder to navigate than she had thought.

A sharp buzz caught Jess by surprise. Flinching, she reached for the pile of books on the coffee table. The buzz continued as she moved them about, searching for the source. The last book to be moved revealed the buzz culprit, complete with flashing lights. Jess tutted to herself as she placed the phone to her ear.

"What's wrong with you? Why don't you just use the buzzer? Yes, I know my phone buzzes. That's not what I meant… Yes, this is closer but it doesn't open… what do you mean *never mind it's open now*? Damnit someday you're going to have to use the actual buzzer and I'm not going to be around to… yes ok if I wasn't here you wouldn't be either… just come up stupidface."

Steven was chuckling away at the exchange.

"I take it Sam's here then?"

Jess replaced her phone somewhere in the books while she disapproved in Steven's general direction.

40

The door swung shut behind Sam, imprisoning the outside behind its glass and steel. It had been a while since Sam had been here. It had been much longer since he had walked in on his own. The whitewashed hallway looked a little faded, or perhaps the lighting was different. Sam moved to the stairs, which seemed grubbier than he remembered, scuff marks and scratches seemed to be combining to take over as the dominant finish of the faux steel and stone wood construction. As he moved up, he felt like each step was sighing under his feet. It was as though they were wearing out under the weight of expectation of each person that had used them over the last year. Sam wondered who they all were, these travellers of Mount Stone Wood. What had their year been like? What things had they seen? What adventures? How had their lives changed as they added these new scratches and scuffs?

His coat lapped the backs of his legs as he wandered the hall. He looked at the walls, the floor… he thought about everyone who walked here before. Those he knew, those from other flats he may never meet, their friends, friends of friends… ghosts of who knows what stories held together by this off beige passageway. And here it was, the door to Jess and Steven's corner of the world. He smiled to himself as he remembered standing here a year before, not knowing what mysteries lay beyond. He couldn't have predicted how that night would go, how the year would go. This time there was no mystery, he had been here many times, and he had agreed with Jess that this anniversary would be best served with minimal people. No need to worry tonight, he knocked on the door and waited to see his friends.

"Press the buzzer."

A muffled Jess yelled from behind closed wood.

"Jess? It's me."

"I know who it is, press the buzzer."

"Why would I press the buzzer, you know it's me, you could just…"

"I'm not going to open the door until you press the buzzer."

Sam stared for a second. He didn't press buzzers. This was his thing. Jess knew it was his thing. This was unacceptable.

"Jess?"

"Buzzer."

Well. Sam pondered his options. He considered knocking, but that seemed incredibly weird. He could wait it out. He was pretty sure he had more patience than Jess. But what would that do? He didn't really want to just stand in the corridor. What if other people saw. Weird. His idea that this would be a quiet and uneventful evening was falling away. Well, that was a bit of an overstatement. Sam considered how this tense stand off was a bit ridiculous, and he reached for the buzzer. He didn't want to spoil his record, but he had a plan. He pressed.

"You did it!"

Jess swung the door open with enough force to nearly blow them both over. Sam's coat flapped energetically at the attention.

"Well, I figured it's not an external buzzer, for the whole building… just a doorbell… therefore it doesn't count under the whole never press buzzers thing. Everybody wins!"

Sam stepped into the flat as Jess considered the argument. Motioning for him to throw his coat in the bedroom, she seemed to choose her words carefully for her response.

"Idiot."

"Thanks. Oh Matt said to pass on that he wasn't going to be able to make it, but good times, enjoyment, etc."

Sam emerged from carefully placing his coat in a heap in the bedroom.

"You could get a coat rack you know?"

"Yeah, we thought about it, but couldn't decide on the style, or the height. Or location. So still thinking about it."

"It's been a year? Like literally a year?"

"Yeah, no need to rush such a decision. Did Matt give the same ridiculous excuse as last time, or a different one?"

"Same one."

Jess nodded in acceptance of Matt's reasoning.

"Go through, you get the special chair. I will be there in a minute."

Sam returned the nod and headed into the living room. Steven waved from the kitchen area. He turned towards the sofa. A woman. A beautiful woman. On the sofa. Sam was a little bit taken aback. He wasn't expecting to see anyone else, Jess had said it was just going to be close friends. He hadn't considered that meant other close friends. Perhaps that was the kind of assumption that Matt often used as evidence when calling him a bit of a dick.

"I get the special chair."

Sam's mouth operated without the proper permits. Who was this girl? She looked a bit familiar, did he know her? He felt like he knew her but couldn't place it.

"Ok… hello…"

Louisa wasn't sure what to make of this guy. He had a certain kind of style, and a certain kind of mess. Like someone had tried their best to dress smartly whilst jumping from a train. She couldn't help but smile at his introduction.

"I mean hi."

Sam sat in the extra chair that Steven had moved across to make up the seating. It didn't match the others. Sam felt a little bit at home in it.

"I'm sorry, have we met? I feel like we've met but I can't think where?"

Sam was still a little flustered. He couldn't really remember why he was flustered.

"Ah, don't let Jess hear you say that, she doesn't like apologies for normal behaviour. I'm Louisa, and no, we haven't met."

Louisa felt a little flustered, she wasn't really expecting anyone else to turn up, well she hadn't really thought about it. And there was something about this guy…

"Oh my behaviour is very far from normal, that's what she tells me. Or is it normal for me and everyone else is weird? That might be it. Oh if we haven't met, then I'm Sam. Well even if we had, I would still be Sam. But yeah."

Sam wasn't really sure what he was talking about and not in his usual way, in a new kind of babbling fool way. There was something about this woman…

"Your lemonade sir, just how you like it. In a glass. There's not really much you can do with it honestly."

Steven presented Sam with a tumbler full of bubbling liquid.

"So, you two finally meet. Only took a year to get you together in the same place. Well, literally the same place I suppose."

Steven threw the comment into the room as he sat back down in his chair, fresh beer in hand. Sam wasn't quite sure what he meant.

"What do you mean?"

Sam's thoughts coalesced in Louisa's voice. Steven looked confused. Sam was a bit concerned they had both just read his mind.

"Oh, you were both here at the party last year, but we didn't think you had talked, so…"

Jess swooped back into her spot on the sofa with ease, completing Steven's sentence as she did.

"So nothing really, it's just you both are awesome, and we are awesome, we get on with each of you, so maybe you will get on with each other."

Louisa looked quizzically at Sam.

Sam caught Louisa's eyes, he felt a jolt, as if she was looking into the deepest reaches of his being. She looked away quickly, but the feeling remained. Who was this woman?

"Well, he does have the special chair."

Louisa smiled at Jess as she spoke. Sam felt a little embarrassed.

"Ah yes he does, special indeed. He likes that chair, but it's not special for the reason he thinks it is."

Jess spoke as though Sam wasn't in earshot.

"Hey, it's special because yours all match in the set, but this one is different, like me, stands out from the crowd."

Sam smiled, pleased with his explanation.

"No, doofus, it's special because although it looks like it doesn't match, it's still our chair. It's still from our home. It belongs here just as much as all the other furniture, it just happens to look a bit different."

Sam was stunned by the description. He had no words to respond.

Louisa looked at Sam. He looked a bit shocked, like Jess had just cut deep inside of him when he least expected it. She knew that feeling. Jess's words resonated in her too. She hadn't thought in those terms, but she did feel at home here, and different everywhere else.

"So before you got here, Louisa was telling us about how last year she cut down that guy Dean who was hitting on everyone, cut him stone dead like a samurai!"

Jess swung her arms mimicking a sword swipe. It cut the weird tension in Sam's mind just as cleanly as a real sword, but with less of the blood and death.

"Dean? Oh was he the bearded hairy guy in the waistcoat? The master dickpenis? He was trying his best. Oh, so very trying. Good job!"

"You too? How did everyone know he was hitting on me except me!"

Louisa blurted out a bit more out loudly than she would have liked, causing Jess to laugh.

"Well, if it helps, I'm really good at telling when other people are flirting, trying to hit on people, but useless when it involves me. It's a purely observational skill."

Sam was trying to be reassuring, but ended up being way more revealing than he intended to. He felt like he could just say anything, weird for him. Especially with someone he had just met. Even though it felt like he had known everyone here for ever. This was turning into a much weirder night than he had given it credit for in the corridor.

"Aww that's so sad."

Louisa spoke without thinking, regretting it immediately. Why had she blurted that out? She just called a stranger sad… what was happening…

"It's true, Sam is great with anyone but himself, that's why I'm here."

Jess beamed her smile before taking a huge gulp from her wine glass.

"And me, I'm also here, but I generally think Sam is a bit rubbish at everything."

Steven was mostly observational, unless given a topic for consideration. Sam was a little concerned by his comment. But he was pretty sure it was a joke. Louisa was laughing. Yeah, joke. Ok. Jess quipped back at Steven, always a good spectator sport. Sam was happy to watch the two of them joke around, and attempt the occasional dig to keep it going. Louisa seemed to be doing the same. The weirdness of the evening seemed to be that special kind of unexpected fun. Sam always liked visiting here. He felt he should be doing it more often.

"So Sam, if you were here last year, did you enjoy it? Did you understand everything that was going on, or miss things like I did?"

Louisa was curious to discover why everyone seemed to have such a better handle on what was going on than she did.

"Yeah it was a fun night, I remember messing with Dean as he was trying to hit on… I don't remember her name, never saw her before or since… anyway, yeah that was entertaining. But then I got caught up in a bit of a mistake."

Mid sentence, Sam had started to wonder about name of the girl Dean had been talking too. He hadn't thought of that conversation since that night. Before he knew it, the sentence had drifted into a place he wasn't sure he was comfortable with.

"A mistake? How so?"

Louisa seemed curious. Sam was still trying to figure out why he had said that in the first place, when he noticed he could hear his voice.

"Yeah, I met someone, and I got lost in it. I didn't handle it very well, and it went badly."

Sam was shocked at his openness. He had only just met this woman, despite claims of earlier proximity. Why had he just started blurting out his past at her?

"Oh that sounds rough. I've made some mistakes in the time since that party too."

Louisa wasn't sure why she had blurted that out. It totally ruined her sense of mystery. This new guy didn't need to know she was a mess.

"Yeah, everyone makes mistakes. Only the good ones recognise they were mistakes and try and learn how to not make them again."

Sam's voice was communicating of its own free will. He felt a little nervous at the lack of control, but also a strange kind of comfort in how easy it was to just talk with this woman. Also, his voice was making more sense out of the quagmire of the last year than his mind had.

"Well I opened a lot of dating profile messages that turned out to be pictures of dicks so…"

Louisa wasn't sure why she was telling Sam this. Or anyone. Ever.

"Wouldn't you see their face on the profile screen? Already be able to tell they were dicks?"

Sam wasn't sure why he was answering Louisa so quickly, without thinking through what he was saying. He always thought it through. A lot. That was his thing.

"Oh no, I don't mean the guys were dicks, well… I mean they were, but I mean the pictures they sent were of their dicks."

"Oh."

Sam saw how he had gotten confused.

"OH!"

Sam realised what the words meant. Wow. No wonder he never got anywhere on dating sites if the girls he was trying to say a nice hello to were getting that kind of thing.

"No wonder I wasn't getting anywhere on dating sites if the girls I was trying to say a nice hello to were getting that kind of thing."

Sam sat back, a little perturbed that his internal monologue had become his external speech. Was Louisa inside of his mind? He always, always struggled with finding the right thing to say to new people. And often with people he had known for ages. Why was he being so open? It seemed so natural. Like he had known her forever, and it was just normal to speak openly. What was going on?

"Oh! I would have liked a nice hello! I never got all the way through the messages, too many pictures. And when I searched myself, all the men seemed to just be married or just looking for sex. Or both."

Louisa shuddered as she spoke. She wasn't sure why she was telling him all of this, she had struggled to tell Jess, and she felt closer to Jess than she had felt to anyone for so long...

"Well, apparently that was another thing I was doing wrong. I spent ages trying to compose the right message, say the right thing, compose the right profile. Huh. Well. Yeah I'm glad I gave up on that. I'm not that kind of person."

Sam wasn't sure which bit of the conversation to be more shocked by. He had assumed every man would use the dating sites in the same way he did, in fact he thought he was probably doing it better after having tried to learn a bit about it. Nope, totally wrong. No wonder he never got any responses. He felt a little sad. Another aspect of interaction he had gotten completely wrong. Perhaps he was going to have to admit he was no good at things like that.

"That's sweet, I gave up on it too. Not that kind of person either. I think I just need to accept I'm not really very good at that kind of thing, can't tell in person, don't like the alternatives."

Louisa felt a little sad, this conversation had started weirdly and got out of hand. She had opened herself up a bit too much, and she didn't know how to deal with where they had ended up.

"Well, ok. In future, I am just going to ask upfront what it all means when I speak to people. And they can just tell me. And I can tell them, there will be no more confusion!"

Sam tried to dig himself out of his hole. Thinking about it, it wasn't the worst idea he had had. Bit odd, but he liked a bit odd.

"What are you two going on about?"

Jess sat back down on the sofa. Neither Louisa or Sam had realised she had gone. They both felt a little shocked that they hadn't.

"Sam was just saying how he gets in messes."

Louisa was quick to respond, before Sam could say a similar thing about her.

"Ah yes, good ol' Sam."

Jess smiled affectionately at Sam, who was struggling to come up with a defence quickly enough to escape being the subject of the conversation.

"The thing about Sam, he overthinks things, gets tangled up in his own thoughts and stuck in them, and they stick him into inaction like his mind is jammed up, he's stuck in the world of jam."

Louisa giggled at the idea. The same could be said about her, but the funny bit was that it hadn't been.

"Hey! Well… yeah ok that's kind of fair."

Sam couldn't really deny it. That was a pretty accurate description of how he spent his time. He tried to quip back at Jess, keen to shift the focus. Steven rolled up his mental sleeves and joined in, nothing like a good banter battle between friends.

Louisa laughed, joining in where she could. She was surprised how comfortable this all was. She had expected to have a relaxed and comfortable evening in the company of friends, but to have someone new here… and still feel the same level of comfort, ease of being… that was a surprise. A welcome one.

41

"Hey, you ok Louisa?"

Steven had wandered off to fiddle with bottles or snacks or something, Jess had quickly decided it was not a good idea to leave him to manage complex tasks by himself and had wandered off to help. Sam had sat, content in the quiet. A few moments passed before he released that he was not alone, Louisa was still here. It was strange, he never usually felt comfortable enough to sit quietly when there were people still around. Looking over to her, she seemed to be a thousand miles away, half staring out of the gap in the curtains at some distant land beyond.

"Huh? Oh yes, sorry I was miles away!"

Louisa snapped back to the room, dream images fading, replaced by the sight of a slightly unkempt face looking concerned in her direction. She hoped she hadn't been ignoring him, she had just felt so comfortable sat there that her mind had wandered away into the darkness and shimmering neon that peeked through the glass.

"That's cool, where did you go?"

Louisa's mind stopped in its tracks. That had never happened before. People had commented on her drifting away, negatively, but no one had ever asked her where she had drifted off too… no one had ever spoken like it was an interesting thing to do…

"Oh, err… the lights…"

Louisa wasn't ready to try and explain exactly what she saw when she drifted, what her mind thought about. But the idea that someone might actually listen…

"Sometimes, I drift into a fantasy world… a magical world. When the real world seems too bad, too scary, or other times… like now… when I was comfortable… it's a happy place, where anything can happen."

Sam shifted in his mismatched chair. Louisa felt she had said too much, he was about to laugh at her.

"Cool."

Louisa smiled. Sam did not seem to be laughing.

"I think I know what you mean, well, sort of. People say I wander into a fantasy world too, except – I don't – not really, it's just how I see the world around me."

Sam felt excited that perhaps he had found someone who might understand what he had been trying to make people see for as long as he could remember. Louisa was smiling at him. This may be his chance.

"See, when I go places, I see things. I see things and I say 'Look at that!' and no one else ever sees. Everyone seems so caught up in what they have been told to do, told to see around them, no one ever seems to actually see anything? Like I walk down the street, and everyone is looking at their phone, or the floor, and I want to stop them and shout 'what was that!' 'did you see that!' 'Is this real?!' Maybe it's not the same, I don't know."

Sam felt he wasn't quite getting his point across. Louisa still seemed to be listening though, a good sign.

"I mean, ok. So I think what you're saying is that you can see the magic in the world, but you see it as a separate thing to move into, outside of reality. I don't think that's true. I think the magic is all around us, all the time, but most people close it off. They don't want to see. They are too concerned with what they have been told to see to actually look around with their own eyes and really see what's there, and what is there, well it's amazing."

Louisa felt Sam's words somewhere deep inside. Was he right? Could that be true? Not only had he not laughed at her, but he had suggested that not only was it not a bad thing, it was the right thing to do… to drift into the magic… was it really all around? She wasn't sure if he was talking about the same thing that she felt, but what if he was? That would mean when she drifted away she wouldn't have to do it alone…

"I like fantasy because I can struggle with the real world, with fitting in with the people round me, what they expect of me…"

Louisa felt compelled to open up to this guy. She had no idea why. It just felt…

"Exactly. Except you're wrong."

Sam spoke with a smile, Louisa could hear the joy in his words. But he said she was wrong? She panicked. If he started to make fun of her now, after all she had said…

"It's not you that's struggling. I look around, I see the world as a fantastical place. I can't understand why all the other people don't. Don't they see the magic? The craziness? Why are they so content to sit in their small self made boxes of rules without ever really looking around, ever really seeing what's around them. People say I live in a fantasy world, but it's them that refuse to look further than what the TV told them to wear, and how to feel. You're wrong to try and fit in with them, it's them that should try and fit in with us."

Sam felt himself shaking inside. He had never felt he could tell anyone this before, without them taking the piss, calling him names. Louisa wasn't doing any of those things. She was smiling, leaning in to hear him. She seemed to understand. He wanted to understand how she saw the world. What she saw when she went to her fantasy place. She spoke with a softness, he leaned in to hear her. The magic of the world was in this room. From the first glimpse of dancing candlelight the year before, Sam had felt this was a special place.

42

"Whoops!"

Sam and Louisa turned, startled by the shout. Jess was sat on Steven's lap, leaning into him. A selection of biscuit crumbs covered her legs, fewer with each brush of her hand. Neither Sam nor Louisa had any memory of Jess moving to that position, let alone there being any biscuits to drop all over the place.

"Oh sorry guys, Just being clumsy! Carry on!"

Jess waved with one hand as she retrieved the larger bits which refused to be brushed.

"Sorry, what?"

Sam was confused as to what was happening.

"You know you've been talking for over an hour, right? You didn't even respond when there were biscuits."

Jess smiled as she collected the last few crumbs.

"There's no biscuits now."

"Oh sorry Jess…"

Louisa felt dazed, an hour? Was that rude? That must be rude. Sam had no words. He just looked.

"No don't apologise! We've been over that! It's nice, to see the two of you getting on. This is a much better party than last year. Much less frantic."

Jess conquered the biscuit crumbs, resting her head on Steven's chest. Sam felt the two of them looked at peace.

"And I think you're spending your time speaking to a much better class of lady than last year Sam."

Steven ruined the notion of peace, why would he say that? Why would he bring up such a wound, right now… when everything was so nice…

"Oh? What lady was that then? Make a habit of this do you?"

Louisa laughed at Sam, although she was curious… and perhaps a little concerned… She remembered something about this being mentioned at the start of the night, but it seemed more real now, and somehow more personal. Jess half heartedly slapped at Steven's arm, seemingly still trying to condition him to not say the wrong thing at precisely the wrong time. It hadn't worked so far.

Sam sat. He thought of what to say. For the first time that night, he thought about what to say. He thought about what might happen if he said one thing, what would happen if he said something else. A different thought sprang up, a different voice than the usual menaces. It raised a new idea. Sam considered it. He had lost himself talking with Louisa. He had said things he never thought he would be able to. He hadn't worried about it. And she hadn't laughed at him, made fun, or left. What if… what if he just told her? Told them all? What if he didn't worry about what they might think, what if he just? His voice agreed, and it began the tale:

"Yeah, so last year, I met someone at the party. Ellie. And to be honest, to be really honest, I didn't meet her. Not really. I saw a woman, and she made me feel something that I felt once years ago. Something I felt for a different woman. Tish. That, meeting Tish, was the first time I had felt a strong attraction. And I never did anything about it. Honestly, I don't think I really wanted to. That way it stayed pure, a perfect idea of a girlfriend, just out of reach. Never at risk of becoming real, with real feelings and real interactions. When I saw Ellie last year, I thought it was a second chance at Tish. It wasn't. I tried to make it something, but it never really was anything. Both of them, they were never really real… they were both just ideas in my head… dreams I was projecting onto women. I never really found out who Ellie was, I just tried to keep that dream alive. And she left, and it hurt. It hurt because it wasn't her that left, it was my dream, it was Tish too. They both left."

Sam felt a huge weight lift from his soul. He hadn't really admitted any of that before, not even to himself. He wasn't sure why it had all come together now. And how he felt he could just say it all. It felt good. Cleansing.

"Ah Hun, I didn't know any of that, you never told me about Tish before."

Jess's words carried a sonic caress, her ability to support even at range was a welcome power.

"It's ok Jess, that chapter is over now. I've actually never felt better. I feel free of it, free of both of them."

Louisa sat and listened. She didn't really know how to respond. She had not expected to feel a little uneasy at the thought of Sam making a habit of spending time talking to women at Jess' parties, but she had really not expected that revelation. She didn't know what to think, it seemed so large, so personal, to just tell everyone like that. To tell her, to not hold anything back… to just say… maybe if he could say that, she could tell them all about her past… maybe… in time. She wasn't sure she had ever met anyone like Sam. She wasn't sure what that meant.

"Yeah, sorry, that was a bit intense. I guess I can mess things up sometimes. I think about it all too much, especially when I'm alone, I have too much time to think about it all, and it all seems fine right up until the moment I realise I've done something stupid."

Sam wasn't sure how to stop, even his attempt at an apology for oversharing had turned into another heart felt revelation.

"Well that's easy to fix… Don't be alone."

Louisa heard herself reply, immediately feeling embarrassed. She couldn't believe she had said that out loud.

Sam smiled.

Louisa smiled.

"Hey so, downer and that, but I think Steven is falling asleep, and I'm not sure how much longer I will last either."

Jess Stood, a few stray crumbs escaping as she stretched.

"Oh right, yeah, sorry."

"Don't you start with the unnecessary apologies Sam, it's been a really nice evening. We should definitely do it again."

Jess helped Steven up, he did look tired. He yawned as he spoke:

"Yes, indeed. And let's not leave it another year before we all do something."

"Yes! Louisa still has to see the club! That was a fantastic night!"

Sam Laughed at Jess's comment, quickly stopping himself. There had been enough tales of his stupidity for one night.

"OK sounds good!"

Louisa got up from the sofa, pleased that her sense of peace and comfort was still with her.

Steven began gathering the glasses as Jess walked with Sam and Louisa towards the coats. She ducked into the bedroom and returned, a coat in each hand. She gave Louisa hers, and threw Sam's at him. Louisa's eyes followed the black fabric as it sailed through the air and into Sam's hands.

"That coat! I remember that coat! I saw that last year, I thought it looked really cool!"

Louisa's memories of finding it lying on the bed returned, how she felt the owner must be interesting, different. She had had no idea. She wondered how different the last year might have been if she had spoken… but then, without all that had happened this year, would she be able to speak the way she had tonight? She watched as Sam put it on, an almost perfect fit.

"Thanks, not many people like it, not very fashionable these days."

Sam made the most of putting it on, letting it swish. It was rare for him to find a fan of his coat. It was his favourite item of clothing. The most him.

"Well goodnight you two, thanks for coming! It's been a lot of fun! I better go and check on Steven, just make sure the door is closed behind you."

"Thanks Jess, really. Night."

Louisa smiled as Jess vanished back up the corridor.

"Cheers!"

Sam wanted to say more, but couldn't really find the right words. He turned, finding himself face to face with the large wooden door once again.

"Huh."

"What's up?"

Louisa was curious as to what Sam had seen, why he was stood there, staring at a closed door.

"Oh, It's just… well. Last year, I stood at this door, and I thought that behind it, was the future. It was unwritten. It could be anything… adventure… and until I opened the door, nothing on the other side was real. I stood here, and I thought about what it could all be. I never would have predicted what happened. I never have any idea what's on the other side of this door."

Louisa looked at Sam. She looked at the door. She put one hand on the door handle and took Sam's hand with the other. He looked at her as the handle clicked and the door creaked open. She looked at him, and then out into the darkness.

"Let's find out."

More Information

Please leave a review

To find out about the author visit

www.duskfall.co.uk

Sam and Louisa will soon return in

Rats

&

Bats

&

Cats

&

Hats

Printed in Great Britain
by Amazon